MADE FROM MAGIC

MARIANNE A. SCOTT

CONTENT WARNING

YOUR MENTAL HEALTH IS important! Please be aware of the following themes in this book:

Anxiety/PTSD

Depictions of Childhood Trauma (magical)

Sexually Explicit Scenes (M/F)

Violence, War, and Death

For the love of my life, my pants.
Thank you for reminding me of my love of writing, even when I didn't remember myself.
Thank you for being my first sounding board, and for listening to all one thousand edits of the cave chapter.
This book wouldn't be possible without you.

Chapter One

ADVICE TO FUTURE SELF. When someone offers you a magically enhanced drink that will "get you fucked up faster," the correct response is, "no thanks." Not, "I'll be the judge of that."

Because of said magical drinks, I don't immediately panic when I hear the water running in my private bathroom attached to my single barracks. I'm quite sure the person in the shower was invited in...but I cannot for the life of me tell you his name, what he looks like or where we met. I do know, however, that he wears an obnoxiously spicy cologne, which I can still smell in my hair and will probably be stuck in my nose for a week.

Even though my head is screaming at me to go back to sleep, I crack one eye open as little as I possibly can to look around my room for clues. My barracks are obsessively neat except for the bookshelf crammed full of fantasy-romance novels written by mortals... my guilty pleasure. Everything looks as it should, all four unadorned walls still standing, the cold tile floor still spotless except for the uniform lying in a heap. This means the bathroom guest is also a soldier...because you better believe my uniform is hanging neatly on the back of a chair. On a positive note, I didn't leave the initiation party for the new privates. However, it *does* mean I had a one-night stand, my first one-night stand, with a subordinate. *Fuck fuck fuckity fuck.*

The faucet turns off, and I tuck the sheet under my arms so that I'm wearing it like a strapless dress. The bathroom door creaks open, and my mystery man enters as I squint against the light that streams in.

"Not so loud," I moan, covering my face with my hand as I get used to the brightness. He chuckles in a deep baritone but closes the door enough so that the light is off my face. He's tall, blonde, and his angular face is set in a smile that's entirely too wide for the hour. He looks a few years older than me, mid-twenties or so.

"Morning, Captain," he croons, and I watch a stray bead of water slide down his muscular chest and chiseled abs before disappearing below the towel slung along his hips. He struts to the edge of the bed, and the mattress dips under his weight as he sits beside me. "How are you feeling?"

I'm sure he doesn't want to know the fact that I'm so hungover I can't remember his name. Or that every word he's spoken, six in total so far, makes my head feel like it's about to split open. So instead, I respond with a non-committal *mmmm.*

His eyes flash as he lies down on the extra inch of space in my twin bed, propping his head up with his hand. He drinks in my body slowly, his eyes not missing an inch of my ample curves beneath the sheet. Boldly, he reaches forward to brush my long chestnut hair off my shoulder and skims his fingers down my side, slightly tugging the sheet lower until my chest is exposed. I'm intrigued to see how far he'll take this.

"Last night was fun," he comments, his blue eyes reluctantly lifting to meet my auburn ones. "I didn't think officers were allowed to fraternize with soldiers."

We're not. But I get away with a lot because of my power, which is more than most witches...okay, more than every witch. Even my mother is afraid of all the power I hold, though she would never admit that. It's why she pushed me through school, making me complete my training in half the time, and why she encouraged me to join the elite group of soldiers called the Dragons that work for the King of Magic.

"Whoops," I laugh, and his responding laugh lights up every inch of his pretty face. He leans in like he's about to kiss me, and I'm debating on letting him when there's a knock at my door.

"Captain." A soldier with a baby face wearing full battle armor pushes into my room. We're only required to wear a black tunic and leggings in headquarters unless you stand guard for one of the generals, which this man definitely does not.

I hastily grab for my bedsheet, tugging it up over my body as his eyes fall to me.

"Oh shit," he says, breaking pretense and snapping his eyes shut. I struggle not to laugh at his expense. "I'm so sorry, Captain."

"You might want to rethink barging into an officer's quarters in the future," I chide, standing to grab a robe that's flung over my nightstand and hastily tie it around my waist.

"Yes, Captain. I'm so sorry, Captain."

"Your name, private?" I bark.

"McNally, Captain." The private in my doorway is practically shaking at this point.

"You can open your eyes, McNally. I'm decent now." His eyes open but don't linger on me in my flimsy robe. Instead, he looks to my bed, and his jaw goes slack.

"Kyle?"

The man in my bed, Kyle apparently, nods awkwardly. "Hey, Sean."

McNally has the audacity to look impressed by his friend, and his posture relaxes. This is why I don't go farther than first base with other soldiers, even if I'm drunk. But I will not lose the respect of an entire incoming class because I made one bad judgment call.

I clear my throat and call my raw magic to my hand, lightning dancing between my fingertips, reminding them that I'm the only Elemental Witch with lightning and that in itself demands respect. McNally snaps back to attention, and even Kyle sits up straighter and clutches his towel. *Good.*

"What is it you want, McNally?" I ask, casually tossing a ball of lightning between my hands before letting it absorb back into my body.

"General Carmichael set a meeting in her office in one hour. She requests that you wear your formals, Captain." I roll my eyes. This could have been an email...or at the very least, she could have used our Mind Magic channel to send the message.

"It's my day off," I say, sitting back on the bed. I run my fingers through my wavy hair, untangling any knots. "Tell her I'll speak to her tomorrow."

McNally fidgets uncomfortably. He starts sweating, his eyes bouncing between Kyle and me pleadingly, and I sigh.

"Fine." I groan. "Tell her I'll be there but do *not* mention I wasn't alone. Understood?"

"Yes, Captain." And with that, McNally sprints into the hallway.

I get up and walk towards my bathroom, circling the bed as Kyle tracks me like a lion with his prey. I won't deny his good looks...I completely understand what I was thinking last night. But now I have one hour to get showered, drink as much coffee as I can, and become a functioning member of society. None of that can get done if I'm beneath a soldier.

"Off you go, Kyle," I pass by him, and he catches the tie on my robe.

"Are you sure?" he asks, using the fabric to pull me back. My body slides towards him instinctively as his hand drops, skimming the hem of my robe, brushing suggestively against my outer thigh.

"Tempting," I whisper, biting my lower lip. I gently trail one hand across his muscular bicep and send a pulse of my electric magic into it. He yelps and pulls back as I chuckle and resume my trek to the bathroom.

"Thanks for the night. Now get out," I say. I shut the door with enough force for him to know I'm serious and wait until I hear the click of my front door before I turn on the shower.

Chapter Two

I RUN DOWN THE sloping halls of the Dragons Headquarters, making my way through the underground helix toward the generals' offices. I only have a few minutes before my meeting, but the labyrinth is so large that I won't get there in time if I don't hurry. The Dragons have strongholds in most major cities, but Headquarters, here in London, is the biggest because we also host the training facilities, where I spend most of my time when I'm not out on assignment.

I grip the sturdy grey stone as I swing around a corner, using the wall to propel me down a familiar darkened hallway. Even though all the rooms have electricity, someone decided it would be better to keep the hallways lit by torches, but I've been stationed here long enough that I'm used to the dark. I slow as I pass four ornate doors, each painted the color representing the element that each general possesses and staffed with a guard in full battle armor.

I'm wearing my formals as instructed. My black leggings are trimmed in gold, and my black velvet tunic hangs to my thighs. The tunic is unadorned, except for the Crest of the King of Magic, three wands that crisscross into a starburst, held by a giant paw.

The crest dates back almost two hundred years when four kings and queens reigned over the entire Kingdom of Magic. Each monarch represented a different section of magic: Light Magic, Dark Magic, Elemental Magic, and Magical Creatures. Two hundred years ago, there was a war between three monarchs, and most of the magical community was dragged into it. Only the Elemental King was willing to step in and put an end to it, so his bloodline has ruled solo from the palace in London ever since.

I approach the brick-red door adorned with golden whorls that represent fire, and the guard gives me a nod to enter. I tug my tunic and tighten my ponytail before yanking the gilded doorknob open and entering the empty office. *Good, I beat her here.*

The office is stifling despite the dropping autumn temperatures thanks to the iron fireplace and the blue flames dancing amongst the coals. I tread across the lush red carpet, my eyes lingering on the floor-to-ceiling bookshelves that cover three of the white-washed walls, before flopping into a golden armchair situated across from an even larger mahogany desk. Scrolls are stacked in a pyramid atop the desk, somehow managing not to topple off the edge, and an open planner lies in the center with a pen neatly aligned to its right. Behind the desk is a portrait I haven't seen before of two of the generals in their white formals. They stare stoically at me as I wait for my appointment to begin.

Voices conversing softly just outside the door have me standing at attention. The door opens, and two generals enter, falling silent when they spot me.

The first to enter is a middle-aged woman wearing the same outfit as me, but her chestnut hair is pulled back so tight that it lifts the creases from her eyes. She would be stunning if she smiled, but she rarely does. Her emerald-green eyes search me, eyeing my formals as if she didn't expect me to follow that order. Behind her is a man so broad he fills the doorframe, the gold seams of his tunic bursting around his muscular shoulders. His head is clean-shaven, but he has a neatly trimmed black beard that obstructs most of his smiling face.

I bow from the waist as the female general moves into the room with power and grace despite her age. She walks towards me and pauses until I stand upright.

"Katie," she leans in and air kisses both of my cheeks.

"Hi, Mom," I smile tightly as she heads to her chair behind her desk. The male general rushes forward and wraps me in a bear hug, forcing the air from my lungs. "Hi, Marcus."

"We've missed you, kid." Marcus releases me, his brown eyes shining with happiness as he heads to stand behind my mother, resting his hand protectively on the back of her chair.

Marcus is my new stepfather. He and my mom knew each other from their training with the Dragons, but afterward, my mom moved to Salem, where she met my dad, had me, and rose through the ranks to eventually head the North American division of the military. When my parents divorced and I graduated from school, my mom took the position at Headquarters to "keep an eye on me" as I went to train with the Dragons. She reconnected with

Marcus, and they finally got married a month ago. They've been away on their honeymoon ever since.

I flop back into my armchair and cross one leg over the other, rolling my booted ankle. My mother purses her lips, and a bad feeling settles in my gut. I crossed a line last night, but the question is whether they know about it.

"How was the honeymoon?" I start.

"Do you know why I called you in, Kathryn?" she asks. I shake my head innocently, which I know won't fool my mother one bit.

"We heard you attended the initiation party last night," Marcus begins gently.

"It was a requirement," I respond coolly.

"Yes, but Katie. You know you need to—"

"Maintain boundaries, yeah I know," I say, exasperated. "I'm sorry, but sometimes it's nice to be with people my age." This is a conversation we've had many times before. The only people I know who aren't soldiers live in Salem, and my quick advancement has made it hard to make any lasting friendships. Marcus tries to cut me some slack, but my mother looks at me like she's unimpressed by my loneliness.

"Being with people your age isn't the issue," she continues.

"And what is, Mom?"

"Did you know that you kissed five graduates before leaving with one last night?" *Shit.* I did not know that. My mom leans forward, putting her elbows on the desk and rubbing her temple. "Kathryn. I don't know what to do with you anymore."

"Have you had any complaints about me in the field?" I ask. My voice is light even though I can feel my blood simmering beneath the surface. "Or in the training ring?"

"No, but it's only a matter of time."

"Then why are we having this discussion now? On my day off." I stand up, my magic crackling beneath my skin.

"Kathryn—" my mother sighs.

"You hated when I dated civilians—" I remind her.

"Well, your choices—"

"And I guarantee if I dated another captain, you'd say they're too old for me."

"Yes, I would."

I step forward and clamp my hands down on the edge of her desk. "Then who's left, Mom? I'm sorry, but I'm not going to lock myself in my room and be celibate because you'd feel better if I didn't date men under me."

She stands to meet me, the anger in her eyes a mirror of my own. Marcus makes a move so that he's beside her as I ball my fists.

"Do you realize how that undermines your authority?" she hisses. "You can't command men who don't respect you."

"They do respect me, *General.*" I work my ass off making sure that my personal life doesn't affect the way the men treat me when I command them, and that she doesn't realize that... The air around me thickens as the lightning surges in my veins.

"Katie..." Marcus warns as he and my mom both reach for their wands. "Breathe."

The portrait behind my mother's desk shatters as my magic slips from my control. I throw up a magical shield over the three of us as glass shards cascade down, narrowly missing my mother and landing on the carpet. I curse before waving a hand to clean up the mess. I guide the shards until they fit seamlessly back into the frame like they never broke in the first place.

"I'm sorry," I mutter, removing the shield and dropping back into my chair. I rarely lose control over my magic anymore, but my mother brings out the worst in me.

Most witches need a wand to channel and focus their magic, but my magic is so powerful that the first spell I cast with a wand snapped the thing like a twig. I usually use my hands to direct my magic, but I don't even need to do that. I barely imagine doing something, and my magic takes care of it. There are only five other known witches in history who have been able to do this, and one of them is my father.

My mother shakes her head. She glances at Marcus, who nods and turns back to me as she sits back down.

"Katie, we have a new position for you," she says wearily. "We need you to guard the Prince of Magic."

The room gets quiet. Only the popping of the fire echoes in the room as I digest this information.

"You're making me a bodyguard?" I ask finally. Even if it is for the prince or the king, being a bodyguard is a huge step-down.

"You will be leading a team of Dragon sergeants to escort the prince on a mission. You will retain your rank and will return here once the threat is neutralized," she clarifies.

"What's the threat?"

"There are rumors," Marcus begins, "of covens of Dark Witches organizing in underpopulated areas. We believe they are using these abandoned areas to grow armies." My mouth drops open. Dark Magic is one of the most dangerous forms of magic and has been outlawed for centuries. Most of what I do entails finding individuals who use it to bring them to prison, but there haven't been organized covens in about twenty years.

"And the *prince* is going after them?" I ask, not trying to hide the shock from my voice. From everything I've heard about him, the prince is an academic, not a fighter.

"He needs his Moment of Valor," Marcus says sternly, and I fight the urge to roll my eyes. Since the first singular ruler, every king has needed to prove himself in some type of battle before taking the throne, which the Dragons refer to as the Moment of Valor. It was a precedent set when Baran ended the Four Kings War, but I find the tradition pointless personally. It's not like there's anyone else to take his place if he fails.

"We've infiltrated a coven that's based in Sicily." Marcus continues. "They're a small group at the moment but appear to be growing. They convinced an entire village to vacate their homes with Mind Magic. The mission is to bring them down before they get the chance to become stronger."

"Capture and question? Or--" Marcus cuts me off with a curt nod.

Mind Magic, the ability to cast your mind out and read other people's thoughts, memories, and emotions, is something I excel at and the reason I'm often asked to run interrogations. It was originally considered a form of Dark Magic because people used it for mind control. However, one king realized the benefits of simply observing a mind and made it the only form of Dark Magic that's not illegal. Mind control, however, will still land you a one-way ticket to jail.

"Katie," my mom says softly, "that's the mission of the group. Your specific mission is to ensure the prince returns alive. The covens want him dead. They know the King is old, so they seek to bring down the next heir."

I sigh but nod in agreement. "When do I leave?"

"The prince will be here in a few minutes for a meeting," Marcus says. "Then you'll head to the palace for two days before the group moves out. You'll be his personal guard until you leave for Sicily."

"How are we getting there?" I ask, unable to keep the smile from my face. *Please say flying.*

"Flying is the safest way." *YES!* My mental celebration drowns out Marcus while he prattles on about why we're not taking a car or something faster. "We have brooms ready for you. It should take you three days to fly down and another three to fly back."

"There's one more thing you need to know," my mother says somberly, standing and circling her desk until she's in front of me. She braces her hands on either arm of the chair so that our faces are even and inches apart.

"Your father has been broken out of prison."

Chapter Three

I'M LAID OUT ON a hard marble slab. The room around me is dark, and I can't see much further than the end of the table, where a pale child sits. She watches me through wide grey eyes that are sunken into her head, gently twirling her finger around a blonde spiral.

"Away from the table," a male voice booms from the darkness. The girl reaches a hand towards me in comfort, squeezing my leg and offering me a weak smile before backing into the shadows. The male figure comes closer, his black hood and cloak obstructing his face so that I can only see his tall shape.

"Begin recording," he speaks into the darkness. There's an electronic click, and a red light appears above me. I don't like that light. Nothing good comes when that light is on.

"Please..." I whisper. My voice sounds small and helpless. The man ignores me.

"Infusion number ten. The infusion will last for ten minutes, followed by one hour of practicing spell work." I whimper. My only thought is that I need to get out of here. I jerk my arms to find them magically tethered to the table. I kick my legs to no avail and let a helpless cry fall from my lips.

"Beginning now," the man says, and he reaches down to place his hands on either side of my head.

Searing pain. My skull erupts in a shadowy fire, my blood turning molten beneath my skin. I buck against the restraints, flailing my arms and legs, trying to get free. I toss my head side to side, and yet the hands hold me, sending more fire down my veins. Black shadows cover my eyes as the magic spreads down, searching for any entrance into my body.

"PLEASE!" I beg, my voice ripping from my throat.

"Made in her image," the man chants. "Made from magic. Made to conquer. Made to rule." He repeats the chant over and over again as the magic courses through my body. The words spur on the magic, making it stronger, allowing it to invade every inch of me. I whimper; the pain is too much.

A spark of sunshine inside my stomach flares to life, and the shadowy flame being pumped into me collides with that bright, pure light. The two sensations dance around each other in a blinding fit of agony as the chanting grows louder still. Suddenly, the pain is gone, and I inhale a sharp breath of air. I feel the shadow and light wrap around each other and surge through my entire body, extending through my extremities.

Lightning bursts from my fingertips, shattering the restraints and illuminating the room. The chanting is cut off abruptly as the man is thrown away when the power surges to my head, shocking him. The magic blasts towards the red light, sending glass and plastic raining down from the ceiling. I sit up, the lightning still flaring at either side of me.

The young girl approaches the table, her blonde hair sticking out at odd angles from the static. I regard her curiously, as a wide smile breaks across her face.

"Made in her image," she says, taking up the chant. This time the magic doesn't react. It feels less like a spell now and more like a promise. "Made from magic. Made to conquer. Made to rule." The girl drops to one knee in front of me. "I'm here to serve you, my queen."

The man appears standing behind the kneeling girl, his cloak thrown back, revealing his gleaming auburn eyes.

Chapter Four

"Katie," my mom calls gently, clearing the memory from my mind until I'm back in the present. Her hands move to my shoulders, her grip the only thing keeping my world from spinning out of control.

My father has been broken out of prison.

My chest is heaving, and tears brim in my eyes as I desperately try to banish the panic racing through my system. I try to speak, but instead, a strangled cry comes out. My mother pulls me into her arms as she kneels to the floor, ripping me from the chair I sit in to be thrown across her chest like a toddler. I break apart in her arms, my sobs shuddering through my body.

"No," I whisper. I look to Marcus as he stands above us, tears threatening to spill from his warm brown eyes. My mother strokes my hair and begins to hum a soft lullaby. It's a tune I haven't heard in years, but one she used to hum whenever I woke from a nightmare or had an explosion of my magic. Its effect is instantly calming. I pull back from her, not removing myself completely but enough that I can see her face.

"Is he...is he there? In Sicily?" I ask, trying desperately to steel my spine.

"No, sweetheart," Marcus replies gently, circling to kneel beside my mother. I shudder in relief.

"We only know of the location of the one coven with certainty," my mom says, the edge of authority creeping back into her voice. "But your father hasn't been identified as one of their members. Which means—"

"The Sicilian Coven isn't the leadership," I finish for her, and she nods. Years ago, when the Dark Magic Covens rose to power, they worked in small units scattered across the world. The coven with the most powerful witches gave all the orders. Unbeknownst to us, my father was their leader, which meant he was the most powerful Dark Witch in the world before we sent him to prison. It stands to reason now that he's been broken out that he'll be in charge once again.

"We suspect all the old covens are back up and running, but we need confirmation on that fact. That's why you're headed to Sicily. Our contact went dark a few days ago."

I nod, sliding off my mother's lap and tugging my hair from the confines of my ponytail. I rake my nails along my scalp before running them through the strands, slowly pulling myself back together. My mother and Marcus are still regarding me like I'm about to shatter, but my father couldn't break me fifteen years ago, so he certainly won't break me now.

"So, my orders," I start, squaring my shoulders, "are to accompany the prince and a small group of soldiers to Sicily to find one, inconsequential coven of Dark Witches. Let the prince be mildly heroic, but don't let him get hurt, capture the members and bring them back here for questioning. Am I missing anything?"

"That's the gist," Marcus says as he and my mother resume their positions behind her desk.

"Then," I continue. Their eyes snap to me and widen. "As my reward for babysitting--"

"It's not—" Marcus begins, but I level him with a look and an arch of my eyebrows.

"I get to be a part of the mission to find the rest of the Dark Covens. And when we find my father...his death is mine." Something deep in my gut calls for vengeance against the man who hurt me. It's a dark, twisted part of myself that I've learned to keep locked away. "I should have killed him that night."

"You were five," my mother murmurs softly. She and Marcus exchange a glance, but I don't back down.

"You deserve that justice, Katie," Marcus says carefully. "But sometimes justice isn't worth the cost."

"I'll be fine."

"You're *my* daughter," Marcus continues sternly. "I just...I don't want you to corrupt yourself any further for that man." Tears brim in his eyes, and I soften.

"Thank you," I whisper, and I rush around the side of her desk to embrace him. His arms fold me in towards his chest in one quick movement, cradling me in the warmth. Even before he married my mom, I viewed Marcus as a father. He was my mentor at the Academy and was always in the front row of every promotion ceremony. I give in to the comfort he offers for a long minute before he pulls back and wipes a stray tear from my cheek.

"The prince will be here shortly," my mother says, retreating behind her walls. "Do you need a moment to compose yourself?" I laugh harshly. Only she would hear me declare to kill my father and ask if I *need a minute.* I shake my head and return to my side of the desk, refastening my hair into its high ponytail.

As if orchestrated, there is a knock at the door, and the guard from outside pokes his head in. "Generals, Captain," he says, bowing deeply. "May I announce His Highness, Prince Archer Baran."

He steps aside, and the prince walks in. For all the time I've been stationed in London, I've never met the prince, and he's not at all what I would have imagined. He is tall, almost a full head taller than me, and his body lean. His midnight hair is rumpled, and the blue-black color is stark against his pale skin. But his most striking feature is his eyes, the hazel hue changing colors as he steps into the red chamber, shifting from a pale green to a muddled brown.

I bow deeply, my action echoed by my mother and Marcus. Archer walks to Marcus, who rights himself and surprises me by giving the prince a sloppy, wet kiss on the cheek before pulling him into an embrace. When they break apart, Archer moves to my mother, pulling her into a hug, to her dismay.

"General Carmichael," he says, his tone lilting in his crisp British accent. "Or is it Weatherbeak now? I'm sorry I missed the wedding."

"Misty is fine," my mother says warmly, extracting herself. "We heard your relay team won the championship. Congratulations."

"Wish I could have been there," Marcus says wistfully.

"You had an excuse!" Archer replies, haughtily hugging Marcus again. *Wow, they're friendly.* Finally, I see the prince's gaze flit to me, still bent over, and I drop my gaze in anticipation.

"Kathryn, you may stand," my mother says. I stand up at attention, and I give the prince a warm smile.

"Wow," he blurts out, and I bite my lip to hold in a laugh. My mother gives an exasperated sigh and very uncharacteristically rolls her eyes. "I'm so sorry," he continues hurriedly.

"She's used to it," my mother says, eyeing me, her glare telling me to keep quiet. "Archer, may I introduce your new guard from now through your mission to Sicily, Captain Carmichael."

"Carmichael?" He looks to my mom, confused.

"My daughter, Kathryn."

I bow my head slightly. "Your Highness."

"Archer is fine, Captain." I smile, and Archer looks like he's about to melt.

"You can call me Katie." I sit back in my highbacked chair, and Archer floats to the one next to me, his gaze transfixed.

"Your Highness," my mom calls, snapping his attention. "Would you prefer to sit behind the desk?" She gestures to her chair, stepping aside.

"Oh, no, thank you, Misty, I'm fine here." He sits next to me, his eyes scanning my legs in a less than subtle way as I cross one over the other. My mom and Marcus exchange a glance that Archer misses.

My god, she's stunning. The words are propelled into my mind from Archer's, which he's clearly unaware of. I try damn hard to school my expression into neutrality, and I focus on an invisible spot on the floor in front of me.

"Great," my mother growls, drawing Archer's attention from me. This is probably for the best because I feel we were about to hear an entire inner monologue comparing my beauty to that of an English rose. Which is super sweet and all, but not appropriate for the situation.

"Sorry?" Archer asks, still unaware.

"Your Highness," I interject, "I'm sorry if this is out of line, but have you ever learned to shield?" He cocks his head to the side, confused. "Your mind?" I press. His eyes open wide as he realizes, and he snaps a hand over his mouth.

"Oh shit," he sinks back into his chair, his face going red. "Did you hear that too?" he directs to Marcus, who nods slowly.

"Sorry, man," he says with a bark of laughter. "Katie is stunning, though; she takes after her mother." My mother shoots Marcus a terrifying glare. Archer groans, and this time, the laugh escapes my mouth.

"I'm sorry," I say, trying to rein it in.

"Kathryn, do you need to leave the room?" my mother asks pointedly. I cough, clearing the last of the giggles from my system, trying to think of something serious to calm my mind as I shake my head.

"I only asked," I say, not quite meeting Archer's eyes, "because it may be necessary on our trip."

"Great idea! Kathryn can teach you," my mother replies, her voice saccharine sweet. Now it's my turn to shoot daggers at my mom.

"I'm not a teacher," I respond coolly. "I was thinking maybe we could bring a tutor—"

"Nonsense, you run training here all the time. And you're one of the best Mind Magic wielders in our realm. Teaching Archer to shield should be easy." Her mind presses against mine, *Agree to this. He clearly needs it,* she says silently.

"That would be great," Archer says, looking at me expectantly.

"It would be my pleasure," I say, gritting my teeth. I should have kept my mouth shut.

"Done. Archer," she says, turning her attention to him, "Is there anything else Katie should know about your mission? She's been brought up to speed on everything that was planned prior to our vacation."

"No new developments," he says thoughtfully. "We leave in two days."

"Is there a healer coming with us?" I ask.

"No, but that's a great idea," Archer says, looking at Marcus. "Can you make sure we have a healer as well? Make our traveling party an even eight?" Marcus and my mother share a look before they both nod.

"Wonderful," Mom says. "Marcus has prepared some training for you to do today and tomorrow if you'd like to proceed to the facilities. I'll help Kathryn pack for the move to the palace, and then we'll join you." Marcus walks to Archer, offering him his hand to stand.

"Let's see if you can best your godfather in your magical training, Your Highness," he says playfully. Archer takes his hand, and the two head out the door, Archer casting a final look at me before leaving.

I wait until the door clicks behind them before turning to address my mom. "I didn't know Marcus was Archer's godfather."

"Yes. He was very close with Queen Elissa. May her soul rest." My mother looks over me.

"Am I moving to the palace?" I ask, fidgeting under her scrutiny.

"For the time being. You'll be stationed in the room adjacent to the prince's suite until the threat is cleared." I nod. At least it should be an upgrade from my barracks. Silence falls again.

"Just say it," I sigh, and she arches an eyebrow. "We both know you've already sent people to pack up my room, so what is it you want to discuss, Mother?"

She clicks her tongue. "You are forbidden to sleep with Archer," she orders, and I scoff. "I'm serious, Kathryn. The boy obviously has a crush on you, and you are not about to take advantage of that. Archer is—"

"Royalty?" I offer. "Expected to marry a courtier? The person I'm supposed to be guarding?"

"Innocent." The blow lands.

"And I'm not?" I snap.

"You are many things," my mother whispers, "but no, you are not innocent. And if you sleep with that boy..." she trails off, but the silence is full of warning. "Don't make me regret giving you this position."

"I won't," I say sternly.

"I need you to say the words, Katie."

I roll my eyes emphatically. "I won't sleep with the prince."

As soon as the words are out of my mouth, I feel a twinge in my gut. A deep-seated part of me wants to defy the instruction because I know it would drive her crazy. But I won't do that...*probably.* I curse myself for being so childish, but I keep my face impassive.

This is a terrible idea, my mother's mind projects. Whether she meant me to hear it or not, I ignore her.

"Let's go meet them in the training ring," she says out loud. "I want you to watch Marcus's training and continue it while you're on the road. And start the shielding lessons today."

I nod and stand, gesturing for her to lead the way. I can't help but echo her thoughts. *This is a very bad idea.*

Chapter Five

WE GET TWO STEPS into the hallway when I feel a brush against my mind that sends a warmth through my entire body. One of the things I can do with my Mind Magic is create communication channels. It's a way to literally reach into someone's mind and deliver a message without the fear of seeing their memories or emotions. Once a channel is set up, you can block it off, but it remains in the recesses of your mind so that the members of the channel can always call through it. It's more personal than texting and great when you're moving in a group. I haven't felt anything from this channel in a long time. I press into the feeling to find a message.

Mirror date? You free? I skid to a halt.

Two minutes. I fire back as I groan and grasp my stomach.

"I need a minute," I announce, pouring my non-existent acting skills into the bit. My mother clicks her tongue in disapproval, but I turn on my heel and sprint towards my barracks.

Ask Edina if she's still coming for Christmas, my mother's voice rings in my ears through our channel. She knows me too well. I chuckle as I sprint up the hallway to my room. When I arrive, I burst into the open doorway to find my room has been turned upside down. Two soldiers are in the process of packing my underwear, one of whom is holding up a lacy thong.

"Paws off, boys," I command, striding into the room. He drops the thong, and they both snap to attention. "Go take a break. I'll pack my lingerie."

"Captain, the General..."

"Is aware I need twenty minutes. Out." They don't dare argue as they scramble out of my room, shutting the door behind them. I trod over to my underwear draw and procure a silver, handheld mirror adorned with ornate swirls that remind me of gales of snowflakes. My hands trace over the swirls absently as I wave a hand over the aged glass. A picture starts to crystalize but stalls until I repeat the motion.

"We could have just FaceTimed," I grumble as the picture finally comes in clear.

My best friend, Edina, is staring back from the mirror, smiling warmly. Her blonde hair, streaked by the sun even in the dead of November in Massachusetts, hangs damp around her shoulders. Her skin is tanned and flawless, and she only wears a hint of mascara on her wide, sapphire blue eyes. She's wearing a sweater that hangs off her slender shoulder, revealing just a hint of her camisole.

"Fuck that," she scoffs. "I didn't pay to learn this fancy-ass magic just to use mortal technology. And you get no service in the bunker." Even though she has a point, I roll my eyes dramatically.

Edina and I met in primary magic school. I was bored and set the classroom carpet on fire, and she doused it with her water magic. We've been inseparable ever since. She's my ride or die, my confidant, and the only person I trust completely. She's the person I love most in the entire world.

"I need all the details of the party last night," she says, leaning her cheek against her perfectly manicured hand. Judging by the angle in the mirror, she must be sitting at her vanity in her dorm, and I sigh, remembering the luxury of the Salem Academy of Magical Arts. We would have been there together if my mother hadn't accelerated my studies, but Edina is graduating this year and then she'll move to London, so we'll finally get to be in the same city again.

"Like I can remember all the details," I deadpan. She lets out a melodic laugh, tossing her hair over her shoulder. "But according to Misty, I had a great time."

"Oh shit, she's home?" she gasps. "How bad was it?" I mimic tying a noose around my own throat, and she chuckles and pouts in sympathy.

"She wants to know if you're coming for Christmas this year," I tell my best friend. "I know you were just here for the wedding—"

"Wouldn't miss it," she squeals. "I'll be there in time for my birthday, so I expect a party with some of those sexy soldiers you've been keeping to yourself."

"I promised Misty I'd keep the fraternizing to a minimum." I groan.

"So, keep your nose clean for the next month and save the slip up for when I'm there. It's my twenty-first! I need a blowout."

"Fine, but if she kills me, it's on your head."

"I can handle that," she smirks. "So why were Misty's panties in a wad about this party?"

"Well," I draw out the word for about ten syllables, which causes Edina to sit ramrod straight in anticipation. "I sort of left the party with someone..." Her eyes bulge.

"Shut the fuck up!" she claps her hands, perpetuating the valley girl aesthetic she gives off. "Your first one-night stand! I'm so proud."

"E, I didn't remember his name this morning!"

"YAS!" She snaps her hands in approval. "You're up to date on your tonic, yeah?"

"Yes." The birth control tonic the healers whip up only needs to be taken once a month, so it's easy enough to keep up with.

"Good." She cackles with glee. "It's really about time you're moving on. You've been punishing yourself long enough for that douche bag."

"I wasn't—" She fixes me with a glare, and I concede. In truth, she has a point. I'm not doing it intentionally, but I have been a little...guarded since my ex dumped me over the summer.

"Did you see the tabloids?" I ask, sounding more vulnerable than I intended. "He's with—"

"A mortal, yeah, I saw. I say we hex the bitch," she quips, although I'm pretty sure she's giving an actual suggestion. I give a half-hearted shrug. "Babes, you're the best witch of our time, and you're hot as hellfire. His loss."

I give her a small smile. "Thanks, E."

"Okay, I have ten minutes before I have to run. What else is new?"

"Actually, I'm moving today." I can't tell her the full details of the mission since she's a civilian, especially not when mirrors aren't the most reliable form of communication. But I do tell her I met the prince and that I'll be moving to the palace for the foreseeable future.

"YOU MET THE PRINCE?" Edina shrieks, blowing out my eardrums. "YOU WASTED TIME TALKING ABOUT THAT MUSICIAN DICKWAD WHEN YOU MET THE FUCKING PRINCE OF THE KINGDOM OF MAGIC TODAY? Is he as hot in person as he is in print?"

I laugh. "Misty has already forbidden him."

"Which only makes you want him more," she says knowingly. I wouldn't have thought twice about Archer until he became forbidden fruit. Honestly, you would think my mother would know better. "Did you read his mind?" Edina asks.

"I didn't have to. He didn't have shields up," I say, a stupid smile breaking across my face.

"What did he think?" She leans forward with intrigue.

"That I'm stunning," I gush, trying to ignore the blush creeping over my cheeks. I'm used to men finding me attractive, but there's something in the sincerity of the prince's thoughts that warms my jaded heart.

"I give it a month," she laughs.

There's a grumble of a man's voice in the room behind her and a masculine hand drops a cup of coffee on the counter. "Thanks," she murmurs, winking to whoever it is.

"Do you have a guy in your room?" I ask and she shrugs nonchalantly.

"Unlike you and Prince Charming, this one *won't* be around in a month," Edina says.

"He brought you coffee?" I offer.

"Yeah, but he didn't bring me to orgasm," the edge in her voice is just enough that I burst out laughing, and she joins me. "Gotta run, babes. Tell me the minute you get back from your mission."

"Love you."

"Love you most."

Chapter Six

MARCUS AND ARCHER ARE in the elevated center ring when I get down to the training arena, speaking in hushed tones. People jokingly refer to this space as "The Pit" since it's at the very bottom of the compound and the fire-resistant, black stones make it feel like a barbeque pit. The arena is all one level, except for the sparring ring, which magically hovers four feet from the center's ground. It doesn't have any barriers around the edges, and I've seen many a soldier sent flying off the side during training practices. The Pit is empty except for the two men I'm seeking, and I'm not sure if it's because Marcus cleared it specifically or if all the soldiers are having a lazy Sunday.

"Katie," Marcus waves me over. I take a running jump into the ring, clearing the awkward height and rolling to my feet in front of the prince. "Take over for me for a minute. Your mother and I need to check in with the other generals."

"What are we working on?" I ask, pulling my hair loose from its ponytail so I can braid it.

"Archer needs some refreshers on his Battle Magic," he instructs. "And I've been showing him some simple spells you may need on the mission." My stepfather claps me on the back and hops out of the ring.

"Right," I turn to Archer who gives me a sheepish smile. "What have you done so far?"

"Umm... we just kind of caught up. He was telling me about the honeymoon." Another sheepish smile. Part of me wonders if he's actually this awkward or if this is a tactic to soften me while I train him. If it's the latter, it's not going to work.

"Okay then. Let's just dive in. We'll start with Battle Magic," I announce, stepping back and calling my lightning to my fingers. "Take the first strike."

Archer pulls out his wand and for a second, I think he's joking. But then he casts a spell and I deflect it before holding up my hand for him to stop.

"Hang on," I call, and he halts his attack. "Have you used Battle Magic before?"

"I have...." he says in a way that lets me know he hasn't. I arch my eyebrow derisively and his shoulders slump. "Okay, I never had to."

"That's...odd."

"I took diplomacy classes during the time allotted for Battle Magic." He shrugs, and I get the feeling there's more he's not saying, but I'm not about to push for his life's story.

"You should still know how to defend yourself."

"I do," he says defensively. "With spells." I grab his wand from his hand.

"Now what would you do?" I ask and Archer looks at me like I have eight heads. "When in a battle, access to your wand might be limited. It could break, be stolen, or be in your pocket when you're flying on a broom. So rather than rely on spells, we rely on the raw magic in our bodies." I call the lightning to my fingers again and show him.

"Call your raw magic to your hand. You can do that right?" I tease, which earns me a glare as he opens his palm to reveal a small flame.

Magic in its raw form always takes a unique shape depending on the caster. Because most are Elemental Witches, it usually shows up in the form of fire, water, earth, or air. Light Witches have a ball of sunshine and Dark Magic in its raw form looks like a shadow that can swallow you whole. Raw magic on its own can be volatile and is rarely used outside battle.

"Good. Now we'll work on shaping it into different attacks." I trot back over to the other side of the ring. "Imagine a weapon that would be helpful in a battle. Then allow your raw magic to pour from your hand into that shape. Start with something simple." He closes his eyes in concentration and the fireball begins to lengthen. I flick my lightning out and it gently shocks him.

"Open your eyes," I command, and he does. "Never take your eye off your opponent." Archer focuses on the shape and then stops when it's a long, coiling whip. He cracks it in front of him and his eyes connect with mine.

"Good, another." I silently curse myself as the command comes out more like a breathy plea than an order. Archer's smirk gets cockier, but he continues.

We spend time bouncing between the different things Archer can make with his fire. Aside from the whip, my personal favorite is a spear which he successfully launches to the back of the room. Once he's gotten a handle on the shaping, we switch to different attack strategies, a subject Archer has a much better handle on.

"Awesome," I praise, and he beams at me. "You think you're ready to spar?" He looks me over, and I can't tell if he's intimidated or if he's underestimating me.

"Could you show me some of the spells you think we'll need first?" Archer asks. *Intimidated it is.* I hand him back his wand.

"Okay, so your raw power can be channeled into spells through your wand."

"I know how magic works," Archer deadpans.

"I mean, you didn't know how Battle Magic worked, so..." I joke, giving him a cheeky smile. He shoots a fireball in my direction, which I easily avoid, cackling as I circle back to him.

"Oh, you want to play?" I ask, searching around for something to help with my lesson. My eyes latch onto the sprinkler system above my head. I send a bolt of lightning to the sprinkler head, and it bursts open. Before it can begin to rain down on us, I use a siphoning spell to collect the water into a giant ball. Then I send it zooming across the room until it crashes into Archer, soaking him completely.

"Fuck," he sputters, and I chuckle.

"Spell number one. Dry yourself off, Your Highness." He glares at me, but I ignore it as I set about fixing the sprinkler system I broke.

Archer luckily knows most of the spells I need to show him. He makes quick work of the warming spells, the siphoning spell for clean water, the cleaning spells, and even creates a shield.

"How aren't you tired?" he huffs after I batter his shield with my lightning until it breaks. He lasted a lot longer than I thought he would.

"I train every day," I respond simply. Magical stamina is a lot like anything else. The more you do it, the easier it is. "Battle Magic also uses a lot of energy, especially when you're not used to it. Grab some food, restore some of your energy."

Marcus strides back into the training arena, followed by my mother.

"Let's see what you've learned!" he calls jovially and hops into the sparring ring. He casts a small cyclone of air in his hand and gives Archer a taunting look. Archer's hazel eyes move to me pleadingly.

"I'm not getting you out of this." I quip, striding to the edge of the ring. "Off you go, Your Highness." Archer grimaces as I jump down and stand next to my mother as the two men square off.

Chapter Seven

SEVERAL HOURS LATER, I am officially settled into my room in the palace, which is easily three times the size of my barracks. Sounds of the city trickle in through my open window along with the fall breeze. The palace is hidden in plain sight, disguised as an abandoned warehouse, and layered with spells that deter mortals from trespassing and seeing its true form.

I'm starfishing across the gigantic four-posted bed, the pale gossamer canopy drawn back so I can see out the open window that overlooks a hedge maze. My clothes were deposited in an oak wardrobe before I arrived, and my little bookshelf was brought up and propped against a wall crusted with gold foil that winds its way to the ceiling like ivy.

My room isn't only adjacent to Archer's room, it's literally connected. We share a sitting room that doubles as a library, a recreation room, and a small dining room. Thankfully, I have my own bathroom, which has a soaking tub that I'm already planning on putting to good use.

I found out Archer has a rotation of Dragons always guarding his door, making my presence here somewhat pointless. I'm expected to shadow him if he decides to leave the room, but since he got his ass kicked by Marcus in training, he's been in his bedroom licking his wounds.

Since it's technically my day off and I'm not needed, I decide to read a particularly trashy vampire novel, basking in the warmth of the sunlight that streams through my window. It's the kind of day you dream about when someone says fall; sunny and cool, with just a hint of chill that promises winter is coming. I absently twirl a strand of hair around my finger as the main character meets the love interest, ignorant to the fact that he's a vampire because she's an idiot. I'd like to think that if I ever meet a vampire, I'll recognize the signs before his fangs are in my neck.

A knock has me jolting upright and locking eyes with Archer as he leans in the doorway. He's changed into a faded t-shirt and jeans; his hair is still damp from his post-practice shower. He stuffs his hands in his pockets and gives me a slow smile that makes my breath catch for a reason I refuse to name.

"Did you need something, Your Highness?" I ask, overcorrecting and sounding more formal than I intend. In truth, I'm not sure how I'm supposed to act here, around royalty. There are procedures and rules that my mother has repeatedly tried to drill into my brain, but that's one lesson that never stuck.

"I have a friend here for lunch," Archer states, and I nod politely, waiting for him to give me more information. "And the chef sent up way too much food. Did you want to join us?"

"Oh, umm—" I pause, my mother's words ringing in my ears. "I'm not sure..."

"No pressure, but if you're hungry..." He starts to leave, and my stomach takes that exact moment to growl loudly. I haven't eaten anything unless you count coffee or the healers' tonic for my hangover. Archer pauses, his eyebrows raising in amusement.

"Sure, why not," I say with a laugh, closing my book and setting it down on the top of my bookcase. I'm about to pass through the door when Archer puts both hands on the doorframe, caging me in.

"One condition," he says leaning in closely, and the scent of cedar and agave envelops me. I look up at him through my lashes and watch as his throat bobs. "You can't call me Your Highness in front of Jai."

"Does he not know you're a prince?"

"Just call me Archer, please," Archer says with a twinkle in his eye.

"Whatever you say, *Your Highness*," I tease, brushing his arm with mine as I pass through the doorframe and head towards the dining room. Archer's groan follows me, and I can't help but laugh.

Archer wasn't kidding. There is easily food for ten people set on the oblong table. Towers of finger sandwiches, platters of pastries, pitchers of iced tea, and carafes of sparkling wine are arranged amongst the place settings, which has already been set for three. The dining room has a balcony attached and the doors are thrown open, allowing the room to be bright and airy, despite the dark wooden walls and the gold finishes on everything from wall sconces to the edge of the table.

Archer's friend stands as we enter, his broad shoulders rippling with huge muscles that continue through his biceps and across his chest. His curly hair is cropped short, and his bright green eyes stand out against his sepia skin tone. He, like Archer, is wearing a t-shirt and jeans which are artfully torn. His mouth stretches into a smile as I cross to him and extend my hand.

"Hi, I'm—"

"Holy shit," he breathes. "You're Kathryn Carmichael."

"Katie," I say tentatively, not recognizing him in the slightest.

"You're a fucking legend," he says, awed. "You saved the king at that wedding last month."

Ahh, that. An assassin tried to sneak into the ceremony at my mother and Marcus's wedding. I picked up on his presence with my Mind Magic and had him apprehended before he even made it inside. I didn't think it was a big deal, but the king sure as hell acted like it was.

"That's why I knew your name," Archer says with a snap of his fingers. "Misty said you were her daughter and it threw me, but I knew I'd heard the name Kathryn Carmichael somewhere else."

"You're our age, right?" Jai asks excitedly and then continues before I can answer. "And you're already a lieutenant."

"Captain," Archer corrects.

"Right, you got promoted," Jai says, practically bouncing in his excitement. "Is your element really lightning? Can you show me?"

"Dude, breathe," I laugh calling my lightning to my fingertips.

"So, fucking cool," Jai says in awe. "I'm Jai by the way. Well Jamison, but everyone calls me Jai."

I take the opportunity to sit at the table, situating myself facing the open balcony and putting myself between Archer and the door. The boys follow suit and Archer pours me a glass of wine from the carafe.

"So, you're guarding Archer?" Jai asks, taking a stack of finger sandwiches before passing them to me.

"Looks that way," I say handing the platter to Archer. His hand brushes against mine long enough to have my heart racing.

"And you thought having a bodyguard would suck," Jai scoffs, and Archer laughs shakily as he finally tears his eyes away from me and focuses on his plate. I take a long drink of wine, the light citrus flavor bursting on my tongue and calming my nerves a bit.

"So, you know each other from school?" I prompt, and they both nod.

"London Magical Academy, top school in the Kingdom," Jai boasts, and I roll my eyes.

"That's cute, but Salem Academy of Magical Arts is clearly better."

"How do you figure that?" Archer asks.

I flip my hair over my shoulder and lean in closer to him. "Because *I* went there."

"And?"

"And they didn't forget to teach me to shield, Your Highness," I tease.

"You don't know how to shield?" Jai asks amidst a mouthful of something meaty.

"I know how to shield..." Archer pouts.

I slip into his mind like a knife through warm butter, creating a private channel for the two of us. *Is that so, Your Highness?* I ask down the channel, amplifying the sound tenfold, so it echoes in every section of his mind, and he winces.

"Fuck that's invasive," he grumbles, and Jai and I both chuckle.

"You're lucky your tutor went to the best school in the Kingdom," I say, punctuating my sentence with a bite of a sandwich, and Archer purses his lips.

"Archer and I are on the relay team together," Jai says out of the blue, drawing my attention away from the prince.

"Wow," I murmur, impressed. Relay Flying is the most popular sport in the Kingdom and it's exactly how it sounds. Archer's team won the championship this year and it was a huge deal seeing as though they're all just out of school.

"Do you like flying?" Archer asks.

"Fucking love it," I respond and he beams at me. "I wanted to be assigned to the aerial division of the Dragons but—"

"But you're too powerful," Jai states, and I nod.

"I'm sure my mother had something to do with it in the end," I say with a shrug.

"She's...ahh..." Archer starts, searching for the word.

"A fucking bitch," I offer, and he laughs, eyes widening slightly.

"I was going to say controlling. It looks like she keeps you on a tight leash."

"She tries," I say with a wink, and Archer's eyes light with promise. *Oh my damn, what is wrong with me?*

Archer refills my glass and I'm so transfixed by his gaze that I let him before thinking the better of it. I should sober up because drunk Katie is full of *wonderful* ideas...ideas that have heat rising to my cheeks and would break at least one important rule.

"You want me to leave you two alone?" Jai asks, the question breaking the tension like ice-cold water. I laugh nervously, dragging my eyes from Archer and take a huge gulp of my wine. Archer just shakes his head and turns back to his lunch.

AFTER LUNCH IS CLEARED, we play some pool in the recreation room. This room, like the other, is all dark wood and gold furnishes, but it has a giant leather sofa in front of a flat-screen, a piano, and of course, the aforementioned pool table. I'm sitting perched on the back of the couch as Archer and Jai finish up their game. Archer is surprisingly good, and I fight the urge to make a joke about him knowing how to handle a cue.

Archer heads to the bathroom, leaving Jai and me alone to play the next game. I hop off the back of the couch and start racking the balls when he comes over to me, dropping his voice.

"Okay listen," he says, sternly, causing me to pause and rise to my full height. "I know you're a soldier, and you're super powerful and everything. But Archer..." he trails off, his brow furrowed. "I told him this shouldn't be his Moment of Valor. The Dark Witch

Covens... Even the generals are afraid of them. And I love Archer, and I'm sure he'll make a great king, but his Battle Magic..."

"Yeah, what's up with that?" I ask and Jai sighs.

"There was an incident when we were kids," he says solemnly. "I think he has more power than most of the Kingdom, but he's... Anyway, that's not my story to tell."

I click my tongue, upset that I don't have more information, but understanding his loyalty. Of course, I'll have to get to the bottom of that at some point, but it will help Archer's training more if he tells me himself.

I can see that Jai is still worried, so I take a step closer to him, lowering my voice so it's barely a whisper. "I'm not supposed to tell you this, but do you know what *my* mission is?" His eyes lock on mine and I offer him a reassuring smile. "To make sure he comes back alive. That's it. My whole reason for being on this mission is to protect Archer."

I pat Jai on the shoulder. "I've got him," I vow.

Jai visibly relaxes, his shoulders coming down from his ears. Then he takes me by surprise and hugs me.

"Thanks," he says after a minute, breaking away and picking up his cue. "Let's see if you can break, Captain." I laugh and grab my stick, removing the rack and bending down to set my aim.

"Oh," Jai says, right before I release my cue. He leans down so he's at eye level with me. "Don't pry too deep into Archer's mind...unless you want to hear filthy thoughts about yourself." I release the stick and the white ball hits into the others with a resounding *CRACK*. I laugh as the balls scatter into the holes and Jai curses.

"You're gonna need to do better than that to throw me off," I tsk as I circle the table. Jai howls, his laugh echoing through the corridor, as Archer comes back in with a newly filled carafe of wine.

AFTER A FEW GAMES, Jai excuses himself, leaving Archer and me alone in the suite. He sits at the piano, expertly playing the keys even though his body is swaying from the liquor. I'm curled on the couch, listening and I have a glass of wine hanging from my hand. Even though I've stopped drinking eons ago, I'm still entirely too tipsy to be considered professional.

The melody Archer plays is light, playful. The music invades my senses and I start dancing in my seat, letting my body sway gently as the runs deftly tinkle from his fingers. Archer looks over his shoulder at me and smiles, his fingers never stopping

"You're really good at that," I muse, wobbly standing and crossing to him. He slides over on the piano bench, moving the melody slightly higher and I sit beside him.

"Piano was always my favorite lesson before my magical training," he says as he slows the melody, and it changes into something I recognize from my own lessons. I reach in my pocket for my phone and pull up a copy of the music, propping it on the music stand when I find it. He circles back to the start of the selection and I take the lower harmony, managing to keep up even if it's not as elegantly played.

I hit a wrong note and it grates on the melody, causing me to wince and Archer to chuckle and keep playing. I lose my place in the music and give up, resigning myself to listen and watch his fingers move skillfully over the keys. When the song is over, I applaud, and he playfully bows.

"Well since you can play..." he gestures to the piano, leaning back. I give him a mock salute and position my hands.

"Don't judge," I warn. "I haven't played in a long time."

I take a deep breath and start to play my lullaby, the only song I know by heart. I allow the music to flow through me, the melody pouring out through my fingers and the rich notes filling the room. I get lost in the calming energy it provides, letting it soothe my soul like a balm.

A light melody takes me by surprise, and I realize Archer has joined me, playing the octave above. His notes add an ethereal quality to the lullaby which makes me smile. We move in perfect harmony, the music wrapping around us like its own form of magic. At the end of the phrase, my eyes lift to meet his as the last notes linger in the air.

"Beautiful," Archer murmurs, and my heart stutters in my chest.

"Thank you," I whisper, my voice breaking. We sit like that, staring into each other's eyes for a long time until Archer clears his throat and begins to play a rowdy song I've heard frequently in pubs.

"This is probably better suited for our mood," he says, and a laugh croaks from my throat. I sing along because I vaguely remember the words of the barroom song. When I'm uncertain, I make up my own, which has Archer howling with laughter. We sit in the game room playing different songs until our buzz wears off and we slink back to our rooms to nap off our mid-day hangover.

Chapter Eight

A WOMAN HOLDS ME as we read a book, her dark hair tickling my cheek.

I zoom through a stone hallway on a broom, servants trailing after me screaming in alarm.

There's a white-hot fire surrounding everything. A female I can't see screams.

I'm leaning in to kiss a girl with spiraling red curls.

The red-haired girl looks up at me, as I'm positioned over her on a bed.

"UGH!" Archer exclaims, and I extract my mind out of his.

I always feel a little dirty after using Mind Magic to see someone's memories outside of work. But it's a necessary evil, especially since Archer *needs* to learn how to shield ASAP. The prince flops horizontally on a golden chaise lounge in the sitting room, throwing an arm over his face.

"I suck," he exclaims. The hand not over his eyes gropes along the floor next to the couch until it finds his glass of ale, which he brings to his lips and gulps down. Alcohol unfortunately can't be blamed for his lack of success because his mind is still completely clear.

"Maybe we're approaching this wrong," I say, folding my legs underneath me in my high back armchair. "Let's go back to the basics," I announce, taking a sip of my drink.

"I learned how to make a shield," Archer glowers.

"Prove it. Tell me how you put it up."

"I imagine a forcefield," he says with a heavy sigh. I pause, waiting for more, but he just stares at me.

"Okay..." I search for the right words, but I'm not a teacher and I don't think anyone has ever called me nurturing. "What does a forcefield look like?"

Archer shrugs. "It's an invisible barrier."

"So how would you know if there are holes in it?" I ask and Archer stares at me blankly. "Okay, next question. Can you feel when I'm inside your mind?"

"Yes," he grumbles.

"That's a start. Sit up," I command using my captain's voice. He swings his legs to the floor and bends down so his elbows rest on his knees. I pull my chair closer to him so our knees touch, and I mimic his pose.

"We're going to focus on one memory, something recent so it's at the forefront of your mind. Let's use lunch today." He eyes me skeptically. "I want you to close your eyes and picture the three of us sitting at the table having lunch." Archer closes his eyes and nods.

"Good. Now, I want you to imagine a stone wall being built, brick by brick around this memory. Just this one. Imagine it circling the three of us, don't leave any gaps. Tell me when that's done." Archer is still for a moment, and then he nods.

I reach out tentatively with my mind. I flit through a couple of different memories, moving around the passages in his mind. I feel him flinch as I see the fire again, but I don't linger there. That's not what I'm looking for. My magic continues to seep through, invading his mind until I find resistance. I hone into that feeling, tracing it to a small solid wall that rises through his mind like a parapet of stone.

Good My mind to speaks to his. *Now, hold that wall.*

I feel his hesitation briefly before I fling my magic at the wall. It clangs around, searching for a way in, a crack in the brickwork. When I can't find one, I use my magic like a battering ram, trying to break it down with sheer force. It remains solid. After a few minutes, I retreat out of his mind completely and he releases a long breath.

"Nicely done," I say, and his eyes open to find me.

"But most of my mind is still unguarded." He still looks incredibly relieved despite this revelation, his body sagging forward.

"We'll get there," I assure him. "For tonight, I want you to put a wall around anything sensitive to the mission. That way the information will be safe if we encounter any Dark Witches that can use Mind Magic."

Archer nods in agreement, and I can see him already starting to work deep within his mind. I take a long swig of ale, the alcohol helping to cure my cumulative hangover. I think I've drunk more in the past twenty-four hours than I have all month.

"So...how much did you see?" Archer asks, tensing.

"Mostly just pictures," I respond, keeping my voice casual. "I tried not to stay in any memory too long. I'm not trying to pry."

"I feel like you know all my secrets now," he says softly, his eyes lowering to his ale.

"I really don't. But if I wanted to, I could. Which is why shielding is so important."

"When did you learn?"

"When I was five," I tell him, and he scoffs. "I'm serious. My mom was obsessive after my dad..." *Tortured me and went to prison.* "She wanted to make sure I was safe, so she taught me to shield my mind."

"Did she teach you to create channels, too?" he asks.

I nod. "She did. I can teach you too once you've mastered shielding."

"And you made one for us today?" I nod. "And it's open?"

Yes. And it will be, I say using the communication line between our minds. *At least until our mission is over. Then I'll close it back up.*

But I can knock if I need you? he mentally asks, and I nod. *How long of a range do you have on these?*

I have one with my friend who's in Salem, so pretty far.

Archer nods, looking distracted. I let it sit for a minute, but then the silence turns brooding.

"Archer?" I say aloud, and he meets my gaze, his eyes dark.

"I haven't seen her face in so long," he whispers taking another long drink.

"The redhead?"

"No...well yeah. But I meant my mom."

I'm an idiot. I know I saw at least one vision of the prince with his mother during my probing. I'm embarrassed to say I don't know much about Queen Elissa, except she died when I was a child and my mother cried...which is a rarity, to say the least.

"Do you want to tell me about her?" I ask tentatively and Archer lets out a short, strangled exhale.

"She would hate this mission. She always thought the Moment of Valor was a stupid tradition." His eyes meet mine, their hue golden in the light of the sitting room. "In a weird way, you remind me of her."

My heart does a little leap, which I pointedly ignore. I lean back in my chair, propping my one arm up on the armrest and cocking my head to the side. "So, she was beautiful? Brilliant? Had a quick wit and was a total badass?"

"Mostly she was incredibly modest," he ribs, but his smile doesn't last. "The fire you saw...that was when she died. I was eight."

"How?" I ask with a gasp. Despite what mortals think, a witch dying in a fire is unheard of. Flames can burn us the same as any other person, but most of us know spells that can control them.

"When my Element manifested, I was so excited," Archer says, his eyes focusing on the amber liquid in his glass. "My parents were also both Fire Elementals, so they encouraged me to play with fire and made sure the staff was armed with extinguishing spells.

"One day, the flames came out white. It spread so quickly that my nanny couldn't extinguish them. I was trapped inside my room. My mother appeared and ran through the fire to get me. Because of her element, she shouldn't have been touched by the flames, but it attacked her skin right away. It...it looked like it ate her alive. She tossed me from the room before it consumed her. For some reason, the flames didn't touch me." He takes a sip of his ale, swallowing thickly.

"I haven't used my raw magic much since. I had such a panic attack during my first Battle Magic class that Father called the school and made special arrangements to have me excused. I was supposed to train with Marcus, but he never pushed it."

"You should have told me. I wouldn't have made you—" he waves me off.

"You were right. I need to know how to defend myself and the Kingdom."

We sit in silence for a few moments, the weight of Archer's revelation sitting between us. After a while, he takes a shaky breath, and when he looks back at me, I can see he's buried that particular memory.

"So, since you saw all my secrets," Archer says, pasting a small smirk on his face, "can I ask you something?"

"You can ask...I might not answer," I flash a smile over my cup as I drink deeply. He leans back putting one arm over the back of the chaise and propping his ankle up on his opposite knee.

"Do you have many friends?" he asks, his gaze locked onto me as if he can bore directly into my head. The question should be light, but it's weighted. I nervously reach to my hair tie and pull my hair loose, running my fingers through it before I shake my head *no*. "Why not?"

I sigh, heavily. "Girls don't like me...they're usually threatened. And guys just want to get in my pants. Combine that with my power, and the fact that I never was in a class or a unit for very long..." I shrug and take another drink, my glass getting woefully empty. "I have a best friend, Edina. She's the one in Salem."

He nods. "I really only have Jamison," he says thoughtfully. "The courtiers are all fake, and honestly I hate spending time with them. Everyone else is paid to hang out with me." I look down into my glass as guilt washes over me. "I didn't mean you," he amends.

"I wouldn't be here if I didn't want to be," I say honestly, and I mean it. I could very easily have declined his lunch invitation, stayed in my room the whole day keeping my eyes and ears open. But there's something about the prince that makes me want to know more, makes me want to linger in his presence. It's warm... comfortable. And probably completely inappropriate but I don't care.

"Tell me about the redhead," I say, waving my hand so that both our glasses refill, and Archer gives me a look that says his mind is blown. "Duplicating spell," I explain taking another sip.

"I'll have to remember that one." He drinks, ignoring my question. I stare him down until his eyes finally meet mine again. "What do you want to know?" he asks with a smirk.

"How dirty would it have gotten if I hung out in that last memory?" Archer chokes on his ale, and I cackle.

"You would have seen some shit go down," he winks.

"Quite literally, I imagine," I quip and Archer shakes his head, his cheeks turning bright red.

"That memory," he begins as my laughter dies, "was our...well my first time." I see a hint of sadness creep in. "Her name is Adeline. We were together for almost four years. We broke up a few months ago."

"Why?" I ask gently.

"She didn't want to be a queen." He says the fact like it's so simple. And at that moment, I realize just how similar our lives are.

"Did you propose?" I ask.

"No. But we both knew that's where we were headed," he says, his eyes clouding over. "Your turn."

"What do you want to know?"

"Hmm," Archer brings one hand up to stroke his chin. "Last relationship or first time...you pick."

"Last relationship or last...fling?"

"Both."

I consider for a moment. "Last fling was last night," I admit, and Archer chokes on his ale again. "One of the recruits I met at a party. Honestly, I still don't remember his name. Do you judge me?"

"No judgments here," Archer says, holding up his hands. Then he points to my glass with his wand and refills it with the duplicating spell. *He's incorrigible.* "Last relationship?"

"My last relationship was with a musician. I was eighteen and my best friend and I took off the summer before I joined the Dragons to follow his band on their American tour. We were together for two years and we broke up in September."

"What band?" he asks and I groan.

"I don't want to tell you."

"Come on, I can't be any more intimidated than I already am."

I sigh. "Nocturn." Archer's face falls.

"You dated Rodger from Nocturn." I feel myself physically cringe. "Holy shit. They're the biggest band in the Kingdom right now. Is it true he's a werewolf?"

"No, but I wish it were. I have a weird fascination with werewolves." I flash Archer a smile, but he is still in total shock.

"Fuck," he swears and downs the rest of his beer. "How am I supposed to compete with Rodger from Nocturn?"

"Pretty sure prince trumps rock star." It slips out before I can stop myself and the breath leaves my body as Archer gives me a slow, cocky smile.

"Not that it matters," I say. "Because we're not sleeping together."

"Of course," Archer says, his smile unmoving.

"I'm serious. I'm your guard."

"And you wouldn't be able to keep an eye on me if we were having sex?" he asks.

"Depends on the position," I shoot back at him.

He stares at me for an eternity before letting out a deep chuckle that clangs through my body. *Fuck me. I need to buy a filter because clearly mine's broken.*

"Relax, I'm joking," he says, his voice somehow lower, and more gravely. I feel the heat flood my cheeks, because even though he says he's joking I know he's not. The tension between us is tangible, and I'm totally encouraging it.

"You know," I begin feigning anger, "you were so awkward when I met you. Where did that go?"

"You can't blame me for that," he chuckles. "Within the first three seconds of meeting you, you heard how hot I think you are."

"You didn't say hot, exactly."

"No," he says thoughtfully, his eyes scanning me making me feel exposed. "I said stunning. And I stand by that." I blush like a freaking school girl. I'm not exactly known for my humility, and I know how to take a compliment. I don't know what it is about this guy that makes me feel all giddy and off-kilter.

"Can I tell you something honestly?" he asks.

"Should I be afraid?"

"I like you," he states, and my breath hitches, but Archer holds up his hand. "I think we could be really good friends. And I—neither of us have enough people we count as friends. I wouldn't want to mess that up, you know?"

I nod. *Good, that's exactly how I feel.* And yet, as the breath settles back in my body, it feels heavy in my chest.

Chapter Nine

THE MORNING OF THE mission, I exit the palace before the sun has risen, stopping on a small patch of lawn in front of the drawbridge. I take a deep inhale and slowly release it, condensation puffing from my lips. The biting wind is already seeping through my crimson leathers and my subsequent layers, and it will only get colder once we're in the air.

I met the team of six who will be escorting the prince to Sicily yesterday, none of whom I've worked with before. Well, except for our invaluable healer, an older man named Coleman, who I met my first week stationed in headquarters.

This is the first time in two days that I've left Archer's side, leaving him in the care of his usual guards so I can make final preparations for our departure. Jacobs, a scruffy sergeant with dark hair brings out an armful of broomsticks and props them against the palace wall behind me. With a terse smile that's hidden beneath a thick mustache, he heads back into the palace, leaving me to magically test the brooms for any signs of foul play.

Across the lawn, Justin and Jared O'Malley, identical twins with pale skin and red hair, are shrinking our luggage so that all our supplies can fit in two backpacks. I unsuccessfully tried to tell them apart earlier, so I have since made the executive decision to call them by their surname. The remaining members of our team are all milling about, adding gloves to their ensembles, or frantically using their cell phones for the last time before we leave.

When I'm almost done attending the brooms, Archer comes out cradling a small flame in his hand, wearing a black cloak so thick and long that I can only see a hint of the leathers he wears beneath. His skin is pale and the bags under his eyes are pronounced, giving away his terror. I fight the impulse to hug him as he brings his broom to me for testing.

"A warming spell will use less energy if you're cold," I advise, and Archer shrugs but extinguishes his flame.

By the time I finish up with the brooms, everyone is ready and waiting on me. I regard the men all wearing the same battle leathers, and the same excited yet wary expression. Our black tunics are designed to protect against the cold, but I can tell some also wear extra layers like me, though Archer is the only one of us in a cloak. I close my eyes, willing this mission to go well before I do a headcount and gather everyone in the center of the yard.

"Remember," I say squaring my shoulders, "we fly for three four-hour blocks, thirty-minute breaks in between flying. We should reach our first campsite tonight before sundown if the wind is with us. Does everyone have the coordinates in case we get separated?" Everyone nods.

I reach into their minds, opening the channel I created yesterday during our first meeting. *Count off in here, please.* Each of the sergeants, plus Coleman and Archer, acknowledges that they can hear me through the channel. *Good,* I reply once Archer finishes the count. *Remember keep this channel free of chatter.*

"If anything goes wrong," I say aloud, "we split off as discussed and meet at the safe house in the Alps. Storms are rolling in over the mountains so we should be able to lose a tail but keep an eye on your six as you approach. Any questions?"

"Captain?" A woman's voice draws my attention, and all the Dragons bow as I turn and find my mother and Marcus striding through the open drawbridge.

"We wanted to wish you all a safe trip," Mom says as I hastily bow as well. Marcus walks right over to Archer and embraces him roughly, whispering something too low for me to hear. When they emerge from the hug, Archer looks much less somber.

"Captain, a word?" Marcus says, directing his attention to me. He takes my arm and leads me to a more secluded spot behind a watchtower.

"Katie there's been a disturbance near Marseille," Marcus murmurs as my attention peaks. "There was an expulsion of Dark Magic late last night. I know the plan was to fly through France and cross into Italy at sea, but you may want to stay inland."

"But the Alps—" I contest, and Marcus gives a heavy sigh. November weather may be mild where we're going, but the Alps could be disastrous to cross by broom at this time of year.

"I know." Marcus runs a hand over his face. "Where are you camping tonight?"

"Outside of Lyons." The plan is to cross the English Channel early this morning and hopefully cover most of the length of

France. Then we'll continue south and cross the Mediterranean into Italy before flying over land to Sicily. But Marcus's nerves are worrying me, so I rack my brain for another solution.

"Should we switch to mortal transportation?" I ask. "A plane or even a car--"

"Too closely monitored," Marcus says, shaking his head. "Even the highways are watched constantly, and you need the element of surprise. That's why you're camping instead of staying in a mortal hotel, and why you're leaving your phones here. If word gets out that you're on the move—" I nod. I knew Marcus would have a reason for the incognito level of travel, even if I didn't hear them when I signed up for the mission.

"Stay the course for now," he says firmly. "Troops are headed to Marseilles to check out the situation, so I'll know more by tonight. Open the channel with your mom and me when you land, and I'll update you."

"Yes General," I say before dropping pretense. He wraps me in a hug, and I lean into the warmth, letting his strength seep into my body and quiet the butterflies that have started.

"Be safe," he whispers in my ear before planting a kiss on my cheek. I return to the rest of the soldiers, where my mother gives me a stiff hug and a nod before heading back inside. *Typical.*

Everyone grabs a broom from the pile, and the twins shoulder the deceptively light backpacks.

"Okay men," I announce, and all eyes turn to me. "Let's fly."

Everyone straddles their brooms and, on my signal, we kick off from the ground, shooting straight into the dark sky. Because we're over London, we rise high above the clouds to avoid prying mortal eyes. My ears pop as we ascend upwards, the wind tugging at my braided hair and already whipping around my layers.

We level off and begin to fly south in a hexagon formation. A sergeant with dark hair and almond-shaped eyes, Soto, and a tan sergeant with blonde hair whose name I'm forgetting lead the group of us. The twins take up right and left flanks, and Jacobs and Jefferson, a behemoth of a man with ebony hair and skin take up the rear. The healer, Coleman, and I fly beside each of the twins and the dead center of our little bubble is Archer. While the rest of the men will rotate positions during the journey, I'll always fly next to the prince, ready to take him to safety if anything goes amiss.

Captain, Soto's voice echoes through the open channel. *There is a plane heading towards us, we should rise a little further until we're past Paris.*

Let's do it—everyone on Soto's lead. I watch as his dark hair juts upwards, and the rest of us follow him higher into the clouds. We push past another layer of cloud cover, misty rainwater soaking me in the process. When we finally level back out, the air is peaceful, and I catch a glimpse of the sun beginning to rise as I perform a quick-drying spell on my clothes to remove the moisture.

We fly in silence, nothing around us but open air and clouds. Even the wind up here doesn't seem as intrusive. My shoulders relax, and I release the tension I've been holding in my brow. The wisps of hair the earlier wind pulled from my braid flutter against my skin, but I don't mind. I'd spend all my time up here if I could; flying gives me a sense of freedom I've yet to find anywhere else. I sink into that feeling and let myself forget my responsibilities for a moment and just become one with the wind.

I steal a look at Archer about an hour in, watching his cloak billowing out around him. He has a look of wild abandon on his face, true happiness, that I know is mirrored in my own. I can't help but smile as I watch him in his element. He notices my glance and flashes me a grin.

How's it going, your highness?

Better now that we're in the air. I cast my eyes forward, nodding to one of the twins who gives me a hand signal before dropping to do a perimeter scan. I'm tense until he returns into formation and confirms that all is well.

You belong on a broom, Archer sends privately. I detect a hint of lust in his tone, which I'm probably imagining, but ignoring either way.

I can take the lead next time we switch positions. Archer offers. *What do you say, Captain? Want to lead the group with me?*

The others wouldn't be able to keep up. I hear his haughty laughter despite the wind and the distance. I know he's probably bored being sandwiched in the middle of the group, but it's what needs to be done.

Ready for training, your majesty? I ask.

We're training? Here? I can feel his internal groan before I throw my Mind Magic at the barriers he's created.

UGHH a little warning next time, Archer whines. I catch a glimpse of a memory of him and his father before his mental shield snaps up tight.

You can do better than that, I taunt as I begin another assault. This time I can't find any cracks that let me in. Archer must sense this and gives me a triumphant smile.

Good work, I say, letting him bask in his temporary victory. *Now I'll stop going easy on you.*

What? he asks, but I don't give him any extra time to react before I blast down one of his mental shields with the force of a charging rhino. He scrambles to try and repair it, but I move on to another, and then another, breaking down each defense.

Force me out, I command.

How the fuck do I do that? Archer throws up a small barrier around a certain memory, and I can feel the importance radiating from this spot. Which makes it the perfect place to make a stand.

What does my Mind Magic look like to you? I ask, pausing my assault.

Like a web of blue light, he sighs.

Imagine your mind is its own color light. Use that to push against mine and kick me out. As you go, resurrect those shields so I can't come back in.

I attack the sensitive memory again. The shield holds against me, but I can feel it weakening against my attack. Suddenly a surge of red-light blasts into me, creating a pulsing in my head.

Like that? Archer asks and keeps hammering at my Mind Magic. I struggle against it until I start to feel lightheaded, and then I withdraw my magic.

Like that, I concede. He whoops and punches the sky, eliciting confused looks from our team. I wait until the thumping in my head quells before I give him a devious smile. *Again.*

Chapter Ten

FOUR HOURS IN, WE stop to stretch our legs and have a bite to eat. Archer's gotten the hang of forcing me out of his mind, but he still hasn't mastered not letting me in at all. It's still great progress for just a few short days, but we still have work to do.

We find a secluded spot along the Seine outside of a town called Melun, settling behind a row of tall bushes that line a walking path by the riverbank. I throw up a quick cloaking shield so that any mortals who walk by won't notice us. It's not good enough to hide us from Dark Witches, but we won't be staying long. Now that we're back on land and the sun has risen, the weather is much warmer. I tuck myself between the hedges to take off my leather vest and one of the tunics I'm wearing, carefully shrinking the clothing so I can store them in my pocket. When I return, one of the twins hands me an apple and a bit of jerky.

"I should have brought coffee," I grumble taking a bite of my apple.

"There's a small town not too far from here Captain," the blonde sergeant says. "Want me to fly over? I could use a cup too." I shake my head; we have a schedule to keep, and we should avoid mortal towns as much as possible. I know we'll have to stop in one tonight for dinner, so even though my head is screaming in protest, I'll skip the coffee for now.

"You can't just...manifest coffee?" Archer asks. I laugh him off thinking he's kidding, but my laughter dies in my throat when I notice the curious glances of the other guards.

There are a few things that witches can't do and one of them is create something from nothing. I could make coffee without heat or a grinder if I had coffee beans and water, but I can't just reach into the air and pull out a cup.

"Can *you?*" My tone is a little more biting than I intend it to be, but I'm honestly a little peeved by the question.

"No...but I also need a wand to do spells," Archer quips back.

"My magic obeys the natural order, just like everyone else's," I say sternly, hoping to squash this conversation.

"So, you can't teleport either?" the blonde sergeant asks. I still, and the other guards' mouths drop open. It's then I realize what they're really asking me, and my blood runs cold.

Teleportation is considered Dark Magic, and it was taught to a select handful of Dark Witches by the Fae. The Fae left the mortal realm almost two hundred years ago and haven't been welcome here since. They're ruthless creatures who murder for sport and delight in cruelty. Manifesting items from thin air, teleportation, flying, and necromancy are all magical qualities of the Fae. Either accusation is tantamount to a prison sentence.

"If I could teleport, why would we be flying?" I hiss, my lightning crackling under my skin. The blonde shrugs.

"Maybe you can't teleport more than one person," he suggests, and the other sergeants give him a death glare. "No offense meant, Captain."

"I'm a human witch, for the record." I don't owe them an explanation, but at this point, I'm so pissed off, I can't control my mouth. "And I don't have Dark Magic. See?" I bring my lightning to my fingertips, proving my point, and the men instinctively back up a step.

I turn on my heel and storm away from the group, trying to calm the magic surging in my veins. I stride past the hedges and take a seat on a bench overlooking the blue-green water of the river. I breathe deeply, focusing on the jagged moss-covered rocks and the retaining wall that make up the opposite riverbank. I watch the mortals in the three- and four-story houses all painted the same weather-stained white with the same sloped brown roofs with cracked shingles. A young girl's laughter drifts across the river, and my magic settles back down as I watch her playing with an older woman.

This isn't the first time someone's questioned my lineage or my power. I've heard all kinds of assumptions about why my magic is so much stronger, why I don't need a wand. I asked my mother once, and she told me I was given a gift and that my job wasn't to question it but to learn how to wield it properly.

A twig snaps behind me, and I throw my mind out in a web to see who is approaching. I'm not really in the mood to talk to anyone, but I also don't discourage him from sitting on the bench beside me. Archer extends his canteen, his gaze drilling into the side of my face as I ignore him, focusing on the little mortal girl playing.

"I'm sorry," he murmurs as I grab the canteen and take a swig without meeting his eye.

"You can shock me if you want," Archer tries, and I cave, glaring in his direction as he gives me a cheeky smile.

"Or I can just use my Dark powers to blast you back to the palace," I monotone.

"I should have talked to you about all that in private," he sighs.

"*All that.*" My head bobs in consideration. "So, you still think it could be true." It's not a question, but I still wait for an answer.

"I don't think you have Dark Magic," Archer says carefully. "I thought you might have some Fae ties. But like...super distantly." He flashes that smile again like this is all some kind of a joke. Like being any part Fae isn't cause to be executed or banished.

"Would you have me thrown in the dungeon if I was?" I seethe.

"Only if you're into that," he goads, and I resolutely swallow the chuckle that tries to escape my lips. Archer sighs. "It's just... I've never met anyone like you before. With your level of power, I mean."

"So that automatically makes me another race?"

"No," Archer huffs. "I guess part of me hoped that maybe you were."

"Why?" I breathe, my anger fading into something akin to hurt, not that I let him see it.

"If you were something...*extra*, then at least there's a reason you're so much better than me. Instead of me just being some sub-par witch." His shoulders droop with self-deprecation, and I soften, the need to comfort him overwhelming my anger.

"My father is a Dark Witch," I blurt, and Archer's eyebrows hit his hairline. "And he...he's not a good man."

"Did he hurt you?" Archer asks, his knuckles turning white as his hands fist.

"Yes," I admit, looking down at my boots. "But that's why what you said, what everyone thought..." I take a deep breath, organizing my thoughts.

"I work hard to distance myself from his legacy," I say finally, meeting Archer's gaze. The hedge beside him is on fire and Archer is practically shaking in rage.

"Fuck," I swear and direct water from the river to the bush, extinguishing the blaze. Archer shakes his head and looks between his hands and me.

"I—I did that?" he asks, and I nod. "Fuck, I didn't even know—"

"When I started training in Battle Magic, the same thing would happen to me," I reassure him. "I still lose control occasionally, but it got better once I was trained."

Archer reaches towards me but thinks better of it and drops his hands back in his lap. "I'm so sorry I ever—"

I push to my feet and take a fighting stance, cutting him off.

"Come on then," I announce. "You said I could shock you, right?"

"Shit, yeah" Archer stands and braces himself.

"Good. Try and stop me." I give him a second to form a shield of fire before I unleash my lightning. I laugh as I get past his defenses and lightly zap his arm.

"You got me," he says, raising his arms in surrender. "Can we go back to the group now?"

"Not until you can beat me, *your highness*." Which of course, he won't. And so, we continue sparring until it's time to head back into the air.

As much as I love flying, hours upon hours spent above the clouds can be a bit monotonous. There's nothing but sky in all directions, and without scenery to focus on, it's hard to keep my mind from wandering to my father. I've successfully ignored the fact that he's out of prison since I heard the news, but with no other distractions, the thoughts bombard me.

How the hell did he get out? The magical prison is a fortress in the middle of the ocean. The iron bars are spelled so that no magic can be used inside, not even by the guards. And the guards themselves are rumored to be centaurs, so they're fast and brutal and don't imprison you again if they catch you trying to escape.

My mother didn't say it, but I could tell she was scared, which means he's coming to finish what he started. I believe my mother when she says my father isn't in Sicily...but I can't shake the feeling that he's close.

What's wrong? Archer asks through our mental channel, and I shake my head, realizing Soto has begun our descent without me. I nudge my broom downwards and fall back in line with the group.

Nothing.

You're crying, Archer observes as a tear slides down my cheek and off my chin.

It's just the wind. I don't want to worry him. My issues with my father have nothing to do with the mission. Archer doesn't press, but I can feel his eyes on me.

We break through the clouds, flying over vast green fields dotted sporadically with brown rooftops. The sun has dipped over the hills in the distance, vibrantly coloring the sky with its dying rays. We continue our subtle descent until we land at the edge of a forest outside Lyons, our campsite for the evening. We move through the trees speckled with occasional russet, yellow, and red leaves, but most have fallen and crunch beneath our feet as we find a spot away from the mortal hiking trails. Even though we're stiff and cold, we begin setting up camp, removing all our provisions and magicking them back to their original size and weights.

The blonde sergeant, whose name Archer tells me is Deavers, and Soto head into the city proper to get us provisions as the rest of us gather firewood and set up the tents. I almost kiss Deavers when he returns from town with a cup of coffee and a croissant for me as an apology. Camp is erected quickly, the four tents we brought with us set up in a semi-circle around the fire pit that Jefferson digs, and bedrolls distributed amongst them. Once I get the fire started, the sergeants and I all sit on benches carved from logs with someone's Earth magic, watching as Coleman cooks the chickens the men brought back from the town butcher.

"Why didn't you buy food that was already cooked?" Jefferson asks the men who went to the market.

"We're camping!" Deavers responds enthusiastically. Soto just shakes his head, and everyone chuckles easily. The mood is marginally less tense than this morning, or even at lunchtime.

"Captain, next time you need to give them specific orders," Jefferson notes, the laugh still echoing in his throat.

"Next time, you're on town duty Jefferson," I say raising my cup of coffee, and Jefferson raises his canteen in return.

I feel a pulse on one of my mental channels, and I excuse myself, leaving my coffee by the fire and heading to my tent. I duck under the canvas opening and crash into Archer, the two of us falling into the tent and landing in a tangle of limbs.

"Sorry!" I breathe, pushing myself up and trying to figure out how to remove my body from his without doing any further injury. His eyes meet mine as I hover over him, and my mind clouds of anything but the sensation of his body pressed against mine.

He props one arm underneath him, reducing the space between our faces to inches, and his other braces my shoulder. But somehow, it feels like he's drawing me in rather than pushing me away.

He swallows hard, and I feel a blush creeping up my cheeks. "Sorry," I repeat. The word snaps us both out of the haze we were in, and I roll off to the side to try and escape him.

"Are we...are you in here with me?" Archer asks tentatively.

"Yep. I'm your guard," I respond, trying and failing to sound professional. He stands, and I struggle to do the same. There isn't much room for both of us to be standing, let alone sleeping in here together later. Our bedrolls are practically overlapping.

"Which one is yours?" I ask. He points to the bedroll on the left side, so I plop down cross-legged on the right.

"I have to talk to Marcus. Can I have the tent for a minute?" I ask as the brush against the channel in my mind comes again.

"Oh, yeah sure. I'll go get dinner," he says quickly, clambering out the tent flap.

I release a heavy breath as I watch him go, making a mental note to expand the tent a little further before bedtime. The knocking down the mental channel becomes more persistent and I swear before opening it.

Katie? His voice flies down, clearly agitated.

Marcus. We landed about thirty minutes ago and set up camp. We're—

Don't say your location. He sounds panicked and my heart does a small jump. The mental channels I create should be completely secure, so I'm not sure why he's so worried. *The troops that investigated Marseille didn't find anything.*

That's good.

No, Katie. There was no trace of anyone ever having been there. Whatever caused the disturbance was cleared and removed.

That means they're crazy, scary powerful, I surmise eloquently.

All magic, especially Dark Magic, has a signature and leaves a residue behind which is extremely hard to remove. For them to completely remove all traces means we can't track their next movements. They could still be in Marseille, back in London, or right outside our campsite for all we know.

The call is yours, Captain, Marcus says. *But there is a blizzard making its way through the Swiss Alps.*

Fuck, I curse, and Marcus echoes my sentiment. Dark Witches or blizzard? Which is the lesser of two evils?

Well, I start tentatively, *if they're not in Marseille then we'll travel that way and hope they've moved on. But I'll tell the team to be on high alert and we'll go over our backup plans in detail tonight.*

That's what I would have done too. Marcus's reassurance makes me feel about one percent better about the odds of this trip. I really hope the team knows what they signed up for. *Keep in touch.* And with that, I feel him close off his end of the channel.

Chapter Eleven

THE SOUND OF ROARING laughter greets me as I exit my tent, and I linger in the opening, hesitant to ruin everyone's fun.

I can wait until after dinner to tell them about the Dark Witches.

I use the reprieve to quickly mutter a shielding spell around our vicinity. The magic shimmers before turning translucent once more, and I breathe a sigh of relief knowing my team is safe for now.

I'm about to pop back into the tent and leave them to their fun when Archer catches my eye.

"Katie, come join us," he calls, and the laughter dies down. I make a sound of protest, but Archer jumps up from his log and crosses the space between us in three long strides.

"Come play with us," he says jovially, and then dips his voice so that only I can hear him. "Let them get to know you." He grabs my hand and pulls me towards the fire.

"I can take first watch—" I say, but Jacobs shakes his head, tossing his empty plate next to the fire.

"I've got it, Captain," he says and doesn't wait another second before rushing off to the perimeter of the camp.

Archer pats the seat beside him, and I hesitantly lower myself to the bench, nodding my thanks when Coleman passes me a plate and Deavers hands me the coffee cup I abandoned earlier.

"What are you playing?" I ask, breaking the silence. I take a bite of my chicken and groan in delight. Somehow Coleman has managed to spice the skin so it's crispy and delicious and keep the meat inside moist. I may never go camping without him again.

"Truth or Dare," Jefferson says.

"So that's why Jacobs hightailed it out of here?" I ask, and the men laugh at my observation. "I don't think I should—"

Archer nudges my shoulder. "Truth or Dare?" he asks, and everyone sits forward on the edge of their seats.

"Fine," I say rolling my eyes. "Truth."

"Oh, I have one," Deavers says. I arch my eyes expectantly and Archer motions for him to take over. "There's a rumor you dated Rodger from Nocturn."

"Yeah, that's true." Everyone always asks that question, even though it's pretty much common knowledge. We were a regular feature in the tabloids, much to my mother's chagrin.

"That wasn't my question," he says, his eyes lighting excitedly. "Was he into anything weird?"

"I mean...he collected mortal video games if that's what you mean?" I offer and Deavers shakes his head.

"I mean like...in the bedroom." I choke on my coffee.

"Oh, yeah definitely," I say amidst a laugh. "And there's no way in hell am I telling you what it was."

Deavers opens his mouth like he's about to ask a question, but decides the better of it and grumbles, "Yes, Captain."

"Deavers, you just asked me about my ex-boyfriend's kinks. You can call me Katie." The men all chuckle, and I allow myself to sink into the camaraderie.

We play for hours, the questions bouncing around, and soon I'm cackling alongside everyone else. One of the O'Malley twins eyes me as he takes out a flask, but relaxes when I grab it from him and take a swig myself, the liquor making things infinitely funnier. My mother would not approve.

"Your Highness," Soto directs to Archer. Archer grabs the flask and takes a swig before declaring *truth*.

"If you weren't born a prince, what would you want to do with your life?"

"Fly," Archer says without hesitation.

"You sound like you've thought of this before," I murmur as the other guards start talking amongst themselves about the relay championship. Archer shrugs.

Jacobs comes back to the fire to switch out with one of the twins.

"Before you go, we need to talk about tomorrow," I say, halting the O'Malley twin. I stand, switching back into my captain's voice, and fill them in on what I know.

"Everyone remembers the emergency plan?" I ask and they all nod, soberly. "We'll be flying with shields up, so I'll need everyone to be ready for confrontation. It'll be hard for me to cast a shield that large and use my Battle Magic. Not impossible, just harder."

"I can barely hold up a shield and walk," one of the twins mutters. I ignore the compliment, but I can tell the other sergeants are also impressed.

"I'll need one other person to travel with Archer and me if we need to separate. Whoever comes with us needs to be fast and good with their wand." Deavers snickers at the innuendo, and soon the group is laughing again. I roll my eyes half-heartedly before joining in. Archer doesn't even crack a smile at the joke and excuses himself to our tent without another word.

I stay with the soldiers for a few more moments, going over the watch schedule and the details of tomorrow's flight. They refuse to let me take a watch tonight, and I finally give in with the promise that they'll wake me if anything happens, even if it's small. I do insist on performing a cleaning spell on the plates before I also excuse myself to the tent.

When I walk in, Archer is curled on his side, facing the outer wall of the small space. I reach my mind out tentatively and find a solid mental wall blocking my way.

"You...you're shielding!" I exclaim, and Archer nods but doesn't turn towards me. I poke around and can find no way into his mind. "Holy crap. Archer, that's...that's an amazing shield."

"You sound surprised," his voice is tense. I strip down to the tank top and leave one pair of leggings on.

"Not at all. I knew you could do it." I tell him as I kick my boots off and climb into my bedroll.

"Then why do I need an extra person guarding me tomorrow?" he shoots at me, bitterness coating his words.

"It's protocol—"

"No, it's because I'm weak." The words hang heavy in the air, and I open my mouth to dispute them, but Archer keeps talking. "You won't let me out of your sight. Hell, we're even sharing a tent."

"We only brought four," I say simply, opting for diffusing the situation rather than rising to his anger. "And it's my job to see you through this mission."

"Exactly," Archer says, sitting up and facing the front of the tent, still refusing to look at me. "When my father performed his Moment of Valor, he slew a fucking dragon by himself."

"It's not the same—"

"But me?" he continues, not hearing me. "Not only do I have an entire team of soldiers with me, but Marcus hires the best witch in the fucking Kingdom to be my babysitter. What else could that possibly mean? How is that supposed to make me feel? Because I feel fucking useless.

"Do you know what my dad told me before we left?" Archer asks, his voice is hollow, and I see him hug his knees to his chest. "Not 'good luck,' not 'come home safe.' He said I should use this time to get to know you because you would make a strong choice for a queen. He said that I could use your strength."

My mouth falls open in shock. The king has been nothing but nice to me, but that's...honestly, that's something my mother would say. I can't help the chuckle that slips out. Archer's eyes are practically glowing with anger when they turn to me.

"Are you *laughing* at me?" he hisses.

"I'm sorry, it's not funny," I say, choking down the laughter that threatens to bubble out of my mouth. "It's just the literal opposite thing my mother said to me." He glares at me until I continue.

"Right after I met you, my mother told me not to sleep with you," I say, the laughter winning and coming out in full force.

"And you're laughing because...?"

"Because what else can we do?" Archer lies back down, probably exasperated with me, but I can't tell in the darkness of the tent. My laughter dies down, and we fall into an uncomfortable silence.

"Your father's wrong though. I'd be a terrible queen," I finally say. "I can barely command six soldiers."

"Are you kidding? They adore you." Archer's tone has returned to normal, the bitterness subsided.

"They're doing all this for you, not me," I tell him, rolling on my side to face him.

"Maybe," he says with a shrug and then turns to face me as well. "But it's because they respect my position. They respect you as a person, a witch."

"They called me a Fae earlier." I remind him. "*You* called me a Fae."

"We all feel bad about that," he murmurs. "Deavers mentioned it again when you were talking to Marcus. You have to understand something."

He reaches out and brushes my shoulder, not even having to fully extend his arms to touch me in the cramped space.

"Most of them have heard hundreds of stories about you," he continues, his fingers lightly moving against my bare skin. "You don't exactly fly under the radar."

"I do crave attention," I monotone.

"It's natural to wonder if any of the rumors are true," he says, and I can't argue with him.

"Truth or Dare?" I ask, and he smiles.

"Dare."

"Tell me one rumor you've heard about me that I don't know about," I say softly.

Archer sighs. "Well, you've heard the ones about your magic..." he stalls, his hand falling away from my arm. "There's another rumor that you're a little...easy."

"*Easy?*" I bark out a laugh because that couldn't be further from the truth.

"Their words, not mine," Archer says. "Are you going to deny it?"

"That sounds an awful lot like a truth or dare question, your highness."

"Truth or Dare?" he asks, and I can hear the smile in his tone.

"Truth. But you have to answer the same question you ask me, so ask wisely."

"That's—fine," he huffs. "How many men have you been with?"

I sigh and fall silent. I can see him arch his eyebrows in the thin sliver of light from the fire outside.

"I'm counting," I tease. "Four...no five."

"Really?"

"I only have sex with men I'm dating monogamously," I admit. "Other than the one-night stand I told you about, but I'm not in a hurry to repeat that. Your turn."

"I haven't been with any men," he chuckles, and I swat at him playfully. "I've been with two girls. My ex-girlfriend and a one-night stand. You're right. It's better when there are feelings involved."

"Truth or Dare?" I ask him quickly.

"Dare." His eyes bore into mine.

"Let me train you," I whisper and Archer's eyes widen. "I know we've done a little but let me train you in Battle Magic when we get back. Real intense military-style training." I reach out and grab his hand in mine. "Prove your dad wrong. I believe that you'll be a great king. You're kind and generous and I swear it's impossible not to like you. But if he wants to see Battle Magic, let me teach you to kick ass."

"You would do that?" he asks, his eyes swimming with emotion that makes me swallow, hard. "You would make a good queen, you know." I start to protest, but he takes the hand I'm not holding and brushes a piece of hair behind my ear. His hand lingers by my cheek and my heart pounds in my chest.

"Truth or Dare?" He grazes his knuckles against my jaw, and I wet my lips. His eyes track the movement and my breath hitches in my throat.

"Dare." It's barely audible, but I see Archer's breath rise in his chest.

He leans forward and presses his lips to mine. It's soft and quick, barely a flutter, but it steals my breath and makes me desperate for more. He bends his forehead to touch mine, and for a moment we just look into each other's eyes as he waits for me to confirm that I want this. Which I do. I *so* do.

"Captain?" A voice comes from just outside the tent. I scuttle away from Archer just as one of the twins pops his head in. "Sorry to...wake you, but you want to see this."

I stare back at the prince, rendered immobile and speechless as adrenaline pounds through my veins. *Holy shit, Archer just kissed me.*

"Captain?" the O'Malley twin calls again, shaking me from my stupor. I'll have time to sort out my feelings on this later.

I give Archer a wistful smile, which he returns before rolling over. I reach for my boots, hastily tugging them on my feet before clambering out of the tent.

"What is it, O'Malley?" I ask the twin. I follow him past the dying fire to the edge of our camp.

"Look." He reaches ahead of him towards the darkness and touches the shield I created. It flares to life in front of him, completely intact before disappearing again to be translucent.

"What am I looking at? It's completely solid."

"Just a minute." He touches the shield again, this time with his wand as if he's adding a layer of magic to enhance the protection. Suddenly, a series of charred marks appear in front of us.

I curse under my breath. *Someone tried to get into our camp.* I step back, looking over the markings, and realize they aren't entry lines, but words.

Made in her Image.
Made from Magic.
Made to Conquer.
Made to Rule.

I read the lines twice, the breath leaving my lungs with every word.

"It wasn't here when I started my shift," O'Malley says. "I went to add extra magic to the shield just now and it popped up."

"I know it wasn't you," I say absently. "Wake your brother. I want two guards on watch at all times tonight. One of you should be stationed behind the prince's tent."

O'Malley nods and heads back into the camp. I turn my attention back to the words on the shield, and I allow myself exactly one moment of pure panic.

My father is in these woods.

Chapter Twelve

I'M ON THE TABLE in the darkened room, staring at the young girl with blonde curls and grey eyes and the dark man with auburn eyes. The entire room is shrouded in darkness, so they are all I can see. Lightning crackles around me, but it doesn't hurt. It soothes away my lingering pain and leaves me feeling powerful, invincible.

"Kathryn," my father says, his voice is revered, awed. I feel the lightning crackle across my eyes, as I narrow them. "Time to test your power, princess."

The girl approaches the table, her head barely clearing my perch. I shake away the heady feeling my magic gives and allow my mind to form her name...Adriana. My half-sister.

I want to show her the lightning, so different from the drab, grey clouds she calls to her hands. As if reading my mind, she nods.

"Show us," she whispers. "Show us your magic. Show father what you've been given."

Given? My brain stumbles over her words. I was born with my magic. It's beautiful and light, like sunshine on the hottest summer day. She's seen it hundreds of times since it first manifested. Why does she want me to show her now?

"Show him on me," she pleads. The lightning crackles under my skin, begging to be released.

"Kathryn, show me on Adriana," father insists, pushing Adriana down to the floor so she's bowed before me. But I know deep in my soul that the lightning will hurt her.

"No," my voice is small but sure. I won't hurt my sister.

My father calls his pitch-black magic to his hands. It whirls and writhes like it's alive as he holds it to the back of Adriana's neck. I try to call my sunshine to my hands, but all I feel is the lightning stirring.

"DO IT!" he bellows. Adriana whimpers as his magic gets closer to her.

"Stop," I beg.

"Kathryn," he intones menacingly and the lightning returns to my fingertips. I roll it around in my hand, watching it skitter along my skin, jumping across the lines in my palms.

"You know how," my father coos.

I desperately call for the sunshine, but where the rays used to exist, only lightning remains.

And at that moment, I know.

He stole my sunshine.

A strangled cry erupts from my mouth as I realize that he's taken my magic. He transformed it to this...electric charge. I want to hurt him, to pump my magic into him the way he pumped his darkness into me.

I don't even direct the lightning. It hears my thoughts and responds, erupting from my small body in a powerful wave. My *father's auburn eyes, eyes that match mine, widen as he realizes the current is rushing towards him. He can't react fast enough, and it delves into his chest. His entire body begins twitching, but instead of easing up, I call forth more.*

He looks to Adriana, who is now cowering under the table. "RUN," he squeaks before I launch another surge towards him. I feel Adriana's skirt brush past me as she runs from the room.

"Princess," he whispers, his body still aloft and flailing.

"I'm not a princess," I say in a cold, cruel voice. "You made me a queen."

His breath catches in his throat before the lightning pulses and he goes still.

Chapter Thirteen

"KATIE! KATIE!"

I jerk upright, gasping for breath, my heartbeat thundering in my ears. I'm drenched, cold sweat and tears dampening every inch of my skin. My whole body starts shaking and a strangled sob claws its way out of my throat.

I don't know how he does it, I didn't even register that he was in the room with me, but suddenly I'm in Archer's lap, nestled into his chest.

"It was just a dream," he soothes.

I reach my arms around his neck, leaning into his warmth, focusing on the steady thumping of his heart beneath my ear. My tears fall freely, halting at my lashes before they get absorbed into his shirt. His lips gently brush against my temple, still murmuring dulcet words as my eyes close and I let him comfort me.

It's been years since I've dreamt of that night. When I was younger, I'd wake up every night in the same cold sweat, imagining myself back in that room, with Dark Magic pumping into my body. I'd remember my sister's eyes, wide and afraid when I began to hurt my father. I'd remember the way his body jerked in response to my magic, and how my mother screamed when she saw him tortured at my hands. I heard his chant in every silence, those words echoing over and over.

A curse.

A promise.

It's been years, and just the sight of those words can still send me into a panic.

I don't know how long I sit wrapped in Archer's arms, but I become vaguely aware of thin rays of sunlight stretching through the canvas flaps of our tent and the muted sounds of the men breaking down camp. I've clung to the safety of this moment for too long, and yet I can't seem to tear myself away.

When I can no longer deny the day is upon us, I pull away, absently rubbing the wet splotch on Archer's shirt before meeting his concerned gaze.

"Thank you," I whisper, removing my arms from around his neck. "I'm sorry I woke you."

He brings his hand up to cup my face, his thumb scoring over my cheek as if he can erase the path of my tears. "It wasn't just a dream, was it?" he asks, and I shake my head, swallowing hard to keep the tears at bay.

"It was a warning."

TODAY'S ATMOSPHERE IS TENSE, and we haven't exchanged a word since we've taken off. Before we left, news of the words etched into our shield spread through our entire traveling party. While no one has expressly asked me the meaning, they can sense my edge, and I'm sure they guess it's related to the Dark Witches. The clouds around us are thick, and no matter how high we fly, we can't seem to escape them.

Captain, Jefferson's voice comes through the channel. *Are you seeing this?*

I ascend to see above the front of the group and see that we're flying directly into a black cloud. Apparently, even though we avoided the mountains, the winter storms have found us. I'm about to tell the group to pull up to avoid it when the cloud zooms towards us.

What the fuck? someone swears down the channel, echoing my thoughts. I push extra magic into the shield, extending it farther around us as we continue forward, slowing our pace. Suddenly the cloud disappears. Everyone is silent, eyes frantically scanning the skies.

Any idea what that was, Captain? Jacobs asks.

None at all, I respond softly. *But I don't want to be around to find out. Everyone increase speed. Let's get out of here.*

We surge forward when the cloud materializes in front of us. Jefferson and Soto in the front of the pack pull back, and all of us quickly do the same.

"Holy shit," I hear Deavers say aloud beside me.

The cloud pixelates until the image clears, revealing an army of witches in black cloaks. *It was a cloaking spell.* The realization dawns on me and a pit opens in my stomach. There are easily fifty witches floating on brooms in front of us, their faces obscured by heavy hoods, Dark Magic pooling in their hands.

Captain, we're outnumbered, Jefferson calls from the front of the pack as the spell dissolves, revealing more and more of their ranks until all I see are black cloaks.

The shield will hold, I say confidently. *Battle Magic at the ready. When you find a break in their ranks, be ready to fly.*

On some invisible signal, the entire contingent forms a giant ball of shadow and launches it at our shield. My magic shudders under its impact but holds tight as it crashes against the barrier. Instantly, the one attack makes way for thousands of small blasts that rain down on us. My men all call their elements to their hands in preparation for a fight, but I won't let these Dark Witches break our shield.

They're on our six, one of the twins shouts, panicked. *Captain, we're surrounded.* Magic blasts at us from all sides, but my shield is firm.

Hold your positions, I call out.

As suddenly as it began, the attack stops. The witches surrounding us hold their magic at the ready, but don't release it. I take the reprieve to wipe the sweat beading across my brow, but I don't allow myself to relax. We haven't seen the worst of the attack yet; I just know it.

We've got movement up front, Soto indicates, pulling my focus back to the front of our group.

A single figure parts the masses, slowly gliding towards our shield. His long hair is a pale silver and whips around his pasty face as he floats forward. His cloak billows around his thin frame, making him look like death incarnate.

He's not on a broom, Soto swears.

My breath catches as my gaze falls to his legs. The Dark Witch is completely suspended in the air, nothing more than a pool of Dark Magic keeping him aloft. It swirls around him, propelling him forward until he stops directly in front of Jefferson. He places one hand smugly on the edge of our translucent shield as if he can see its exact location. He raps his knuckles against the shield, a sinister smile spreading from his lips.

Remember your pairs, I remind them, not feeling nearly as confident about my shield now. *Stick with your partners and meet at the safehouse.*

The man extracts one long fingernail and drags it down the shield, and I feel my magic being torn apart. Rather than putting more power into the shield, I call my lightning to my hands.

Soto and Jefferson waste no time in blasting strong gusts of air through the gap, but it doesn't so much as flutter the man's silver hair. He reaches to either side of his claw mark and sends a pulse of Dark Magic so powerful I feel it rattle my teeth. The shield shatters, and the rest of the Dark army fires, launching balls of shadow at every one of us.

ARCHER, WITH ME I bellow down the channel, rocketing straight up in the sky.

Archer and Deavers follow behind me, but soon Archer is surging higher, exactly how we discussed. I spare a look below me as I rise and see the group peeling off in different directions. Entire battalions of Dark Witches follow each pair, outnumbering our groups twenty to one. But in pairs, we'll be quicker, and hopefully, the cloud cover will help put some distance between us and the huge army.

We level off and begin furiously flying east, heading for the mountains rather than the sea. Archer slows slightly to be next to me, and Deavers flies directly behind us as we head in the direction of the safehouse. A small group of Dark Witches is trailing us, but there's no sight of the silver-haired man who shredded my magic. Deavers sends spells over his shoulder as often as possible, and he takes out three of the witches following us. When they fall, more replace them. His accuracy is good, but not as good as mine.

Deavers, switch. Guard the Prince I instruct, and I begin to drop back. Once I'm beside him, he nods to me before flinging one final spell over his shoulder. As he leans forward on his broom to move forward, a blast of magic connects with his back. Our eyes connect in mutual shock before he plummets from the sky.

"DEAVERS!" I shout. Archer turns at my scream, and I throw up a quick shield between the Dark Witches and us, just in time to deflect another blast of magic. Archer's eyes dart between the witches and me, and then he nosedives after Deavers.

Archer, stop! I scream down the channel, but I'm greeted with a brick wall.

The Dark Witches notice Archer's motion, one that only an expert flyer could perform, and they take off after their prize. I curse and turn my broom into a dive, urging it down as I streak through the clouds after them. My stomach floats into my throat as I drop closer to the earth, but my eyes remain on Archer and the witches that trail him. Archer is gaining on Deavers' body, but at the rate he's diving, I don't think he'll be able to stop in time before he hits the ground. I take out the witches closing in on Archer with a well-timed blast of lightning.

When he gets within an arm's reach, Archer's hand stretches out and winds up with a fist full of bristles from Deavers' broomstick. I let out a whoop of joy as Archer secures his grip, but it's premature. A black cloud materializes beneath them, the illusion clearing to reveal a group of twenty Dark Witches with their magic all poised at Archer. In shock, he pulls up too hard and loses grip on the broomstick, and Deavers disappears as he plummets beneath the witches. I throw out a spell to hopefully slow his descent, but I lose track of him beneath the army.

ARCHER, FLY. I'll hold them off. I fling lightning at the witches, trying desperately not to hit Archer, who hovers in front of them, face pale with shock. I pull my broom next to him and ram it into his, almost throwing him off but jolting him out of his daze. His eyes meet mine, wide in terror.

"GO!" I scream and he takes off towards the mountains. Two witches begin to follow him, but I'm not letting that happen. Lightning explodes from my body, seizing every member around me. They all freeze, their bodies completely immobilized. The cloak falls off a girl close to me, her purple hair glittering as my lightning pulls it out in static. Her eyes pop out of her head when she sees me.

"It's *her*," she mouths. I send an extra jolt of magic and she jerks before going silent. I keep the lightning attached to them and I streak through the sky after Archer. He's not going at full speed; he's waiting for me.

Archer, faster. I'm right behind you. He picks up speed and I release the witches from my magic with a final pulse of electricity.

Archer and I serpentine through the skies, ascending and dropping, doubling back and sprinting forward. Doing everything we can to make sure we aren't followed. After we put more space between us and the army, I finally allow myself to take a breath and assess the damage. My thighs shake as I clench the broomstick, the release of that much magic leaving me feeling drained. We're lucky to have gotten out of there as quickly as we did. Any longer and I don't know that I would have been able to hold them off.

We reach the mountain range, and I hold my breath. Soto and Jefferson were the first to head to the safehouse, their mission to head directly there to make sure it's safe for us to converge. They should be there by now, but our channel is silent. I'm too afraid to reach out to ask everyone's location.

I can't help but replay the moment Deavers was hit. Over and over, I see him fall from the sky. I send up a silent prayer to whoever could be listening to let him be okay, but I'm not an optimist. Surviving that kind of fall would be a miracle, and we have no idea what kind of spell he was hit with. He could have been dead in the air for all we know. One glance over at Archer and I know he's thinking the same thing.

The clouds around us darken and my heart drops. Instead of turning black with Dark Magic, they turn charcoal grey, and the temperature instantly plummets. Ice begins to crystalize my broom handle, making it hard to grip even with the leather of my gloves. The wind picks up, slowly at first and then in sharp gales. We found the blizzard.

Brace yourself, I tell Archer as the snow begins to fall. The wind is wicked, tossing us around like helpless ragdolls. Heavy flakes coat my hair and land on my eyelashes, obscuring my view. The snow starts coming down sideways, pelting my cheeks and making them raw.

Archer and I descend, flying closer to the mountains on my signal. The snow is thicker down here, and the cold is seeping through all my layers, but the mountains will block the worst of the wind. At least that's the hope.

How much farther? Archer asks, losing altitude from a particularly strong gust of wind. I point ahead past a steep ridge that towers above us like a fortress.

It should be just over---

SAFE HOUSE IS COMPROMISED! Soto's voice echoes through the channel, and Archer's eyes widen as they find mine. *ABORT. ABORT.*

The channel cuts off abruptly.

Chapter Fourteen

I CURSE AND DESPERATELY try to reach down the channel to Soto. I've never experienced a channel going completely dark before. Before I can spend another second panicking about my lack of communication, I'm abruptly thrown upwards by a gust of wind. It spins me until I'm disoriented, and I lose track of Archer as I fight to regain control of my broom. A hand grips my broomstick, righting me and I shake my head to clear the vertigo that ensues. I vaguely hear the prince yelling something that's swallowed by the storm.

We need to find shelter, I send through our private channel, but there's no response. *Shit.* I try screaming, but the wind absorbs my voice. Following my lead, Archer angles our brooms towards the closest mountain. As we dive down towards the base, he keeps hold of me, but the air currents are so strong that we can only descend in short bursts.

Archer points ahead of us to a ledge carved into the mountainside. I squint through the flakes to see the mouth of a cave mostly obstructed by a pile of snow. We begin streaking towards the hole in the rock as fast as the storm will allow us. My depth perception is thrown off by the white-out, and I land roughly, crashing through the drift. I stumble across the opening as Archer tries to slow my dismount. Once I'm on my feet, Archer releases my broom and sets it down in the opening of the cave.

I slump against the jagged rock, pulling away once I realize the slate is covered in a thin layer of ice. The cave is so dark that I can only see a short way past the opening, but what I can see glimmers, encased in rime. The ice crunches beneath my feet, breaking to reveal loose dirt and rocks as I take a step further to observe our shelter for the evening.

As I slowly make my way further into the cave, the darkness surrounds me, making it impossible to see an inch in front of my face. I halt and I cast my mind out instead, letting it flow into the cavern. Using my Mind Magic, I can sense the cave curves at the back, and it goes deeper than I initially thought. Luckily, I don't sense any other presence with us, human or animal. I force myself forward, allowing my mind to guide me. My gloved hand brushes against the wall until I find the curve, the wind subsiding, and the temperature rising as I round it. *This is where we should camp for the night.*

My brain can't even begin to unpack the danger we've seen today, mostly because I know it isn't over yet. The Dark Covens know our movements and seem intent on hunting us down. But I can't shake the feeling that Archer was a secondary target today.

I can't focus on that right now. I need to focus on surviving the night and making it out of these god-forsaken mountains before we starve to death. Or dehydrate. Or freeze. And of course, we don't have a single canteen or blanket with us. If--*not if, when.*

When we meet up with the rest of the team, I'm going to insist on dividing up the supplies more evenly.

I head back to beckon Archer to the spot I've picked out for us, and find him sitting on the floor, his knees brought into his chest. His hands run through his raven hair, melting the flakes clinging to his locks. He stares hopelessly into the storm, not acknowledging my presence. I rest my hand on his shoulder and he cringes, causing me to pull away. He's cold and wet. For that matter so am I. We need to get our soaking clothes off and warm up.

"We'll rest here until the storm breaks," I announce. I try to use my assertive captain's voice, but it comes out wary and exhausted. I shed my leathers, gloves, and two of the tunics I wear until I'm only in a black tank top and leggings in front of him. Archer watches me curiously as I ball up the wet clothing. My skin is chapped and pimpled with goosebumps from the cold. "As soon as we can, we'll head to the rendezvous point. Hopefully, the others headed there when they heard the safe house was compromised."

"They could be stuck in this storm. Or killed by the Dark Witches," Archer grumbles, despair heavy in his voice. "Have you been able to reach them yet?"

I shake my head. I've never felt anything like this before. Usually, when a channel is blocked, it feels like I'm encountering a wall similar to a mental shield. That only happens when a person doesn't want to use the channel, and they make the active choice to close it temporarily. This feels like our channel was obliterated.

The thought that someone could outdo me in Mind Magic, a skill I consider my best, is sobering and disturbing.

"They have to be okay," I murmur, more to myself than to Archer. A gust of wind pushes into the mouth of the cave, but Archer doesn't flinch.

I block the wind from him, dropping the clothes balled in my hands to the floor. I stand there until he finally looks up and meets my intense gaze. I see it almost immediately. The grief swirling beneath his eyes is intense and it's swallowing him. He's breaking right in front of me, and that thought chills me more than the gusts of wind at my back. I swallow thickly, trying to suss out what he needs from me.

I reach out again, gentler this time, cupping his cheek with my raw hand. Despite my exhaustion, I perform a quick warming spell, willing the heat to flood my arm and transfer to his ice-cold skin. He doesn't push away this time but continues holding my gaze. Slowly, I position myself over him, sinking to my knees so that I'm straddling his lap. His hands instantly fall to my hips as I brace myself on his shoulders.

"Ten minutes," I whisper. "We can feel it all for ten minutes. And then we need to put it away until we're back home and safe. Can you do that for me?"

"I can try," he responds honestly, his hands shifting to my lower back, urging me closer.

"Okay." I pull him into my body, wrapping my arms around his neck. He buries his face in my shoulder and I feel a sob shudder through him.

I swallow my own sob as I picture Deavers falling from the sky. I've been in dangerous situations with teams before, but I've never lost a soldier. And what hurts the most is that we went into this mission unprepared. We had no idea just how strong the Dark Magic Covens are, which means this mission was a failure before we even set off on our brooms. It doesn't matter that I was added to the mission late. They're my men. My team. And their blood is on my hands.

"This is all my fault," Archer chokes out, his voice raw. "I had him. He slipped right through my fingers."

"You didn't do this. You tried to *save* him. It isn't your fault," I say sternly, pinning him with my stare once again. His eyes well, but don't spill over as his guilt crashes against me.

"I needed the Moment of Valor. If it weren't for me, Deavers would still be—"

"You can't think like that." I'm trying desperately to pull him back from the pit of despair, but it's hard because I feel the exact same way. "You are not to blame," I insist, both to him and myself. Archer brushes a rogue piece of hair behind my ear. His hand lingers at the nape of my neck as his eyes brim with emotion again.

"I thought..." He releases a shaky breath. "At first I thought it was you falling. I thought you were the one hit." He wraps his arms around me again, his grip so tight it's bruising.

"I'm okay. We're okay." I whisper, rubbing soothing circles across his back as he shudders into me.

"We've just met," he murmurs into my hair. "And I already know I can't live without you." I balk at the intensity of his words, and the pure desperation in which he clings to me. And somehow, I feel the same way. I ignore my instinct to shy away from his affection and instead lean into it.

"The moment they cornered you was the scariest moment of my life," I tell him sincerely, returning the intensity of his embrace. If I'm honest with myself, I know that my terror at Archer being trapped wasn't related to the mission. My violent display of magic had nothing to do with protecting the prince. It had everything to do with protecting Archer, the man who held me after I had a nightmare, who could make me laugh, and who could calm me down when I was losing control of my magic.

I pull back, my auburn eyes finding his hazel ones. I can't help but feel exposed as I've just offered him a piece of me. A sharp wind blows, breaking the moment and reminding me quite forcefully that we need to get dry. Archer takes out his wand, and I hold still as he gently pulls my hair from its flight-torn braid. He begins siphoning the water from my chestnut hair like I did for him. The tender act rivets me, and I take the moment to memorize the angles of his face.

"We're both okay," I murmur, and Archer sends a warming spell over my skin.

"We're okay," he echoes. His eyes are momentarily mesmerized by his hands on my bare flesh. "Why are you practically naked? Not that I'm complaining." I chuckle and maneuver off his lap, instantly missing the warmth of his body against mine.

"Have you ever tried to clean and dry clothes when they're on?" I ask, and he shakes his head as he stands. "No matter how thorough you are, the magic always misses one freaking spot."

"Nothing worse than a wet spot," Archer chides and I feel my cheek heat at the double entendre.

"Can you dry our clothes and do a cleaning spell? I'll make a shield." I say, quickly maneuvering the conversation back to our survival. He scoops up my clothes and our brooms and heads towards a curve in the cavern. I watch him go before I turn my attention to the mouth of the cave.

I'll have to get creative with this shield; we need to see out, but I don't want anything to give away our position. Shimmering magic blooms from my fingertips as it spreads across the opening. I carefully weave a cloaking spell into my shield so that it'll appear to be an empty cave if anyone passes by. I briefly think I should leave a marker in case our team finds us, but my magic protests. My reserves are running low, and I know I'll need sleep before I try any other complicated magic tonight.

Once I'm satisfied the shield will hold, at least against a normal witch, I make it invisible and retreat towards the back of the cave. My eyes slowly adjust to the lack of light, and I keep to the middle of the path as I notice the jagged grey rocks jutting out in a sharp, uneven pattern.

I turn the corner and find Archer, shirtless, with his wand in his hand. He moves it slowly over each piece of clothing, first siphoning the water off, then muttering the cleansing spell, and finally warming the item. My mouth drops open as I take in his thin frame. I didn't expect it, but every inch of his torso is cut with lean, sculpted muscles. I swallow hard as my skin flushes despite the cold.

"Your clothes are clean and dry," Archer nods in the direction of a small pile. I try unsuccessfully to tear my eyes away from the perfect V peeking out from above the waistband of his pants. "Change into them and give me the ones you're wearing. I'll do your boots too if you want."

He catches me staring, and returns my gaze, scanning down my body. The wintery light from the mouth of the cave illuminates the fire in his eyes as he's distracted by his task. My mouth dries as his eyes flit back up, pausing on my lips as I suck my bottom one between my teeth. His throat bobs and I'm completely ensnared by his gaze, the memory of his lips brushing against mine sending heat through my body into my core. It was barely even a kiss, and yet the memory is making me tingle.

God, there's something wrong with me. *Why am I focusing on this now?* Clearly, there are more important problems to be worrying about.

I amble towards where he mentioned my clothes are and grab the small pile. "Don't look." I wink, before slipping away behind him. I move just far enough into the dark so that he can't see me while I change. I keep my eyes on Archer's back, watching his muscles tense before he releases a frustrated breath that I feel in my soul. To his credit, he doesn't turn around, but I can tell he's thinking about it.

Once my tank is off, I slide the warm tunic over my body and sigh at the heat pressing against me. I do the same with my leggings and return my wet clothes and boots to Archer. I can't help but whimper when my bare feet touch the cold floor. He takes them silently and continues working. I turn away from him, so he'll have privacy enough to take his pants off. There's enough to do before we rest that I can get started on. Water is my next priority. I'm debating braving the storm to get snow when I hear a faint dripping sound coming from the deeper in the cave.

I trot through the dark, my fingers skimming the porous rocks along the walls until my feet sink into a muddy bank. I test my magic by calling forth a ball of light. It flickers but remains lit. With a groan of effort, I throw it ahead of me and it illuminates a large lake within the cavern. Ice-covered stalagmites hang from the ceiling, dripping their melted droplets onto the obsidian surface. I inch deeper into the mud and scoop up a handful of the water. It's pale green color and smells foul.

"That water isn't clean," Archer's voice from behind me makes me jump. His clothing, now dry, is back on and he's carrying my items in his hand. He tosses them down at my feet, and I quickly set about putting them on, brushing the mud off as I go.

"No shit," I jab, though my tone is light. He chuckles and comes to stand beside me. "You remember how to purify water, your highness? My magic is running low."

He nods, removing his wand from his pocket. He scoops up a mouthful of the water using a siphoning spell and removes the silt and algae. He sends the removed bits back into the lake until he's left with an orb of cleansed water hovering in the air before us.

"Open your mouth," he murmurs and sends the water in a stream towards my lips. I swallow greedily, not realizing how thirsty I am. The groan that I release is nothing short of sexual. Archer chuckles and begins the process again, giving me enough until the liquid fills my empty belly. I finally wave him off, and he takes a drink himself.

"What else needs to get done?" Archer asks once he's finished.

"We need..." I break off, trying to decide if our need for warmth is worth risking a fire. Neither of us has eaten in hours, but there doesn't seem to be anything we can eat here. The day is weighing on me now, and my head is beginning to pulse. Archer must sense my exhaustion because he grabs both my arms.

"You need sleep." I shake my head. But Archer wraps one arm around my shoulders and walks me back towards the first curve in the cave. When I approach, I find he's made a fire and his cloak is laid out on the floor like a blanket. "Lie down."

"One of us needs to stay awake and keep watch," I protest as Archer eases himself down onto the ground and beckons for me to join him.

"Will the shield stay up while you're sleeping?" he asks and I nod wearily, releasing a weighted sigh. Shields are one of those spells that, once set, will stay until someone physically breaks it. "You didn't sleep last night. Lie down." My brows arch over the command, but something about him being assertive is super sexy. He holds his hand out to me as a wave of exhaustion washes over me, negating any thoughts about him using that tone in other ways. Ways that will keep us *plenty* warm.

"Katie," his voice deepens when I don't immediately take his outstretched hand. "Let me take care of you, please. Let me keep you warm." My pulse quickens at the tenderness in his tone, the gentle look in his eyes.

I take his hand and lie down on my side, facing the opening of the cave, even though the cave wall obstructs it. He curls his body around me, one arm sliding under my head and the other slipping over my stomach. His leg threads between mine and he pulls me so that every inch of my back connects to his front.

"Did I thank you today?" he murmurs, his breath tickling my ear.

"For what?"

"Saving my life." He pulls me in closer. My back is soaking up the heat pouring from his body into mine. I shake my head, meaning to protest that he shouldn't thank me, but he nuzzles into me. "Thank you," he breathes, placing a kiss where my neck meets my shoulder. My eyes flutter closed, and a soft moan breaks my lips.

"It's my pleasure, your highness," I say sleepily.

"Sleep, I'll keep watch," Archer commands against my skin.

"Wake me in an hour," I instruct. Sleep is already calling me, my eyelids drooping heavily as I fight to keep them open. The harder I try, the more difficult it is.

"Okay," he says, but I feel his lips turn up into a smirk.

"I'm serious, Archer. One hour and I'll be good." My eyes drift close and I allow the oblivion to wash over me.

MUCH LONGER THAN AN hour later, I wake to find I've rolled over. My face is buried in Archer's chest; his hands are idly stroking my back. I tilt my chin, sleep still clouding my eyes, and blink up at him.

"My turn," I whisper. He smiles down at me and shakes his head.

"Don't you dare move." His hands pull me in closer.

"Archer, you're exhausted. It's been a long day for both of us. You need to sleep, too."

"We'll both sleep." He tucks his head down to the top of mine. "Your shield will hold." I'm hesitant, knowing we should have one set of eyes looking out for danger, or our team. But I know the shield will alert us if anything approaches us, so I concede.

"Okay," I whisper. Sleep is already dragging me back under. Suddenly there's faint music in my ears. I lean into the melody and realize Archer is humming the lullaby I taught him on the piano.

"You're...that's my lullaby," I whisper breathlessly.

"I figured you might need help sleeping," Archer whispers, tilting my chin up gently so I look into his eyes, which have a silver gleam in the darkness. I can feel his breath tickling my lips and the urge to close the distance between us is overwhelming.

"Will your mom be mad?" Archer asks, his hand tracks up to the base of my neck and plays with the wisps of hair that hang down from my topknot.

"About what?"

"Us sleeping together." He winks and I laugh, dipping my head so it's hidden in his chest again.

"You're an idiot," I say against him, and his laugh echoes mine.

"Goodnight, Katie," he says into my hair, placing a kiss on the top of my head. I fall asleep to the sound of my lullaby, wrapped in the arms of my prince.

I awake the next morning to a bone-chilling voice calling my name, and the sound of nails scraping down my shield.

Chapter Fifteen

KATHRYN. My name echoes through my mind and I jerk upright, disrupting the bubble of warmth and safety Archer and I have encased ourselves in. I know that voice. I recoil, my body breaking into a cold sweat as I feel another scrape down my shield.

"No." The plea slips past my lips as the breath leaves my body.

"Katie?" Archer reaches for me. His eyes find mine and widen as I try to get control of my breathing. It's coming in too shallow, too fast. "What is it?"

Archer grabs my balled fist, running his thumb along my knuckles until I unclench. His touch grounds me, bringing me back from the brink of panic. Pushing down the bile rising in my throat, I take a deep breath and brace myself.

I need to get Archer to safety.

I surge my magic to reinforce the shield while I rack my brain for a way to get us out of this.

Very clever shield, the voice caresses my mind, invading it and looking for the source of my magic. He wants to take down the cave's shield from the inside. *Let me in, I won't hurt you.*

How the hell did he get into my mental shields? I focus my Mind Magic, imagining it in the shape of a whip and I connect to the magic creeping into me with a resounding *CRACK*. It rears back, wounded and I take the brief reprieve to slam down a thick brick wall on top of it, locking it out.

"Archer, you need to go." I pull him to his feet and stumble towards where we left our brooms. "It's the Dark Witch from yesterday. Their leader."

"Fuck." He locks onto both of my wrists, pulling me to him. His eyes are set with determination. "I'm not leaving you."

"Yes, you are." I break his hold and thrust his broom into his hands. "I'll be right behind you. I'll create a distraction, and you need to fly to the next meeting point. Don't wait for me, don't look back. Just fly as fast as you can."

"Katie—"

"That's an order, *your highness.*" He bites his lip, whether in frustration or fear I'm not sure but I find myself reaching towards him. I halt my hand an inch from his skin, suddenly unsure. He steps into my touch, pressing his lips to my open palm.

"You'll be right behind me," he pleads, his eyes hardening, the color shifting to a beautiful deep blue. I nod, even though we both know I can't make any promises.

"If I don't..." a scrape down the shield sounds hitches my breath. "If I'm not there by tomorrow morning, fly straight back to London. Take whoever is at the rendezvous point with you, but go home. Don't stop until you're with Marcus and my mom. Tell Marcus...tell him the witch's name."

"Katie, how do you know his name?"

Another scrape sounds down the shield. My magic is about to break. I wave my hand over Archer, coating him in a level of protection and invisibility. His hand on mine is the only indication that he's still in the cave with me.

"His name is Seth Carmichael. He's my dad." Archer gasps. "When I bring the shield down, count to ten and then fly out of here. Fly fast and silent. Don't look back."

I turn on my heel before he can respond and, grabbing my broom, stalk around the corner of the cave. The light reflecting off the snow-covered mountains is blinding, and I squint against the harsh daylight.

Tucked in the shadow of the cave's mouth is the silver-haired man. I didn't recognize him when we were in the air yesterday; his hair is longer, and his face is creased from the hard years we've spent apart. But I'll never forget that voice, the penetrating feeling of his magic.

He's leaning against my shield, using the magic to prop himself up like he doesn't have a care in the world. Somehow, he must be able to see through my illusion because he tracks me with precision. The wind pulls at the silvery strands of his hair gently lifting its edges away from the strong jawline. His lips turn up in a sinister smile, showing off a mouth full of yellowing teeth. His black cloak hides the shape of his body, but I can see what once was a dominating figure is now thin and frail. As he lifts his arm, his sleeve falls back revealing scarred, pale skin. He takes one long fingernail and draws idle circles over the shield.

"Princess." His voice creaks, devoid of warmth. There's no melody or cadence, it's just rough sounds that are forced out from years of disuse.

"Seth." The choice to ignore his parentage is clear, the first blow I'll deal him this morning.

I look him over. People always say I'm my mother's twin, which I'm exceedingly grateful for now, seeing the other person who gave me life. I share her hair color and texture, we have the same build, the same look crosses our face when we're pissed off. I'm hers in every way except for my eyes. Those were given to me by the monster in front of me.

"You look like shit," I comment, bringing the magic to my fingertips. "How was prison?"

He laughs, but it doesn't reach his eyes, and his nail sinks deeper into my shield. The lightning beneath my skin pulses, but I hold it down. *Soon*, I silently promise the force surging in my veins.

"You have quite the control over your magic, princess." His eyes turn molten, and I can see I'm getting under his skin. I send my mind out to his, a golden spear that pierces right between his eyes. It collides with a black obsidian wall, but the intent wasn't to break into his mind. It was to show him that I could. He gives me an impressed smirk.

"Your mother has taught you well, I see." His eyes flit to my tunic, to the embossed crest of the kingdom that lies over my chest. "Molded you to her image. But tell me, does my magic still call to you? Do you feel the darkness begging to be released? Is—"

I don't let him finish the question. "NOW!" I call into the cave behind me.

In one swipe I bring the shield guarding the cave crashing down. Seth stumbles forward into the shelter now that the wall holding him up has disappeared. But I don't want to fight him in here. Archer needs to get out of the cave, not caught in the crossfire. I need to take this fight where I might have the upper hand, the air. I hop on my broom in one fell swoop and barrel towards him. I crash into his chest, knocking him backward and the two of us go careening into the valley of mountains.

As we freefall, I grip his cloak and release my lightning. It crackles around me, dancing on every inch of my skin, flickering across my eyes. The current flows from my hand into Seth's chest for just a moment before his black magic rises around him like wisps of smoke to combat it. With the aid of my lightning, I toss Seth into the air above me, and he jerks from the electricity. I level my broom out and rise to meet him, aiming to take another blow, but he wrangles the shadows around him to hold him aloft.

"I'm not here to hurt you," he says, his voice booming in the valley, scattering and repeating his words back to me. I let out a cruel cackle.

"Wish I could say the same."

The magic inside me feels savage, unchecked. For years, whenever I released my raw power, I was quick to clamp it down. But no more. I unleash everything I have, every inch, every fiber of magic pours into my fingertips, waiting to be directed. I'm going to shred him apart, to make him feel every bit of pain he's made me feel. The power is heady. It swirls around me protecting me while simultaneously lashing out. It connects with his body and my father is thrown backward towards a jagged mountainside.

"Kathryn," he screams, his magic trying to cushion the blows, to slow the electricity. But it's no match.

"Do you remember it all?" My voice has taken on a quality I've never heard. It's cold but powerful.

"Do you remember every session? Every moment you pumped me full of your poison? Do you remember the time I fought back? I was only five and I was able to best you. What makes you think you could come back all these years later and take me on?"

He collides with the edge of the mountainside, the snow cushioning the impact, and begins to slide down. I see his panic as his hands grapple for a rock, a crevice, and instead find nothing but snow and ice. His eyes seek mine, pleading as I zoom forward on my broom. I push an electrified hand into his chest, and bindings made of pure lightning wind around his hands and pin them above his head to stop his helpless sliding.

I float back far enough that I can take him in. My anger flares as I remember his fault in the battle yesterday. He is at fault for Deavers' death, for the possible death of my other men whom I've had no contact with. Part of me wants to end it quickly, snap his neck and fly off after Archer. But there's another voice, something singing in the pit of my stomach, telling me to make him suffer. My magic strokes one of his cheeks, leaving a trail of burn marks.

To his credit, Seth doesn't scream, doesn't try to lash out, just stares at me, his auburn eyes alight with something I can't place. As if he reads my thoughts, the emotion surges against my mental barriers, and I catch the faint glimmer of it before it recedes...*pride*. He's proud of me. *Well, that's all kinds of fucked up.*

"Answer my question," I command.

"I remember the day the magic took hold," he begins thoughtfully like he's not dangling off the side of a mountain at my mercy. "I remember you sparing your sister and torturing me instead. I remember feeling the agony as your magic unleashed itself. And all the while, despite the pain, I remember dreaming of the wonderful things we'd accomplish."

"And how did it feel to know a five-year-old thwarted your plans?" His laugh echoes through the canyon again.

"Not thwarted," he says with a terrifying smirk. I swallow hard and my magic tightens around my body as if it's trying to shield me. "You are more powerful than I could have imagined, and you've only scratched the surface."

"What do you want from me?"

"How often does the darkness creep in?" he asks, his eyes locking on mine, and I feel a familiar tug of his magic on me. This time I don't swat it away, and instead of invading me, it embraces me. It wraps me up, whispering dark thoughts in my ears. The thing singing in my stomach for suffering perks up as if coaxed to life by the darkness. "I'd be lying if I said I hadn't heard things."

"Like what, Seth?" I ask, my body relishing in the darkness around me.

"I've heard tales that you're rebellious. That you pick fights you have no business taking on. Your verbal battles with your mother are legendary."

"Mothers and daughters fight," I say casually, my jaw tightening. "And I'm naturally aggressive. It's understandable considering my parentage."

"Do you find yourself searching for wild abandon? Perhaps with the drink, or with men." My eyes narrow, and I know he sees the slight shift. "Do you allow yourself to relish in those moments, or do you clamp it down and deny your instincts?"

He takes my silence as his response. "That is your gift. The darkness I gave you," he hisses, his eyes turning cold. "And you turn your back on it because *they* have convinced you darkness is evil."

I swallow hard. In truth, I do feel his darkness inside me. It's there every day. But I have learned to rein it in and make it no more than a whisper of temptation.

"I never asked for your gift." I clench down. His face begins to turn red under my power. I can end this today.

"This is bigger than you," he wheezes. "It was told in the stars. *Made from magic--*"

"Enough," I roar, my voice loud and commanding but cold. "What does that even mean? It's a spell, right?"

"Release me," he whispers. I oblige, letting him slide down the mountain further until I snap him back up with my magic. He glowers at me, panting from his sickening drop.

"It's a prophecy," he spits at me. "The magic I gave you is from Queen Carman. And you are her heir...and the rightful Queen of the Dark Magic Covens."

My magic slips, but this time my father is ready, and he floats on his magic, staying level with me. It's all I can do to stay on my broom. When there were four rulers, Queen Carman was the ruler of Dark Magic. She was said to be cold and cruel, and she was killed by King Baran, the Elemental Witch, for the war she started in the Kingdom.

"She had no descendants," I murmur. He has to be lying.

"She had one," he breathes. "One who was not born of Carman but made from her magic. Just as you are." My eyes are rapt on him as he continues, my magic now coiled around me like a cocoon.

"When I was no older than you are now," he begins, "I received a vision from Carman herself. She showed me a baby girl with my eyes, and she showed me infusing her with my magic to make her the most powerful witch in existence. She told me the prophecy, which had been spoken long ago, would come to light with my daughter.

"I had high hopes for your sister when she was born, despite her grey eyes. I convinced myself that I had seen the vision wrong. But when I infused her with the magic, it wouldn't take. Because she resulted from a union with another Dark Witch, her Dark Magic wouldn't accept mine. I knew then I would need to find a witch with Light Magic to complete the prophecy."

"My mother is an Elemental Witch," I glower.

"Is she?" I open my mouth to retort but I stop. I realize my mother has never shown me her magic in its raw form. I gasp as realization dawns on me.

"My sunshine..." I whisper. I'm so awed I don't notice the tendrils of Dark Magic that float around my waist.

"I infused your Light Magic with the Dark, and when it took, the prophecy came into effect. You are the Heir of Carman, and you will come with me—"

"Never," I seethe.

"Enough of this Kathryn," my father commands. "You will come with me to the Highland Coven and take your rightful place on the throne." I chuckle darkly. I needed to know where he and his coven friends were hiding, and he just told me.

"No," I call upon the scary cold voice that appeared before. "I will never be your queen. I will fight against you at every turn. I will destroy anyone who threatens the throne I am sworn to protect." His magic crushes me. I inhale a sharp breath as it ties around my middle, securing my arms. I thrash against the binds, desperately calling for my magic, but it's subdued.

Seth pulls me closer to him, and I have a feeling deep in my gut that once he lays his hands on me, he won't let go. I scour the depths of my magic, all the while desperately trying to remove myself from his clutches. I desperately try to coax my lightning to surface but get nothing. Then I see it. Deep in a corner, a small kernel of flickering light. Seth reaches for me at the same time I reach for the kernel.

White light blasts out of my skin, searing the Dark Magic, ripping me from his hold. It sparks silver and gold and is as brilliantly blinding as the snow on the mountains surrounding us. It rushes towards my father, and his eyes widen. Just before it reaches him, he disappears and the magic crashes into the side of the mountain, sending snow cascading down its slope. I shoot up into the sky, not stopping until I crest the peak. I spin frantically in the air, searching for signs of the man, but he's gone, and I'm alone in the mountains. *Great. He can teleport.*

As if it knows the threat is gone, the light floods back into me and retreats into the corner, barely flickering once again. My small kernel of sunshine that stayed with me all these years.

Chapter Sixteen

I FLY FAST, DESPITE my exhaustion. The weather has warmed, but that causes the snow on the mountains to melt. It batters the earth as it falls, and the collisions send vibrations high into the sky that threaten to dislodge me from my broom. After I almost get taken out by an avalanche, I fly over the clouds, abandoning my search for the other members of my team, hoping they're long gone by now.

My thoughts keep circling to Archer. I can't shake the feeling that my father was a distraction so the Dark Magic Covens could abduct him. But when I try the mental channels, they're obliterated.

I finally leave the Alps behind as the sun is setting. The rendezvous point is in the hills of Northern Italy, tucked into a small forest near a lake. I perform a navigation spell and dip beneath the clouds when it reveals I'm close to my coordinates. The snowfall didn't reach here so the hills are lush and green and scattered with evergreens. I fly over a few small towns, then a grove of olive trees before approaching the lake near the meetup. I scour the area for any sign that Archer made it here, praying that he met up with the rest of the team.

When I don't see anything for several miles I start to panic. I must have passed over it somehow; because the other option, that no one is here, is too terrifying. I'm about to double back when I see a tendril of smoke weaving up from the edge of the tree line. I lower my broom slightly and catch a flash of blue-black hair sitting beside the flames. My heart leaps and my broom plummets towards the camp.

I land roughly, somersaulting off my broom which shoots away from me before crashing into the side of a tent. Archer jumps to his feet at the commotion and his eyes meet mine for exactly one second before I barrel into him. I sag against him, releasing a breath I hadn't realized I'd been holding. He pulls away, scanning me from head to toe, and then wordlessly pulls me back into his arms.

"You're okay," I whisper into his shoulder.

"*You're* okay," Archer sighs, tugging me impossibly closer. "How did you... Is he... Holy fuck Katie, how did you get away?"

I chuckle and pull away, tossing my hair over my shoulder. "How did *he* get away you mean. Apparently, he can teleport," I tell him.

"Well, that sucks."

"Is that your professional opinion, *your highness?*" I tease, but Archer's eyes quickly grow sad, and he cups my face in his hands.

"I thought—I didn't think I'd ever see you again," he murmurs, his eyes tearing as his thumb brushes my cheek.

"I'm not going anywhere," I promise. My palms drift up to rest against his chest, feeling his heart pound beneath my fingertips.

A cough draws my attention away from the prince, and I break away, my eyes scanning the perimeter of the camp, the tents...

The tents.

"O'Malley?" I call tentatively. Two fire-red heads of hair pop out of one of the tents, one on top of the other.

"Hey, Captain!" They rush from the tent towards me, and I wrap them both in a hug, laughing in relief.

"We heard the noise, but..." one of the twins starts.

"Justin thought you and Prince Archer might need a minute," Jared winks and Justin's face turns beetroot. I get the feeling Justin was the one who walked in on Archer and me kissing that first night.

"Jacobs and Coleman are here too," Archer says from behind me, and another strangled cry comes out of my throat. His hands snake around my waist, pulling my back flush against his chest. My body goes taut and the twins make themselves busy with the fire.

"Archer—" I start, trying to break from his hold.

"I am quite literally never letting you go again," he whispers in my ear. "They'll get used to it."

My heart pounds against my ribcage and every bit of energy I've spent fighting off these feelings evaporates. Archer leans down, placing a kiss on the small of my neck, and a soft moan escapes my lips as I let go of all the walls I've put between us. Life is too short of denying something this potent. Hell, we've almost died twice in the past two days, so fuck protocol or what my mother will think, or any of the other flimsy reasons I've been using to deny this chemistry between us.

"Do you want dinner?" he murmurs, his knuckles brushing against my waist, leaving goosebumps in his wake. I pull away slightly, gazing into his ever-changing hazel eyes, which are currently as green as the surrounding trees.

"Actually, I saw a lake when I was landing," I say, gesturing in the general direction. "I think I'm going to take a bath." Archer's pupils dilate and his eyes dip, scanning my body.

"The water is going to be freezing," he remarks. "You sure you don't want to just use a cleansing spell?"

"No, definitely not," I grimace. "Cleansing spells are fine and all, but I need to wash off this day. The past two days really."

"Do you want me to come with you? I promise I'll keep my hands to myself," he says, a devilish grin taking over his face.

"Liar," I tease as I head to the bag with supplies, fishing around until I find soap and a towel. "I know we have a lot to talk about, but I just need a minute...to process everything. Is that okay?"

"Of course," he says, kissing the top of my forehead. "I'll just wait here, definitely not thinking about you naked." I roll my eyes, trying not to laugh as I cast a ball of light to my hand before heading into the forest towards the lake.

THE LAKE IS SET in a small clearing, the trees and lush grass of the forest giving way to rocks and sand before the crystalline water. The moon isn't full, but the reflection on the lake's surface magnifies the pale light, and I'm able to banish my magical light. I head to the shoreline and kick off my boots next to a large rock. As I undress, I perform cleansing spells on each article of clothing to remove the layer of grime that's accumulated from the cave and an entire day of flying.

Once I'm done attending to my clothes, I wade into the frigid water with soap in hand. I perform a quick warming spell to protect my body from the cold and dive under, sighing as the water washes over me. I send the web of my Mind Magic to check for other beings that might be lurking in the depths. Thankfully, there's nothing, not even fish.

I try not to think of my father's words about the prophecy, but they echo my mind as I scrub the soap into my hair. *The magic I gave you is from Queen Carman, and you are her heir.* And I'm not the first if my father is to be believed. Two hundred years ago, another witch was tortured until her body accepted Dark Magic. But how do I go about finding her? Does it even matter? She has to be dead if she lived in Carman's time...so why would he even bring it up?

My nails dig into my scalp, my frustration causing me to draw blood beneath my fingernails. I curse and sink beneath the water, staying under until my lungs burn. My father is a master manipulator. He would have said anything to get me to go with him, to be *Queen of the Dark Magic Covens.* I need to forget about him and our conversation until we finish this mission, then I'll talk to my mom and get some answers.

I lock the events of the past day up tight in my mind as I resurface. I wipe the residual water from my eyes, and my breath catches. I'm not alone.

Standing on the beach is the most attractive man I have ever seen in my life. Black hair pools around broad shoulders and his shirtless torso is chiseled perfection, the moonlight only enhancing every defined line of muscle. He draws his hand over a stubbled chin as he watches me with rapt attention.

"I thought I smelled humans," he remarks, his words colored with a faint accent I can't identify.

"Well, that's not a normal statement," I respond dipping low enough in the water that I'm mostly covered. His eyebrows arch, his face transforming into surprised amusement.

"But you're not just mortal...are you?" he asks.

"I'll show you mine if you show me yours," I shoot back with a shrug, my voice sounding sultry, curious, and entirely more confident than I should be given the circumstances.

He smirks, his eyes practically glowing in the moonlight as he begins to pad along the shoreline. Even from this distance, I can tell he's unnaturally tall; his faded jeans stretch on for a long while before stopping above bare feet. He should be freezing, but he shows no sign of any kind of discomfort despite wearing practically nothing. *Definitely some kind of Magical Creature.*

"These woods are dangerous for humans," he muses. "Your worst nightmares live in this forest, some in the very lake you swim in. You should come out of the water."

"You're blocking my clothes," I remark, crossing my arms over my chest.

"So I am." He picks up the towel I brought with me and holds it out. I scowl, which only makes him smile wider, revealing gleaming white teeth. No fangs, I note...so not a vampire.

"I won't bite," he teases.

"Somehow I doubt that," I deadpan, making him laugh again.

"Not unless you ask for it, little witch," he says.

"How did you know—"

Something soft brushes against my leg. It's probably just kelp...is there kelp in lakes? Maybe it's an eel or something. Either way, it's not a reason to panic, but it's enough to get me moving, trying to figure out how to get out of the water without giving this non-human a free show. His entire body tenses and his eyes flash in horror as they lock onto mine.

"Get out of the water."

I feel the silken touch against my leg again.

"Right now. Get out of the water," the man growls and I don't hesitate in scrambling towards the shore. He rushes to the edge of the lake, halting before he steps in, but extending the towel towards me.

I don't make it one step before the touch completely wraps itself around my leg. I scream as I feel claws dig into my leg.

I thrash, kicking out and connecting with soft flesh. The water around me bubbles but the grip only tightens, the claws sinking deeper, penetrating the muscles in my calf. I struggle against the grip, but it's no use. It begins to pull me towards the center of the lake.

I lower my hand beneath the water, prepared to cast a spell that will blast away my attacker, but when I call my magic, it doesn't respond. *What the fuck?* I cast again, and nothing happens. My chest seizes in panic as another hand curls around my other leg. This one pulls me straight down, and my head is jerked under the surface before I can take a breath. I don't dare open my eyes to see what has me ensnared, but I keep fighting my way up. I punch and kick and thrash until my lungs are burning and my limbs start to feel heavy.

Large, calloused hands grab under my arms, and I'm suddenly yanked above the surface. I gulp down air, barely able to fill my lungs before I'm ripped back under. The tug-of-war with my body goes back and forth several times before I'm finally heaved from the water, but not before the creature that has my legs slashes across my entire calf. I moan in agony as I'm hauled over the man's shoulder like a sack of potatoes, and he hurtles us both towards the shore.

When we reach the beach, he drops to the sand before swinging me off his shoulder and cradling me across his lap. I breathe heavily, the desperate need for oxygen my only focus. When I finally open my eyes and look at the lake, I see a black iridescent tail splash water angrily in our direction before sinking beneath the surface.

I look back to my savior, ensnared by his rich golden eyes, flecked with an even more vibrant sunflower yellow. I search for the words to thank him for saving me, but his gaze is fixed on my leg. I follow it and gasp when I behold the shredded skin and muscle. Claw marks run along every inch of my calf, but the center mark is so deep I can see bone. Purple pus oozes from the cut, and I try to lift my leg to blot away the pus, but I can't move.

"Hold still," the man says, and shifts me carefully, gently setting me on the beach and slowly sliding down my body to my leg. He prods the edge of the slash and I wince, even though I can't feel his touch. He pulls back and tests the pus between his fingers. The smell is rancid, like rotting fish, and I struggle not to heave up the non-existent contents of my stomach.

"It's spreading," he growls, a hint of fear in his voice. I look down and I see purple veins spreading from the cut, creeping over my flesh up to my knee as I watch.

"We have a healer at camp," I tell him, but he ignores me, pointing to a dark mark in the center of the wound.

"I believe that barb is releasing the venom. I need to get it out before we move." He reaches up and grabs my jaw, forcing me to stare into his eyes, which are now completely yellow. "No matter how much it hurts...You. Cannot. Scream."

I nod, but he holds my jaw tighter. "I mean it. If you scream, it will alert monsters much worse than the mermaid, and I won't be able to help you. What's your name?"

"A mermaid did this?"

"Yes. Focus. What's your name?"

"Katie," I squeak out. His eyes darken, and then glow until his entire iris is alight.

"Okay, Katie. Here we go," he murmurs and removes his hand from my jaw. I watch as it ripples, and I feel strange magic settle over us. His hand flexes and his bones start snapping and spreading out in odd angles. Claws shoot out where his fingernails once were and white fur shoots down his hand.

"You're a werewolf." The breath is knocked out of me by the realization. He tenses and the transformation stops at his hand...his paw. He ignores my shocked observation, focusing on the task. Keeping his eyes locked on mine, his paw skims down my leg, gently at first, until his nail sinks into my cut.

I bite down on my lip as pain sears through my body, pushing me back onto the beach. I feel every stroke of his claw, pulling, rooting. My hands fist into the sand, looking for anything to grab onto, to transfer some of the pain. His voice is soothing, repeating my name over and over as if reminding me of who I am will get me through this. The world is nothing but this pain-- this intense writhing, soul-crushing pain. And I can't help it, my mouth finds its way open, and a shriek rises in my throat.

His spare hand, the one that's not a paw, wraps around my head and pulls me into the crook of his neck. My open mouth clamps down on his flesh as his body muffles my scream. He grunts as my teeth dig in, but I back off when a coppery taste floods my mouth and I realize I've broken his skin.

"I'm sorry," I pant as he removes his paw again and tosses a black needle-like structure to the beach beside us. His jaw brushes against my ear as he turns towards me, his stubble scraping against my cheek and sending a shiver down my spine, as he leans in to inspect the bite mark.

"You bit me," he says curiously, and I brace for his anger, for him to withdraw his help and tell me to fuck off. What I don't expect is laughter. He keeps it quiet, but it's a light, hearty sound and I can't help but join in. "Fucking animal," he murmurs, and then I'm laughing harder, and I hide my head against his chest, noticing the small crescent moon tattoo over his heart.

"We need to get you to your healer now," he says as his paw shifts back into a hand and the glow from his eyes fades. In a seamless maneuver, he scoops me into his arms, mindful of my throbbing leg. "I'm going to run. I suggest you close your eyes."

"Wait, my clothes." I reach my hand out to summon them, but they don't budge. "Why isn't my magic working?"

"The venom immobilizes magic," the werewolf responds, and without further warning, begins to run.

And holy crap does he run fast. The entire forest passes by in a blur of green and I instantly regret not listening to his advice about closing my eyes. A millisecond later, he slows and we're standing on the outskirts of the camp, just out of view of the men sitting by the fire.

"Fuck," I swear as I swallow down bile. "I thought vampires were the ones that ran fast."

He scoffs. "Where'd you hear that, little witch? A mortal fairytale?" He gives me a knowing look, but I cover my embarrassment with a cough of derision. "Call your healer."

"Coleman?" I call once, then again louder, causing everyone at the fire to still.

"Katie?" Archer responds as the werewolf steps into the firelight, draping his arms so that most of my naked body is covered. I give him a thankful nod as Archer runs over to meet us and assess the stranger holding me. "What the fuck is going on?"

His eyes fall to my leg, and he pales. "Get Coleman," Archer orders, and the men all jump up, Jacobs running in the direction of one of the tents. "What happened?" he asks.

"I got attacked in the lake," I state, calmer than I probably should be. The werewolf drops onto one of the seats by the fire, not relinquishing his hold on me. One of the O'Malley twins comes over to me with a blanket and extends it, trying to keep his eyes averted. The werewolf snatches it from him and delicately drapes it over me.

"What the hell did this?" Archer demands, flashing accusing eyes at the werewolf. He positions himself in front of me and begins examining my leg.

"A mermaid," the wolf responds, his tone matter of fact.

"Why are you naked?" Archer asks, ignoring the man. "And who the fuck is this?"

"I was bathing," I snap, not appreciating his judgment. "This is..." I look to the man for his name, but he doesn't answer. "Well, he pulled me from the water, but not before the mermaid got me. I need Coleman."

"Quickly," the werewolf growls, his eyes locked back on Archer. "The longer she goes without her magic the worse it'll be."

"What happened to her magic?" Archer growls, which elicits a challenging growl from the werewolf. I roll my eyes, but then a wave of dizziness overtakes me, and my hand slips from the werewolf's shoulder as I tip forward.

"Katie," his strong arms wrap around me tighter, keeping me upright. "Katie, look at me."

"Holy shit, Captain." I'm aware of someone approaching, but everything around me is getting fuzzy. My head sinks into the wolf's shoulder, and my eyes drift shut.

"She needs pure Light Magic immediately," his voice rumbles into my head where we're connected. "Whatever you have in that bag won't do shit against this type of venom. Use your healing magic and then a wand to siphon it out." I see something bright behind my eyelids, but don't open them.

"This might hurt," Coleman's voice says gently.

"You can go," Archer's voice sounds. My savior growls again just as a sharp pain attacks my leg. I whimper and bury myself further into the werewolf's chest.

"I know, Captain," Coleman murmurs. "She needs to stay awake through this. Give her something to focus on."

I'm so tired and in so much pain. Why do I need to stay awake? That doesn't make sense. I should totally be allowed to fall asleep right now.

A blast of freezing water over my head has me sputtering and sitting upright. "THE FUCK?" I choke out, brushing strings of wet hair from my eyes.

"That's right, little witch," the werewolf murmurs, tossing the canteen aside. "Eyes on me."

"Was that necessary?" I glare at the werewolf as Archer uses a siphoning spell to remove the water from my now drenched head.

"Would you have preferred I slap you awake?"

"Only if you aren't attached to your hand."

"Katie are you okay?" Archer draws my attention from the werewolf, whose laughter makes me smile despite the ridiculous pain in my leg.

"I'm okay, Archer." I go to reach for him, but my body is exhausted. I look down at my leg and find Coleman using his wand to extract purple goo from my body. It comes out in a long strand. I gag, but the werewolf moves his hand, so it locks around the base of my neck.

"Eyes on mine." His eyes begin to glow softly, not as noticeably as they were before he shifted, but still glowing. He leans in close, and his voice drops to a whisper. "I can help with the pain. Do you trust me?" I'm vaguely aware that Archer has inched closer as I give the wolf a curious look. *How the hell can he help me with the pain? And why hasn't he done it already?*

"Okay, venom is out," Coleman announces, and I breathe a sigh of relief. "Captain, this part will be worse. I need to patch up your leg. Brace yourself."

I look to the werewolf and give him a nod. His eyes begin glowing again, stronger this time, although no one reacts to them but me. I feel the connection immediately, like a golden tether that snaps in place between us. My skin burns when Coleman's

Light Magic touches it, but almost instantly it fades to mere discomfort.

"How?" I whisper, and I notice the werewolf wince slightly as Coleman's magic flares again.

"You think only witches have magic?" He smirks. "I can share your pain, direct some of it away from you into me, by creating a bond."

"Seriously? That's handy." We both wince in tandem as another pulse of Coleman's magic flares around my leg. "So, we'll be...bound now? Does that mean you'll be able to track me or something?"

"Or something," he says, amusement dancing across his face. I open my mouth to ask exactly what that means when--

"Katie!" Archer calls loudly. "I've been talking. Did you not hear me?"

"I'm sorry, I was..." the werewolf arches his eyebrows conspiratorially. "What did you say?"

"I said the twins ran to the shoreline and got your clothes."

"Right. Thank you." I direct to the O'Malleys. I wince as another round of the magic radiates from tingling to a twinge. I can't imagine how bad it would have been if my savior hadn't been sharing in my pain. Archer's brow knits together in worry.

"I'm okay," I reassure him.

"You're so brave," he murmurs.

"That she is," the werewolf agrees. I turn back to him, and my eyes lock in on his lips, which are a hairsbreadth away from mine.

"Why are you still here?" Archer asks the werewolf, who smiles tauntingly and pulls me flush against his body. I don't have the energy to fight him off, and honestly, there's something about being in his arms that's super comforting.

"He saved my life, Archer," I reply, and Archer just narrows his gaze to where our bodies are connected.

"Your boyfriend's more possessive than most wolves I know," the wolf murmurs, his mouth so close to my ear that his breath flutters my hair. "Then again, if you were mine and you were naked in another male's arms, I'd probably tear his throat out."

"He's not...We're not technically..." I sigh. "It's new."

"Good luck with that then," he scoffs.

"That's the worst of it," Coleman tells me, sitting back on his heels. A sheen of sweat is covering his face. "Let's get you dressed and then I want you to try walking on it."

"Thank you, Coleman." My leg has a visible scar, but the cut is now closed.

"Try your magic," the werewolf instructs. I call a ball of lightning to my hand and breathe a sigh of relief when it comes. The wolf tenses.

"Your magic is lightning?" he asks, looking at me like that just put the last piece of a puzzle together. I nod, giving him a questioning look, but he doesn't respond. He carefully stands with me still in his arms and places me down on the seat where he was.

"Thank you so much," I murmur. "I don't know how to repay you."

"I'm sure you'll think of something." He leans down and gently kisses my cheek. Faster than humanly possible, the werewolf is in front of Coleman.

"Healer, can you look at this? Make sure it isn't infected?" He tilts his head to the side, showing off the bite mark.

"Is that a hickey?" Archer asks, and Coleman glares at the werewolf in solidarity.

I give him a glare that I hope says, *why are you trying to start shit?* The werewolf winks at me again and then bursts towards the edge of the campsite. Archer turns a shade of red I've never seen before in my life and I'm pretty sure his head is about to pop off.

"Don't linger in these woods," the werewolf warns. "Witches aren't welcome here." He flashes a toothy smile at Archer and my wide eyes ping pong between the two of them.

"Wait," I call as the wolf turns to leave. He pauses, glancing over his shoulder, only giving me the profile of his face. "I still don't know your name."

He smirks. "We'll meet again, Katie." And then he disappears into the forest, completely absorbed by the trees and the darkness.

Chapter Seventeen

AFTER I GET DRESSED and Coleman makes sure I can put weight on my leg, Jacobs hands me dinner. It's bland, tasteless, and probably some small animal they discovered in the forest, but I eat it greedily. More than the food, I'm grateful for the company, although I still worry about the unaccounted-for men.

Archer sits by my side, not speaking but holding my hand, his thumb absently rubbing over my skin so often it chafes. When Jacobs and Coleman excuse themselves to get a little sleep before they take over the watch, we're left alone by the fire...in silence

"Any word from Soto and Jefferson?" I ask, desperately trying to break the tension. Archer shakes his head. "I think the Dark Witch Covens must be using Mind Magic to scramble the signals or something. It's the only explanation I can think of." Archer nods and stays quiet. After another long awkward moment, I stand.

"I'm going to go to bed," I murmur, but he tugs on my hand.

"We need to talk." His voice is cold, distant. "Who was that?"

"Of all the things that happened today, you want—" His eyes meet mine, imploring me to dismiss the werewolf. "Why is it bothering you?" I ask and, his mouth tightens into a line.

"Why isn't it bothering you?" His eyes narrow accusingly. "This shirtless stranger parades in and saves your life--"

"Would it be different if he was wearing a shirt?"

"I'm not fucking around Katie." Archer stands and moves so his body is only a breath away. I stick my chin up in defiance, refusing to back away. "We're being chased by Dark Witches, one of whom is your *father,*" he hisses the word and I wince. "And suddenly this random guy shows up. Doesn't that seem odd? Don't you think maybe he could be reporting to them? Or that he could be *one* of them?"

We have no records of the Dark Witches working with any Magical Creatures, but I don't want to tell Archer that the man who saved me is a werewolf. In some weird way, I feel protective of my savior.

"He said witches aren't welcome in the woods." I point out instead. "So no, I don't think he's working for my father."

"What did he say to you?"

"When?" I ask wearily.

"When he was whispering in your ear, and you were giggling like a schoolgirl," Archer clenches his fists and flames burst from his palms. I jump up, my own magic springing to my hands.

"He was trying to help me with the pain. That's all, I promise." It's not technically a lie. I don't need to tell Archer he magically transferred my pain.

The flames dissipate and he begins pacing. "And what was with the hickey on his neck?" he asks. "And the fact that he wouldn't let go of you while you were naked?"

I can't help the chuckle that escapes. "You sound jealous."

"I am fucking jealous!" Archer reaches around to the back of my neck and clamps down on my hair and I inhale sharply. My hands fist in his shirt to push him away, but then he tightens his grip, forcing my gaze to meet his and a moan escapes my lips. I watch as his tongue darts over his lips, my fingers aching to reach up and follow its path.

"I should be the one who saves you," he says softer. He's so close I can feel his breath on my lips, and I almost give in to the temptation to close the distance between us.

"Wait, what?" I ask, pulling back as his words sink in.

"You saved my life twice," he says stroking my cheek with his other hand, the difference in his touches clouding my mind.

"And?" I demand, trying to keep my head about me.

"The girl always winds up with the guy who saves her," he says, looking away.

"I'm sorry, but that's ridiculous," I scoff, and he releases me roughly. "You realize that I'm your bodyguard, right?"

"That's not—"

"And I don't even know who the hell that guy was."

"But he'll see you again," Archer says pointedly, and I roll my eyes.

"He was fucking with you," I say, exasperated. "But what does it matter? He's gone."

"Because I need you," Archer says charging at me again. "Do you know how it feels to rely so heavily on someone? I've needed you this entire trip, and the one time you need someone else, I'm not there."

"Archer..." A wave of exhaustion has me swaying on my feet. "I don't need saving. I'm not that girl."

"Except tonight. When you did."

"I can't handle this right now," I sigh, turning my back on the prince and heading towards the tents.

"We're not done," he calls after me. I hold up a hand and keep walking.

"Archer, I've almost been killed three times in the past two days. We can talk tomorrow when you're not having a pissing contest with someone who isn't even here. I'll take Jefferson's tent tonight."

I pop into the tent and close the flap behind me. I hear Archer's grunt of frustration, but he doesn't follow me. I roll my eyes at the alpha-male bullshit he just pulled, but I don't have much time to let it bother me. As soon as my head hits the pillow, I'm asleep.

I'D BE LYING IF I said I didn't expect Archer to come crawling into my bed during the night. I'd also be lying if I said I wasn't a little disappointed when he didn't. Despite being on the hard floor of a cave, our sleeping arrangement the previous night is something my body is craving again. It's almost enough to make me apologize, but I don't even think he's mad at me. He's mad at the werewolf, so he'll have to get over it on his own.

When I finally give up on sleep, I exit the tent somewhere around dawn to find Archer already by the fire. His gaze tracks me as I sit next to him by the early morning flames. He's cooking some kind of sausage on a stick that wasn't here last night when I was forced to eat that unidentified meat.

"I found a small town just over there," Archer says, reading the question in my eyes and nodding in the direction of the lake. "I figured we'd need a real breakfast. It'll be a long day."

He pulls a cup from the ground next to him and hands it to me. The scent of coffee hits my nose and I moan, eagerly gulping it down.

"Thank you," I murmur. Archer just nods, focusing on the flames. "We need to talk about yesterday—" I start, but halt when Jacobs returns from his watch. Archer silently hands him the sausage before procuring another to put over the flames.

"When do we need to head out, Captain?" Jacobs asks between bites, and I take another gulp of my coffee.

"Jacobs, wake the others," I sigh. "We all need to talk." He nods and saunters off to the tents. By the time the next sausage is ready, everyone is sitting at the fire, eagerly awaiting my orders.

"We've been through so much in the past three days," I start, looking over each of their faces...faces I thought I'd never see again just twenty-four hours ago. "So, I'm going to speak candidly."

"We can't linger here." I continue slowly. "Which means even though Jefferson and Soto aren't here yet...we have to move on." Coleman dips his head solemnly, but the others murmur in agreement. "We'll figure out a way to leave them some kind of signal in case they make it here after we leave."

"The channels are still clogged?" one of the twins asks, and I nod.

"The Dark Witch from the battle...he's a known criminal who recently was broken out of prison. He found Archer and me yesterday where we were camped in the mountains, and I subdued him for a time, but then he escaped. He teleported."

"Fuck," Jacobs swears, shaking his head.

"But because of that, I think we should abandon the mission and head back to London. The Dark Witch Covens are too many steps ahead of us." I keep my voice firm. "The Sicilian Coven could be another ambush, and with only six of us, we won't be able to take them all as prisoners."

"No," Archer insists. "We finish this."

"Archer..."

"If we leave now, everything we've lost is for nothing," he says and Jacobs nods in agreement.

"It's not for nothing," I counter, pushing back at him. "We live to fight another day. We come back with a bigger army and make sure we have the upper hand."

Archer stands, throwing his shoulders back and peering down his nose at me.

"We finish this. That's an order, Captain."

My mouth drops open as Archer's eyes find mine. There is no trace of the fear I saw in him when we left London just a few days ago. The sergeants all look away, avoiding our confrontation.

"What's the plan?" I implore. "We get there and then what? They've anticipated every move we've made so far."

"I'm sure you'll think of something on the way," he says, dismissing me.

"Well, if that's the order, *your highness*," I grit through my teeth, venom dripping from my words. I stand and my lightning crackles in my hand freely. "Let's pack up camp and get going." Archer ignores me as he heads to our tent and breaks it down. I follow him, right on his heels.

"If you're going to pull your position out, you better be able to back it up," I say, grabbing his elbow. The light shock from my loosed magic zaps him enough that he turns to look at me. I pull him in close, trying my hardest to be intimidating.

"Is this about last night?" I whisper when I'm sure I can't be overheard. "Is this some kind of way to prove you're a strong man? Because you're not winning any points by ignoring the advice of *your captain*."

"Not everything is about you, Katie," he deadpans, returning to his task.

"I will not lose another person to this mission," I vow, and Archer ignores me. I turn to leave, but I pause, glancing over my shoulder. "This is a mistake, and you know it."

"Be ready to leave in five, Captain," he orders.

I flip him off over my shoulder as I walk back to my tent. I throw my magic at it, and it breaks itself down and begins to shrink. I do the same for every other item in the camp, except Archer's tent. He's still breaking his tent down when I grab my broom and shoot into the sky alone.

Chapter Eighteen

WE LAND ON A rocky hillside in Sicily in an abandoned village later that evening, and I'm instantly struck by how eerily quiet it is. The only sound is our boots clicking across the cobblestones as we hike our way up a mountain masquerading as a hill. Everything around us is stone, which would be charming if it wasn't falling apart. The ledge that serves as the barrier between the road and the cliffside has giant chunks blown out of it and the road itself is missing pieces so large that you'd disappear if you fell in. We trudge along, following the cloying feel of Dark Magic that coats the air.

The sergeants all have wands at the ready as we move through the lifeless town on high alert. All around there are signs of a quick abandonment. A line of laundry hangs from a dark window, mold clinging to the clothes from being left in the elements for so long. An open door reveals the remnants of dinner that the mortal family never finished. Every one of my instincts are screaming at me to turn around, but we forge on, driven ahead by Archer, who is steadily turning a putrid shade of green.

As we approach an old church, the feeling of Dark Magic intensifies. I take a moment to appreciate the irony that a blessed place is being used something so sinister, before signaling the group to move to the back of the plot. We duck behind a rusty fence into a graveyard. I steer the group as far away from the building as possible, ducking behind large headstones of white and grey marble that date back hundreds of years. We position ourselves along the fence, crouching behind a wilted line of shrubbery.

The church looms above us, made entirely of brown stones and iron accents. The bell in the steeple hangs limp and unmoving, probably disabled by the witches inside. I survey the two doors on either end, made of solid oak. A line of stained-glass windows faces the cemetery, depicting scenes of saints performing miracles. I notice a figure inside, cloaked in black, moving through a hallway.

"Stay here until I can figure out how many people we're dealing with," I whisper to the group. I tested my Mind Magic on the flight over, and even though our channels are disrupted, my magic itself seems to be intact. I brace myself to stand, but Archer grabs my wrist.

"Let me," he whispers. I wave him off, but his hand tightens around me.

"This is not the time for a lesson, your highness. You only know shielding."

"So, show me. This is my mission, Katie." He fixes me with a cold stare.

"Fine," I hiss. "But you should know that this type of magic is considered Dark and is illegal unless you've been given clearance."

"I'm the prince. I think I have clearance," he sneers.

"Keep your shields up," I acquiesce. "You don't want them realizing we're here. Imagine your mind is a web seeping out from behind your shield." He closes his eyes and I do the same. I'm not solely trusting his judgment when there's so much at stake.

"Allow your web to find other minds. They'll feel like orbs. Don't touch them. Just let your magic float over and past them." I briefly brush my mind against Archer's as I feel his web seep out. I push mine along too and marvel at the lack of creatures outside. I'm not even picking up on bugs in the ground, which is ominous at best.

"When you pass the wall," I continue, my web seeping through the stone walls, "cast your web out farther, imagining it covering every corner of the church."

We fall silent as we work. My mind travels through the basement, the living quarters, and finally arrives in the sanctuary before I feel the faint pulse of another mind. I back off, throwing my Mind Magic around the room.

"How many do you see?" I ask Archer, whose brow is furrowed. He starts shaking his head emphatically.

"There are six," I say gently, both to him and to the men. "Not great, but enough to be a challenge. They're in the sanctuary. I'm not sensing a mind I recognize." There should be one man who was sent in undercover, but I don't know if any of these people are one of the Dragons.

"Orders, Captain?" Jacobs asks, and I open my eyes to instruct them since Archer is still not responding.

"There are two entrances. We'll split between the two, so they don't have a chance to escape. Remember, we subdue and capture unless your life is directly threatened. If anyone teleports in, get the hell out of there and meet at the rendezvous point."

The men nod and stand, readying themselves for the ambush. Archer is still crouched shaking his head wildly. His mouth is moving but no sounds are coming out.

"Your highness, it's time." I gently tug on his shoulder. "Archer…" He begins rocking back and forth. I lean forward and kneel next to him, so my mouth is almost against his ear. "Archer, it's not too late to call this off."

Archer's eyes pop open and I stumble backward. His hazel eyes are glowing bright orange, and flames dance through them. His jaw tics as he grinds his teeth together. The look on his face is concentrated, determined, but sure.

"Archer?" I gasp as he stands and takes three steps beyond the shrubs, pushing past the men, and stopping at the closest headstone.

There's a flash of light and a wave of oppressive heat, and then I'm blown backward and pinned to the fence at the back of the church lot. A gust of white-hot fire is streaming from Archer's fingertips and making a beeline for the stained-glass window.

It spills inside like magma, shattering the glass in a rainbow downpour.

"Archer, stop!" I yell and drag myself towards him, but the force of the magic flattens me against a headstone. One of the O'Malley twins rushes over to me and pull me back as Archer releases another pulse of the white heat.

I send my mind out, racing the flames towards the sanctuary. The minds in the church are frantic. They're screaming as the fire attacks them. I can feel their thoughts as one by one, they're engulfed in flames and wink out.

One orb breaks out the front door. I throw lightning in its direction and lasso the witch before she can flee. She screams but I yank her hard, flinging her towards us just before an explosion rocks the church. Her grey eyes meet mine in panic as she realizes how close she was to being in the blast zone.

"Grab and bind her," I call to the men. The O'Malleys are closest, so they run over to the witch and snap magic-absorbing handcuffs around her wrists. As soon as they're done, I release my lightning and turn my focus back to the prince, pushing into his mind.

His shield is completely obliterated, and what I find is terrifying. There's nothing inside his mind that reminds me of the man I've spent the past few days with. All that's there is an otherworldly rage and a desire to prove himself.

Archer, my mind caresses his and his fiery eyes dart to me. I carefully wrap my lightning around his ankles, rooting him to one spot. For one minute I'm afraid he'll turn that rage on me, but the feeling ebbs as he takes me in. *You're done.* My lightning encases his body as I stroke his mind with gentle calming. I whisper a cooling spell, and it replaces my lightning, dousing his flames.

"What the hell was that?" I whisper as he blinks rapidly. Jacobs rushes into the church now that the flames are extinguished. I send my mind one more time into the church but come up empty. There are no survivors.

"Captain," Jacobs says reappearing, his face as white as a ghost. I leave Archer, who slumps to his knees and stares uncomprehendingly at his hands. As I pass our prisoner, she gasps. Her grey eyes, brimming with tears, find mine. She opens her mouth like she's about to say something but stays silent.

"Captain, you want to see this." Jacobs gulps. He leads me through the empty doorway, the wooden door since destroyed in the blast. We walk through a stone hallway that is encased in black soot. There's no light, and I note that the sconces have melted and are a puddle of molten iron.

We head through an archway, and Jacobs summons a ball of light with his wand. He sends it out into the vaulted ceilings of the sanctuary and my breath leaves my body as I take in the carnage. All the windows have been blown out due to the force of the heat, and some pews are still smoldering with licks of fire. But what draws my attention is the front of the room. I pick my way through the burnt debris until I'm standing at the base of an altar, which is cracked in half.

Atop the altar is five sets of remains arranged in a circle. Five blackened husks that once housed life. Their skin is completely melted away, revealing gleaming white bones marred with scorch marks. Bile rises in my throat as the stench of burning flesh fills my nose. Pools of wax surround them, and I absently wonder if Archer was able to tap into the flames already in the room to end their lives faster. Five magical lives were lost when the mission was only to capture and interrogate. *Holy shit.*

"Oh god," Archer's voice rings out from the back of the sanctuary. His eyes widen as he takes in the scene, and he looks at his hands in dismay.

I'm completely numb as I stare at the remains. Even though I know that these are enemies, it didn't mean they had to die.

Archer wretches, whether from the scene inside the church or his display of magic, I'm unsure. I numbly approach him and brush his hair from his eyes where he's bent over. His body is shaking and his lip quivers as he spits out the remnants of his stomach.

"I did this." His voice croaks out as he stands and faces me, wiping his mouth with the sleeve of his cloak.

"Yes," I say solemnly. He nods, his eyes focusing on the altar where the dead witches lay burned to a crisp.

"Let's go home," he dictates, and I can hear him walling himself off from his emotions. His eyes grow cold and detached, and his shoulders square. "Prepare the prisoner."

"Archer..." He holds up a hand to me to silence me, and it's like a slap across the face. I look for the signs of remorse he showed upon entering the sanctuary, but whatever was there has been replaced by steely resolve. I turn to leave, pausing just as our shoulders brush.

"I hope it was worth it," I sigh, the grief heavy in my voice.

As I move past Archer, I swear I hear him whisper, "It was."
I don't turn back around as I leave behind the smoldering
sanctuary.

WE FLY BACK HARD and fast, flying straight through the night until
we reach the south of France sometime in the morning. Our
prisoner rides the first leg of our trip with Jacobs, but I watch her
like a hawk. The last thing I need is her throwing herself off the
broom in a self-martyring act. Her blond curls flutter softly in the
wind, and her pale skin is smudged with soot everywhere except
in lines down her cheeks where the tears washed it away.

When we crash down on one of the beaches, we don't even
bother setting up camp. The morning is grey, echoing our mood.
A drizzle comes down, coating my leathers, and causing the sand
to stick to everything.

"We leave in two hours," I announce as everyone groans. "If you
can sleep, I suggest you do so. I'll keep watch."

"Captain, I can take the watch--" one of the O'Malley's starts,
but I silence him with a glare. He doesn't argue, instead taking
out the bedrolls and throwing them to the remaining members of
the party. He hands me a canteen and I drink deeply, allowing the
water to clear the taste of smoke and charred remains from my
throat.

The crew starts to drift off, sleep claiming them all until Archer, the prisoner and I are the only ones awake. The girl watches the two of us, her pale grey eyes wide as they bounce between us as we ignore each other. When I offer her the canteen, she just stares at me skeptically.

"It's safe," I say, taking a drink in front of her to prove it isn't poisoned. I hold it out to her again and tip it back up to her mouth. Reluctantly she opens, her eyes unblinkingly watching me as she drinks deeply. Once she's done, I move to the other side of the camp, where I can see her and keep an eye on the far end of the beach.

"Katie—" Archer starts, having followed me silently. I ignore him. "Katie, please just talk to me."

"Now you want to talk?" It comes out much weaker than I intend. My fury is palpable, but there's something else there that seems to be winning out.

"Katie, I wasn't trying...I couldn't hear you. It was like I was possessed or something—"

"I don't want to hear it," I snap, whirling around to face him. "You annihilated those people."

"I'm not sorry about what happened," he murmurs. My mouth drops open.

"You--Even if you don't care about--" I will myself to calm long enough to get the words out. "We had someone undercover in that coven. One of our own. Even if you don't care about the Dark Witches or the information they could have given us, how—"

"I got us out of there safely," he says, holding out his damn hand to silence me again. This time I can't control myself, and I slap it away.

"Don't for one second pretend you were thinking about the rest of us," I seethe. "I gave you the option to retreat multiple times. You needed your Moment of fucking Valor. You needed to prove that you could be the hero. Well, congratulations, your highness. I hope it was everything you wanted."

"I'm not looking for your absolution."

"Then why are you here right now?" His mouth opens, and for a second, I think I see a flash of regret cross his eyes. But whatever emotion it was is quickly squashed, and he shakes his head and trudges back to his bedroll. I release an exasperated grunt as I struggle to contain my magic, stuffing it back down into the pit of my stomach before I electrocute Archer.

"Your man wasn't there." I jump and find the prisoner on her feet behind me. Her voice is light, lilting in an ethereal quality.

"Sorry?"

"I overheard," she continues, regarding me curiously. "Your undercover agent, he wasn't there when..." She swallows heavily and I don't need to use Mind Magic to know she's replaying the scene inside that church.

"We discovered him weeks ago and released him outside of Naples. We performed a memory spell on him so that wouldn't remember his time with us, but he should be returning to you shortly." She smiles crookedly, the smile not quite reaching her eyes.

"Why are you telling me this?" I ask softly.

"Because you mourn them too." Her eyes pierce me, the weight of her words sinking into my skin. *Is that what I'm feeling? Am I mourning the loss of my enemies?*

"You mourn innocent lives," she answers my unasked question. "If we had attacked, you wouldn't be feeling so guilty. You're upset by the senseless violence." She drops her voice to barely a whisper. "It's an admirable quality. It makes you a good leader."

She turns and walks back to where she was sitting, leaving me to digest that information. She's right. I didn't spare a second thought for the witches I hit with lightning in our aerial battle. Those witches attacked us; I was defending myself and my men, and I would do it again one thousand times over. What makes me so angry at Archer is that he didn't even try to capture anyone first. That, and the lack of remorse he's showing for the lives he took.

I've only killed one man in all my time with the Dragons. He was a criminal wanted in our realm and the Fae realm; a truly despicable vampire swapping mortal children with Fae children. He tried to kill me when we cornered him, but I got him first. Even though it was a completely justified kill, and I was given a medal, it haunted me every day for years. There are still days when it bothers me.

Archer just killed five people, and he doesn't seem to care at all. It makes me wonder what kind of a person he is, and what kind of king he'll become.

Chapter Nineteen

WE FLY THE REST of the day and make it back into London by nightfall. I physically can't be in Archer's company any longer, so I send the sergeants with him and our prisoner to the palace and I head back to Headquarters to debrief the generals. The prisoner will be sent to the dungeons underneath the palace while she awaits interrogation, and then she'll most likely be sent to prison.

I land in the outdoor pad of the compound and find the place in utter chaos. Several aerial units rush around readying to take off on broom while foot soldiers pile into giant tanks. I pause in the middle of the commotion and manage to snag a private as he rushes by me, grabbing him by the hem of his tunic. He squeaks when he sees me.

"Captain! You're back!" He struggles out of my grasp so that he can bow and then keeps moving, rushing over to one of the commanding officers, a captain I don't recognize. The private makes a few hasty remarks to him and then the captain rushes over to me. A few strands of grey hair sweep over his bald head, but they don't do much to hide the fact that he's glistening with sweat.

"What's going on here, Captain?" I ask as he approaches me.

"Captain Carmichael is Prince Archer with you?" he asks, and I notice the other commanding officers taking notice.

"He's currently on his way to the palace with Sergeant Jacobs and the O'Malleys. What is going on here?" I repeat. He physically relaxes, closing his eyes. All at once, everyone around us stills.

"Thank goodness you're back safe," the captain says, his voice softening. "Three of the sergeants returned from your mission an hour ago saying you were separated. We were about to begin a search party. General Weatherbeak said you went dark a few days ago—"

"Did you say three?" I stifle the cry that threatens to burst from my throat.

"Yes, Captain," he says with a smile. *Three sergeants.* They all made it back. Tears sting my eyes and for the first time since our group has split up, I can take a full breath. "One was gravely injured. They're all in the medical bay now with General Carmichael and General Weatherbeak."

"Thank you," I nod. He returns the gesture as I turn and sprint into the underground compound. I never thought I would be so happy to see these dark stone hallways, but something in my chest eases as I spiral down and down towards the medical bay.

I skid to a halt when I reach a wooden door with a beautiful golden carving of the sun. The door is already ajar, and I can hear several hushed voices and see the white light of the healers inside. I push into the white-tiled room, so bright with its fluorescent electricity compared to the sconces of the hallway. The first few beds are empty, but the third has a pale blue curtain drawn around it.

I throw back the curtain and find Marcus and my mother in a deep conversation with Soto. My eyes scan him and I visibly relax to see nothing overtly wrong with him. Both Jefferson and Deavers on the other hand are lying down in hospital beds. Deavers has two healers working on him. His skin is pale and waxy. My breath catches as his chest rises in a breath and all eyes turn to me, seeing me enter the room for the first time. I turn to Jefferson, whose eyes are brimming with tears.

"Captain," he croaks, a large smile breaking out across his face. All the emotion I've suppressed the past week bubbles up, but I force a smile and rush towards him. I ignore all protocol and throw my arms around his neck. He winces audibly.

"Oh, shit." I pull back and examine him, my eyes scanning for the source of the injury. That's when I see the black mark on his neck, marring his otherwise flawless ebony skin. "What happened?"

"Ambush, Captain," Soto answers for him. He approaches me and bows, but as soon as he's standing to his full height again, I wrap him in an embrace, which he tentatively returns. I turn back to Jefferson and inspect the injury.

"It's nothing, Captain," Jefferson murmurs. "Barely hurts. I told them to focus on Deavers first." The healers both nod towards me, their soft smiles silently assuring me Jefferson is fine.

"Our channel was cut off," Soto continues. "The safe-house was compromised, the entire thing was swarming with Dark Witches when we got there. We didn't land, but they spotted us as we were retreating. We got out of there as quickly as we could, but not before we took some heavy fire."

"You flew into the blizzard?"

"The lack of visibility allowed us to lose them like you said, but the storm pushed us north. Since Jefferson was hurt, we decided we'd get Deavers and meet you back here."

"We thought it would just be his body—" Jefferson says, his eyes flitting to the two healers. I push past Soto and position myself between the two beds. I clasp Deavers' hand, which is ice cold.

"But he was breathing," Soto whispers, his eyes falling to their comrade. "It looks like someone cushioned his fall. Was that you, Captain?"

"I...I sent off a spell. I think it was to slow his descent." I try desperately to remember the spell I sent towards Deavers as he fell, but it's a blur. I turn to the healers. "How bad is it?"

"We're not sure, Captain." The one healer, a small witch with mousy brown hair that blends into her skin tone shakes her head in despair. She pauses her glowing white magic and wipes her hands on her pristine white tunic. "We've never seen this kind of spell before. We're not even sure what it did to him."

"But don't worry Captain," the young male healer says, his hand running over Deavers' blonde hair with his blindingly bright hands. "We'll get him set."

"Kathryn," my mother steps forward, drawing my attention from my injured sergeant. Her eyes search me, looking over me for injury, and when she doesn't see one, she nods once. "Where is the prince? The rest of your team?"

"Everyone is okay. We all made it back. They're on their way back to the palace." My head drops, and I rest it on the hand I currently use to hold Deavers'.

"We need to debrief," my mother says, her voice completely detached. "My office, one hour. I'll call the prince in—"

"No." I stand as she balks at my refusal. "We need to discuss this now. Just us."

"We need to finish with Sergeant Soto--"

"Mom," I plead. I turn to Marcus, my eyes burning.

"Misty, let's go," Marcus says, and my mom opens her mouth to object, but he puts a hand on her elbow. She nods and leaves the room. Marcus turns to Soto. "Get that frostbite looked at, and we'll be back shortly to finish up."

"Yes, sir." *Frostbite.* I shoot a worried look to Soto, who simply smiles. "I'm okay, Captain. It's just a toe." I shoot a look to the healer, who gives me a nod of encouragement as Soto sinks into a chair. Satisfied that he'll be taken care of, I push the curtain back and leave the medical bay.

A MINUTE LATER I'M storming into my mother's office. I push past the armchairs and sit behind her desk, sinking into a black leather chair that swivels slightly from my momentum. For once, I'm not mad about the fire that makes the space stifling hot. I'm convinced that after this trip I'll never be warm again.

My mother follows me and sinks into the guest's armchairs, her face set in her usual unreadable mask. Sometime during the flight, I managed to convince myself that Archer's goal was always to annihilate the coven and that it was kept from me on purpose.

"I need to know," I start, my voice calm despite the storm brewing under my skin, "what was the goal of the mission?" My mom and Marcus exchange a confused glance.

"Find our contact in the Sicilian Coven," Marcus begins. "Capture all others present and bring them back for interrogations." I swallow hard. I'm not sure if I believe them yet so I stare them down.

"Katie, what happened?" My mother's voice is tired. I'm sure she's been worried since we haven't been checking in, but I can't think about that right now.

"The order wasn't to exterminate?" I ask, carefully measured. My mom gasps and Marcus's mouth practically falls to the floor.

"What the hell happened out there?" he demands.

"I need to hear you say the words," I whisper, tears threatening to fall, quickly replacing the rage I was feeling just moments ago.

"Fuck no, the order wasn't to exterminate." Marcus crosses behind my mother's desk and spins my chair so that it's facing him. A wave of relief spills through me. *They didn't know. This didn't come from them.* I sink forward and Marcus catches me in his arms. I melt against him, and tears start flowing freely as the horrors of the mission replay in my mind.

"Marcus, it was so bad," I gasp as he gently strokes my hair. "We were so unprepared. The Dark Witch Covens...they're organized and powerful. They blocked my Mind Magic, all my channels. We barely escaped with our lives. And then Archer—" A sob rips through my body and Marcus holds me tighter as it works its way through me.

"Tell us everything," my mother says softly.

And I do. I tell them every detail, starting with our ambush and ending with Archer incinerating the Sicilian Coven. I even tell them that a mermaid attacked me, but I leave out that my mysterious savior was a werewolf. They don't speak, but Marcus keeps shaking his head in disbelief as I tell him of Archer's savagery.

"We have one prisoner," I inform them. "She told us they discovered our man undercover and returned him to Naples a month ago without his memory of his time in Sicily. I believe it, but someone should interrogate her." My mother nods. By interrogate, we both know I mean someone should use Mind Magic to invade her memories to see if she was telling the truth.

"I can't believe Archer would do that," Marcus mutters.

"He basically said he wasn't even sorry about it," I say, my rage quieted by the sheer exhaustion taking over. Now that the story is out, I can barely keep my eyes open.

"Did he give you an explanation?" Marcus asks, and I shake my head. My mom turns to him, and the two have a private mental conversation. I take the moment of silence to close my eyes, propping my elbows on my mother's desk. I press my hands into my sockets until I can't see the lights of the world behind my fingers.

"Katie," Marcus's voice is timid. "I need to finish up with Soto. Then I need to talk to Archer. Is there anything else you need from me?"

"No," I say, keeping my eyes closed. "I actually need to talk to Mom alone." He nods and exits the office quickly.

I wait until I hear the click of the door and then I open my eyes, setting them on my mother. Her usual cold mask has completely dropped; she looks scared shitless.

"How much do you know of what my father did to me when I was a child?" I ask her.

Tears, actual tears, well in my mother's eyes. We never spoke of the experiments he performed on me, so I always hoped that maybe she didn't know. And even if she did, maybe she didn't understand, like I didn't understand until just this past week.

"Show me your raw magic," I command her, my voice growing cold. Her throat bobs for a moment and then she calls a blinding white light to her hands. I suck in a breath of disbelief. My father wasn't lying. My mother's magic is Light Magic.

"Did you know," she begins slowly, "that Light Magic is almost as feared as Dark Magic?"

"No, it's not. Healing—"

"Is the only acceptable form of Light Magic," she whispers, sadness creeping through her voice. "As you can imagine, I was never meant to be a healer. I simply don't have the temperament for it. When I was about to start my magical training, my mother asked me if I wanted to learn to heal. I told her I wanted to be a soldier, and she said the only thing I could do would be to conceal my raw magic under another form."

"Why?"

"It's the way of the world." My mother stands, flaring her magic so it completely encases her body, showing it off to me for the first time. The white light sparkles gold and silver as if she's completely trapped in starlight. With a heavy sigh, she banishes her magic back beneath her skin.

"Light Magic is the second most powerful form of Battle Magic. Can you guess the first?" Even though she asks, I know she doesn't expect an answer. Of course, I know. I just fought against an entire army of them. "Back in the days of the Four Kings, Light and Dark Magic users were the most sought-after soldiers in the Kings' armies. Elemental Magic users were rarely in charge of defense because their magic could never stack up.

"The first King Baran used the war between King Darius and Queen Carman to his advantage. He let the Light and Dark Magic wielders wear themselves down until they were broken and weak. Then he struck, killing both the monarchs and taking the throne. Since Queen Aldonza, the Queen of Magical Creatures, had already been killed, he was the only choice to assume the throne. As soon as the war was over, he issued decrees making Light and Dark Magic illegal to practice and he banished all Magical Creatures to remote areas of the world. The kingdom was so torn by war that everyone just obeyed. So other forms of magic began to weaken."

"That's fucked up," I breathe.

"Many hid their magic, silently protesting the King's wishes and trying to revolt against him, but none ever succeeded. At some point, the world almost ran out of healers and a group of Light Magic users came forward and offered to use their magic for healing only. The first King Baran accepted."

"How didn't I know this? We never learned--"

"War is never pretty, Kathryn," my mother replies sadly. "King Baran did what he thought was right, and it led to centuries of peace within our Kingdom. When I met your father—" she releases a steady breath. "He believed all magic users should be free to use their magic as they saw fit. As a girl with an illegal form of magic, it was freeing. But he was radical, and I believed there were other ways I could help make the world a better place. It's why I enlisted in the Dragons, to protect those who couldn't protect themselves."

"Did you know he was working with the Dark Magic Covens?"

"No," she answers. "I thought he was working with an underground group of activists. I didn't even know he had Dark Magic. I was so in love with him and his ideals that I never even thought to ask. It wasn't until—"

My mother rushes around the desk, her movements frantic. She kneels in front of me, her eyes locking with mine.

"Katie, you have to believe this," she pleads. "I had no idea what your father was doing to you until that day I found you torturing him. After...when you set him down and I subdued him, I found countless notebooks on the prophecy and on the magical conversion experiments he was performing on you. It made me sick to my stomach; I couldn't believe the man I loved was such a monster. I sent him to prison, and I never looked back. He deserved that and much, much worse for what he did to you.

"But when I discovered he turned your Light Magic to lightning, I was..." she chokes off a sob. "I was relieved." She buries her head in my lap, and I tentatively pat her head in response.

"Because that meant I wouldn't have to hide, like you did," I surmise. "Lightning could be Elemental."

"There's one final thing you need to know." She lifts her head again, sinking back onto her heels. "Our family are descendants of King Darius." The King of Light Magic. *Holy shit.* "The Baran line thought they eradicated Darius's line when they killed his daughter, but he had a bastard son with a servant who was kept a secret."

"Did my father know?"

"I don't think he knows about the royalty in our line," she says thoughtfully. "But I do believe that's why you're so powerful. You have the magic of two monarchs." Her face falls. "It also makes you incredibly dangerous to the King, Katie. No one can know."

I lean my head back in her desk chair, tilting it up to stare at the ceiling. "They're going to come after me. They want me to be their queen."

My head is spinning. I can't believe all the carnage and terrible things that the Elemental Witches have unleashed against other forms of magic over the years. What Archer did was just one more brick in a long road of injustice. Thinking of Archer reminds me that I'm supposed to be returning to his chambers tonight, and the thought makes me shudder.

"I can't be the one guarding Archer anymore," I blurt out.

"I'll assign another guard to stay with him and have your things brought back," she says, her mask fitting back over her face, the concerned look disappearing.

"The men from the mission need a weeks' vacation at minimum," I tell her, putting my mask back on as well. "And they should be promoted. They went above and beyond for his stupid Moment of Valor."

"I'll put in the paperwork today. Would you like some time off as well?" she asks, and I shake my head.

"Put me in charge of training the new soldiers." She gives me a wary look. "Whether you like it or not, they're unprepared for the Dark Magic Covens. And I'm the best we have, so I'm the one they should be sparring against." I see the decision pass over her face before she has the chance to agree. "I'll start training them tomorrow."

"Do you still want to interrogate the Dark Witch?"

"No." I stand up and make my way to the door. "I don't want anything to do with that mission."

Chapter Twenty

I STUMBLE INTO MY barracks, kicking off my boots and not caring when they don't land in their usual space. I groan when I realize all my stuff is still in Archer's suite, I don't even have anything to change into. But I cannot stand to be in these clothes for another minute, so I strip them off and hop in the shower.

Wrapping a towel around my body, I'm trying to decide on using a cleansing spell on my travel gear or sleeping nude when I notice a small pile on my bed. I walk over, finding a few clothes, the book I was reading before the mission, and my phone. A note sits on top in a scrawling script.

I sent Jacobs ahead with some of your things, they said they'll send the rest tomorrow.

~~*Please come see me*~~

~~*I'm sorry.*~~

Give me the chance to explain.

-Archer

Give me the chance to explain. He didn't even have the decency to add a *please* to that request. I crumple the paper and toss it in the wastebasket, determined not to spend one further second thinking about the prince.

I throw on a tank and leggings before sitting cross-legged on my bed, running my fingers through my wet hair, and turning on my phone. As soon as the screen lights up, it's vibrating in my hand, and I answer the call immediately.

"Thank fuck," Edina swears into the receiver, and I can feel her tension a continent away. "I tried to use our mental channel, but it wasn't working. It felt like it wasn't there at all."

"I know, I'm sorry," I breathe, reclining against my pillows. "I ran into Dark Witches on the mission, and they did something to my Mind Magic."

"Katie, holy shit. I thought—" her voice breaks.

"I'm good, E," I say softly. "I'm not going anywhere."

"You're in the fucking military and the Kingdom is on the brink of war," she says, her voice thick with emotion.

"We're not...Who told you there's going to be a war?" I ask.

"Not important," she says, and I narrow my eyes. Even though she can't see me she huffs as though I've worn her down. "Fine, I slept with a Dragons officer who was chatty as hell."

"Did you seduce him on purpose to find out about my mission?" I ask dryly.

"Of course, I did!" she exclaims. "I went full honeypot for your ass."

"You could have called my mom."

"Well, I didn't think of that," she says quickly, and the two of us dissolve into laughter. I laugh until my side hurts, some of the tension from the last few days finally dissipating.

"You doing okay?" Edina asks after we both can breathe again.

"No," I admit, not bothering to hide my fear. "We ran into my dad."

"The one in jail?"

"Not in jail anymore. In Europe. Flying around like a fucking supervillain."

"Damn," she breathes. "And you...I mean did he try—"

"We fought. I won," I tell her, a smile tugging at my lips. "Well, he ran away so I'm counting that as a win."

Even though I'm not supposed to, I tell her everything about the mission, about Archer, about my father. Every confidential scrap of information. She listens quietly for a while, promising not to repeat a word, then sighs heavily when I finish with the tidbit about Archer's note.

"What could Archer say that would justify his actions?" she asks.

"I don't know," I say honestly. "If it was a legit reason, wouldn't he have told me already?"

She hums in derision. "You can be pretty intimidating when you're...breathing," she chides, and I'm sure she can hear my glare through the phone. "But seriously, babes, crossing you when you're pissed isn't easy."

"Maybe," I offer, reluctantly.

"You should probably hear him out," she advises. "It's not like you'll be able to avoid him forever. Eventually, he's gonna be your boss."

I groan, swiping my hand over my face. "Why you gotta come in here using logic?"

"I know, right? What's wrong with me?" Edina deadpans and I chuckle. "Let's talk about the werewolf instead," she says, the excitement in her voice barely contained.

"It was a one-off," I tell her. "There's nothing else to talk about."

"Umm just because you're never going to see him again doesn't mean we can't talk about it," she presses. "A sexy, half-naked werewolf saves your life, and you have undeniable chemistry...it's like the plot of every romance novel you've ever made me read."

"Hey. Some of them are about vampires," I retort, and her infectious laugh trickles through the phone.

We talk for hours until I fall asleep holding the phone and Edina wakes me by playing screamo music at top volume into the phone.

I STEP INTO THE training arena wearing a new pair of leather leggings and a lightweight tunic, my long hair plaited in my battle-ready braid. Despite my exhaustion, sleep was hard to come by last night. My thoughts were constantly running, going over every moment of the mission, every anger-soaked word Archer and I shared, and every bomb my mother dropped. But one thing my mother said stuck with me. She joined the Dragons to protect people with all forms of magic, and that's exactly what I want to do. I want to continue to work hard to protect those who can't protect themselves.

The newest soldiers are the ones I'll be training first, but after my conversation with my mother yesterday, she and the other generals decided it would be best to train all levels under me. I welcome the distraction of having classes all day, less time for me to think about Archer. I'm so mad at him I can barely see straight, but there's a part of me that misses him too. I want to cut that part out of my body and douse it in kerosene. Short of doing that, I don't know how to process these mixed feelings, so I'm opting for avoidance.

I watch absently as some of the privates notice my presence though most are completely oblivious and talking amongst themselves. I groan when I recognize a blonde head of hair working its way towards me. He is clearly cocky, his walk slightly leaning backward like he's pulled through the world from his pelvis. He gives me an impish smile and sketches a bow.

"Captain," Kyle, my one-night stand murmurs, a smile turning the corner of his mouth.

"Private," I bark, the picture of a cold, commanding officer.

"Glad you're back," he winks. *My god, this guy has balls*. He sidles up next to me, leaning his head down so it's inches from my ear. "My shift ends at six tonight if you want..."

"ATTENTION," I call, using an amplifying spell to send my voice out through the cavern. Kyle jumps back from me and tugs at his ear as the rest of the room goes quiet. Everyone stands at attention and then quickly bows once they realize it's me commanding them today instead of their usual trainers. "My name is Captain Carmichael, and I'm here to get you ready to face one of the biggest threats the Kingdom of Magic has seen in decades."

I stride to the center ring and leap into it in one graceful bound. The privates all gather around one end of the ring so that they can see me. "The Dark Magic Covens have some of the most sophisticated magic we have ever seen. They're organized, highly trained, and because they're using Dark Magic, can do things that defy the natural order."

"Like what, Captain?" a voice in the crowd asks.

"The spells they use baffle our healers, they can shatter shields with ease, and at least one of them can fly and teleport." Murmurs break out across the crowd. "Today is an assessment. We'll be working with Battle Magic first, then adding in spells. You'll break into teams of four; I'll be your opponent."

"Just you?" Kyle says, his eyes hungry. *Oh hell no.* This douche bag isn't going to undermine me on my first day of classes.

"You know, you're right," I purr, swaying my hips seductively as I walk to the edge of the ring closest to him. "It should be one on one. Thank you for volunteering." I hold out my hand and Kyle pales.

"I didn't mean—"

"You absolutely did, Private." My hand stays steady, extended to him. "Come on, let's see what you've got." Kyle puffs out his chest and approaches the ring, ignoring my hand and attempting to scramble into the ring on his own. When he struggles, I use my lightning to lift him and set him on his feet across the ring from me. The crowd snickers.

"I'll give you a ten-second head start where I won't do anything but dodge your attacks," I announce to the crowd. "Whenever you're ready." I motion for him to begin. He squares his shoulders, and a ball of water appears in his hands, quickly solidifying to ice.

"One," I begin counting out loud. Kyle makes a series of predictable strikes, all of which I avoid easily. I don't even move towards him, and he's in a sweat by the time I reach nine. "TEN."

The number I call out unleashes a crack of lightning that quickly works its way around Kyle's middle. Because I'm feeling particularly bitchy, I hoist him high above the ring and flip him upside down, my magic binding him completely. He screams as I shake him up and down and the crowd roars in laughter. I set him down in a puddle of his own making, releasing my lightning a second too late. He spasms on the floor for a minute and then rolls to get to his feet, his head ducked in shame.

"Teams of four," I order to the others. The crowd starts breaking off, and a completely breathless Kyle makes his way to the edge of the training ring. I grab him by the elbow and pull him close to me.

"Make no mistake, Private." I drop my voice to barely a whisper. "Any personal relationship between the two of us ended the second you left my barracks. Undermine me again, and I'll end your career."

His eyes catch mine, and I watch as the flare of defiance is snuffed out. "Yes, Captain."

176

"UGH," Kyle screams as my lightning reaches out and gently flicks against his arm, tagging him out of the exercise.

"That was better," I tell him, and he gives me a soft smile that says he doesn't buy it as he joins the rest of his group on the far side of the training arena. "But you all need to be working together. You're still viewing yourself as individuals, work as a unit." The soldiers nod as they climb out of the ring, making way for the next group.

It's been a week of classes all day every day. The privates are in worse condition than I thought, so I doubled their training time, but I'm happy for the distraction. When I'm not teaching, I sit in the medical bay with Deavers, who is still unconscious. The healers believe that he was hit with a sleeping spell, but because the Light Magic didn't work and they can't pin down the correct spell, they haven't figured out how to reverse it. I try to help with the research, but we've come up empty.

"Who's next?" I call when another group doesn't immediately come up to meet me. I take a swig from my water bottle when I see a lone figure emerge over the lip of the ring.

The first thing I notice is the bags under his ever-changing hazel eyes, which are bloodshot today. Archer gives me a tentative smile as he tugs on the hem of his black tunic with the golden crest. He bows deeply as he enters the ring.

"This is a closed class, your highness," I say as the privates all gather around to watch.

"I know, Captain." His voice is hoarse as if he's been screaming. He runs his hand through his rumpled hair. "You offered to train me; I was hoping that offer was still on the table."

Figures begin appearing in the doorways to the arena. I catch a glimpse of Jefferson leaning against one of the open doorways, and one of the O'Malley twins walks past him, clapping him on the back before taking up a position against a wall. They nod when they see me staring, and Jefferson gives me an encouraging smile.

"Please," Archer continues. I can't put my finger on it, but he looks beaten.

"You took out an entire coven," I respond coolly. "Surely you're beyond my training." His head hangs.

"Katie." His voice breaks and he starts to step forward, but I hold up my hand.

"Fine. You want to fight? We'll fight." I unleash my anger and lightning so that it surrounds the ring, obstructing the view of the onlookers.

"Katie," Archer calls, bringing his fire to his hands but not releasing it. I don't waste any time using one of the bolts behind him to snap at the flame. He maneuvers away, keeping it lit. "I just want to talk to you."

"We're training," I say, sending a bolt straight at him, and he deflects my attack. "Good defense. Now attack me." I send another blast towards him and this one knocks him off his feet.

"You want to talk?" I ask, throwing more magic at him. "You win this match, and I'll listen. Otherwise, I have nothing to say to you, your highness."

He stands, anger flickering over his eyes. I see the decision in his eyes a split second before a fireball is blasting towards my head. I duck and it rips a hole in my lightning shield. The other soldiers outside the rink rush forward to peer through it. We're a blur, my lightning versus his fire. We dance around each other, evading, striking, blocking. We each get a few hits in, me more than Archer.

"ENOUGH," he bellows after a strike flicks his ear. His magic surges forward and surrounds me, trapping me in a circle of fire. The fire is hot, but it's not the crazy white-hot fire from Sicily, and I don't know if he can't tap into that power or if he's choosing not to. His eyes widen as the flames get closer to me and a maniacal laugh escapes my lips. With a flick of my wrist, his flames betray him, now bent to my will. Commanding someone else's Battle Magic is a maneuver that I know he's never seen because I'm the one who created it.

I feel a caress of magic against my mind, not an invasion, but a request to open a channel. I clamp my mind down around the tendril of Mind Magic he sent towards me, and I feel him shudder at the rejection.

"Katie, please." His magic struggles to extinguish his flames as they get closer and closer. At some point, my lightning shield shattered, and I can vaguely hear alarmed screams coming from the outside of the ring. But no one interferes.

Does it even bother you? I shatter Archer's mental shield, so my words ring out in his head. I drop the flames, replacing them with my lightning as it ties around his waist. *Do you even have any remorse? You* killed *five people, are you even phased?*

"Of course, it bothers me!" Archer screams as his magic shoots out in a blaze. I barely get a shield around myself as his magic destroys my lightning and explodes out of the ring, sending the soldiers dropping to their stomachs or throwing up their own shields.

Archer sinks to his knees as the flames dissipate. "Jefferson, get everyone out of here," I command, not taking my eyes off the prince. Archer waits until every last person has cleared the room before speaking again.

"You think I don't hear their screams every night?" he almost whispers. "You don't think I felt it as my magic took each one of their lives? Every second of every day I feel that loss, and fear what I was capable of.

"But I did it for you," he says, meeting my eyes.

"Explain," I command. Archer stands slowly and makes a move to approach me, and I visibly flinch. He halts his progress and runs a hand through his hair.

"When I sent my mind out like you told me to," he begins slowly. "I accidentally went past someone's defenses."

"You went into someone's mind?" I ask and he nods. "Did you see memories or their present?"

"Their present." A breath whistles from my lips. That's advanced Mind Magic, and very, very illegal. "I don't know how I did it. It just kind of happened. And once I was in their mind, I heard everything." He swallows hard before continuing. "They knew everything. They planned to wait for us to enter the building, and then call your father. He was going to teleport in and take you with him."

He closes the remaining distance and takes my hands in his. "I just lost it," he whispers, his voice breaking with emotion. "I didn't even...I knew what they wanted for the rest of us. I knew that we were all as good as dead. But when I heard they wanted to sacrifice you to that *psychopath—*"

He releases a hand and cups my face, his thumb gently brushing over my cheek, and I don't pull away. "I couldn't lose you. And my magic, it just reacted. The next thing I knew the building was on fire and you were calling my name, pulling me out of it."

I swallow thickly as I stare back at the prince, my insides jumbled in confusion. Archer uses his hand to guide my face closer to his until our brows are touching. He closes his eyes and I gently brush away the tear that falls down his cheek.

"Katie," his voice cracks and it shatters my resolve. If I were in his position, if I knew someone was going to hurt him, I would have done the same thing. I did do the same thing. I lit up an entire battalion to keep them away from the prince. I place a finger across his lips, gently stopping him from continuing.

"Seth tried to take me with him when he showed up in the mountains," I whisper, and his eyes pop open to find mine. "I was going to tell you...but then I got attacked by the mermaid and we were fighting..." I step back and curse, rubbing my palm across my face. "I should have given you all the facts. This is my fault."

"It was my magic."

"And if I had been professional and told you everything instead of—" I let out a strangled cry of frustration. "You drive me so crazy. It's like I have no control over my emotions around you." Tears spill down my cheeks as Archer prowls closer to me.

"I was so mad at you," I murmur as he invades my space and wraps me in his arms.

"I know."

"You killed an entire coven for me," I speak against his skin, and he nods. "I'm still not okay with that. My life isn't worth—"

He grabs my chin, tilting it up to his face. "You are worth *everything.*" I gulp as his hands hold me still.

"Archer—"

"I'll do anything to keep you safe. I will burn the world down for you." His eyes turn molten, and my heart jumps into my throat.

His hand slides along my jawline to the back of my neck, threading into my hair at the loosened base of my braid. He gently guides me closer, leaning down while I press up on my toes to meet him halfway. The kiss is soft, tentative, sweet. His tongue brushes along my lips as I open for him, sighing as he gently sweeps in, and we cautiously explore each other. His hand lowers to my waist and fireworks explode through my body as he pulls me flush against him.

We break apart only long enough to breathe each other in before we frantically collide again in a clash of lips, teeth, and tongues. It's bruising, claiming, and desperate. My fingers thread into his silken hair, digging into his scalp, begging him to give me more. My entire body is on fire, wanton need burning through me as we deepen the kiss. I unforgivingly tug his bottom lip between my teeth and his resounding groan turns my legs to jelly.

My chest heaving, I step back. Archer watches my moves, his eyes hungrily scanning over my body in my skintight training tunic.

"You'd burn the world for me?" I breathe. He nods slowly, his tongue darting out to wet his lips in a motion that makes my core tighten. I bite my lower lip and call my lightning to my hand. "You better be able to back that up."

"We're training...*now?*" he asks, an edge of desperation in his voice.

"Think of it as foreplay, *your highness,*" I give him a wink before I launch my lightning at him.

Chapter Twenty-One

EVERYTHING HURTS. NO LESS than twenty-four hours after Archer and I kissed, I was hit with the worst cold of my life. I guess flying non-stop for a week, through a blizzard, and then jumping straight into teaching classes all day will drain a person.

I absently swipe at my nightstand for my box of tissues to find it empty. I meant to use a replicating spell before using the last one, which is now full of snot in a crumpled heap on my stomach. I shiver and pull my comforter higher before resorting to wiping my nose with the sleeve of my flannel pajamas, a set that my mom gave me one Christmas, that I only ever wear when I'm sick. I pick up the novel that's propped open on my chest and read a paragraph eight times before laying it back in its spot. I whimper as my head gives another pulse against my skull. The whimper causes my throat to seize, and I cough...which then makes my head start to pound harder. *Fuuuuuckkkk.*

A gentle knock taps against my door, and when it creaks open, a box of tissues is thrust through.

"Come in," my voice is a hefty baritone and I cringe at the nasal quality that distorts my sounds.

Archer, looking entirely too fucking cute for words, pops his head around the door and gives me a wide smile. He's wearing a fitted tunic and his slacks for training, but his hair is neat and unrumpled. His eyes are bright and clear as they rake over my body in all its glory. I groan loudly and attempt to hide under the covers as he leans against the threshold.

"Stop it," I groan as he chuckles.

"Stop what?" I can hear his smile from under my blanket and my heart does a little skip.

"You look too sexy to be in here," I peek just my eyes out of the covers, and I see him step into my room, the door clicking softly behind him. He emits a throaty chuckle as he slowly prowls over to me with long, easy strides.

He reaches me and waves his wand, burning the used tissues around me and then guiding the ashes towards my garbage pail. He sits on the edge of my bed and gently reaches to pull the covers away from my face, and then smooths my hair down, which I'm sure is sticking out in all directions. He gives me a goofy smile, and I see my affection mirrored in his eyes.

"You're so beautiful," he whispers and leans in to kiss my forehead. "And so hot."

"I'm a mess."

"No, babe--" he murmurs, his brow furrowing.

"Babe?" I arch my eyebrows defiantly, and it hurts all the way to my hair follicles.

"What's wrong with babe?" he asks, giving me a tender smile, his hand replacing his lips on my forehead.

"Edina calls me babes, might be weird."

"Is she from Britain?" he asks, curiously.

"No, she just watches a lot of T.V."

"Right. Well, we can talk pet names later," he says, standing abruptly. "You have a fever. Do you want me to call the healer?"

"She came by." I shift under my blanket, my body aching in protest. "I have a tonic I'm supposed to take." I gesture vaguely to the bathroom, where I left the medicine.

"Did you take it?" I nod, which doesn't seem like the right answer since he heads to the bathroom. "When did you take it last?" he calls.

"Um...when she was here?" I offer.

He pops his head out, giving me a comical scowl, and brings out the bottle of tonic and a small cup. He hands the cup to me as he uncaps the bottle and pours. I down the thing and grimace. *Why can't healers find a way to make tonics taste better?* I decide to ask that question the next time one visits as I sink back on my pillow, handing Archer the cup back.

"How did you know I was sick?"

"I went to training," he kicks off his shoes and sits on my bed, this time leaning down so we're almost eye level. "And when Marcus was there and not you, I ditched."

"You should go train," I say, even as my body moves over to his and my head nestles against his chest. He laughs and wraps his arm around me, tugging me to his side.

"No way, I'm here for the long haul." I hum against his chest, as he strokes down the back of my arm. I feel him shift slightly and then reach down between us.

"Did you just try to grab my boob?" I ask, cracking one eye open. His laughter rumbles against my body as he pulls out the book that was on my chest. It must have fallen between us. "Oops."

"Darling, I'd never try to cop a feel when you're this sick." I glare at him. "No to darling? Is it the accent? What if I try to say it in American, *darlin*?" he says in possibly the worst attempt at a Western Accent that I've ever heard. I giggle and give him a quick kiss.

"You're an idiot," I say as I snuggle back into his arms. He takes my book, keeping one thumb to the page I was on and flips it over to read the cover.

"*Love Bites?*" I can feel him trying to contain his laughter as I playfully swat his chest. "Please tell me this is a trashy vampire romance novel."

"Not only is it a trashy vampire romance novel," I say pausing to sneeze. "It's a trashy vampire romance novel written by mortals."

"Shut up," he says eagerly flipping the book to the back and reading the synopsis.

"They're my guilty pleasure. I love hearing what they think about us magic-types."

"And what do they think?"

"Well," I start, rearranging myself so I can look at him. "In this book, vampires can walk in the sunlight."

"Stands to reason."

"And they prefer human blood but can survive on animal blood if they're feeling particularly humane." Archer scoffs. "And of course, there's the fact that they frequently fall in love with humans."

"Why would they not?" he deadpans, opening the book to the page I'm on, and clearing his throat.

"You're not going to read to me," I command weakly, attempting to swipe the book, but Archer wraps his hand around me and flattens me to his chest.

"Shhh, you close your eyes, I'll read." He clears his throat again and I groan in mortification but settle back into his arms.

"*Chapter Three. I was cornered, in a broom closet, with a man I wasn't entirely sure was a man.*" He gasps dramatically before continuing. "*He pins me back with one hand and I struggle against him, but he's unnaturally strong.* Well, at least they got that part right."

"Keep reading. It's about to get sexy," I murmur.

"How do you know?"

"I read a lot of these."

"*He grabs my jaw between the fingers of his other hand and tilts my chin up to him.*" Archer shifts the book so it's directly over my head and uses his other hand to grip my chin. "No laughing," he insists in response to my giggle. "This is serious vampire-y stuff.

"*His hand slowly falls to my neck, lingering there as my pulse flutters.*" Archer's hand gently slopes down my neck and I tilt my head to give him access. "*His knuckles travel lower, skimming along the side of my breast before his hand opens and he cups them, rolling my nip—"* Archer pauses, his hand still at my neck, and his eyes flit down to mine before skimming the rest of the page. His breathing quickens.

"Told you it was about to get sexy," I whisper. His breathing quickens as he continues silently reading, his pupils dilating as he flips the page. "You need a cold shower, your highness?"

I smile up at him, and he swallows hard. He tosses the book across the room and flips me onto my back, positioning himself over me. His head dips and he kisses me, groaning against my mouth as I open my legs wide enough for him to seat himself between my thighs.

"I'll get you sick," I protest, breaking away to steal air as his lips move across my jawline. He kisses just under my ear, sucking on my lobe before pulling it down with his teeth.

"I don't care," he murmurs against my skin as he continues down, stopping at the spot where my neck meets my shoulder. As he kisses the tender spot a moan escapes my lips, and his hands find my breasts over my pajamas.

"Fuck," he hisses against me when he realizes I'm not wearing a bra, and his thumb skims over my nipple. He grinds his hips into me as his mouth finds mine again, and I can feel every inch of his hardened length through the thin material separating us. I inhale sharply as a line of fire shoots straight into my core.

And then my body betrays me. I begin coughing so hard Archer jumps off me as I struggle to force air into my lungs.

When I finally compose myself, Archer sits beside me again, rubbing my back in soothing circles. I'm not ashamed to admit that I pout when I realize the moment has passed; I full-on stick my bottom lip out like a child at the fact that I ruined what was proving to be an incredibly sexy moment. Archer laughs and catches my bottom lip between his teeth before pulling me into another kiss.

"I'm going to get you some tea, and then you're going to sleep while I read the rest of that book," he says with a mischievous look.

WE SPEND THE REST of the day lying in bed together while Archer takes care of me. When I'm awake long enough, we talk about anything and everything until I can't imagine knowing a person better than I know my prince. Even though my chest is heavy with congestion, my heart is soaring by the end of the day, when he cradles me in his arms, the book forgotten on his chest. He looks at me like I hung the moon.

"Sweetie?" he murmurs against my hair. "Honey?" I shake my head.

"I use both of those sarcastically."

"Is there a pet name you don't use sarcastically?"

"You tell me, *your highness*," I deadpan. He laughs and kisses the top of my head.

"Love?" he whispers softly. I look up at him to find his eyes looking at me with such longing.

"Only when you mean it," I tell him. He nods and pulls me in for a slow, passionate kiss. His lips move gently, coaxingly, as if he's memorizing the feel of me against him. And that one kiss wrecks me. He doesn't need to say anything. I feel it all, every ounce of love he feels for me floods my body. My eyes water and my breath hitches as he pulls away slightly.

"Can I ask a favor?" he whispers against my lips. "The Winter Solstice is in two weeks. Well, you know how we have the Solstice Ball every year?"

"Yeah, I usually work it," I respond.

"Are you working it this year?" A look of pure terror washes over his face.

"No, not as a Captain. I think I'm supposed to attend. I have an invitation here somewhere."

"Well," he looks down as if afraid to meet my eyes. "Will you go with me?"

My eyes widen. Asking anyone to a palace ball is a huge deal, but the prince asking someone... I know for a fact that Archer has never taken a date to any of the balls, mainly because I would have overseen finding security for the bitch. The prince bringing someone to a palace ball is a statement to the Kingdom of Magic that they might as well get used to calling the girl 'your majesty'. *Whoa.*

"You don't have to answer now—" he says, still avoiding meeting my eyes.

"Yes," I answer instantly. I'm not sure whether it's the cold medicine talking, or the fact that he's nursed me back to health, but I feel the answer in my gut.

"Really?" His eyes light and a smile breaks across my face as I lean forward to kiss him. He traps me in by wrapping his hands through my hair, and I feel the relief flood through him. He pulls away to look at me and his eyes are glistening.

A thought crosses my mind, shattering the perfection of the moment, and I groan.

"What am I going to tell my mother?" I whine. Archer laughs and kisses me again.

"Rest, love," he whispers, guiding my head back to his chest and hugging me tightly to him. If he didn't, I'm pretty sure I'd float away. "We'll tell her and Marcus together."

"Whatever you say, *your highness,*" I murmur against his chest, and I feel it bounce as he tries to hide his laughter. I fall asleep with a stupid smile on my face.

Chapter Twenty-Two

I PACE THE LENGTH of the palace hallway in front of the throne room, my hands alternating between tugging down my burgundy sweater dress and running through my hair. Archer is annoyingly calm, watching me from his spot propped against one of the marble pillars, looking decidedly more formal than I am in his button-down and slacks.

I'm mentally calculating how long it would take me to get back to my barracks to change when Archer appears in front of me and takes hold of my hands.

"Have I told you how beautiful you look today?" he asks, pulling me into his arms. I whimper as he envelops me, letting his proximity soothe my pounding heart. He rubs my back in circles and I nuzzle into his chest, stealing some of his calm and surety.

Archer stayed with me for two days in my room, nursing me back to health. We watched movies, talked for hours, and he cuddled with me the entire time. I've never felt more cherished in my entire life. I honestly can't remember the last time I was content to just be held by someone. All my past relationships were passionate, but it was passion driven from drama. This--Archer and I—it's warm and fuzzy, which is not something I'm used to, but am trying to enjoy.

I break our embrace and give him a weak smile.

"You're so cute when you're nervous," he murmurs before stealing a quick kiss.

"I don't know how you're not freaking out." I break away and resume my pacing.

"Marcus will be here. He'll be our buffer," he assures me, and I nod absently. Marcus is usually the one who steps in between my mother and me, but now he needs to protect us from my mother *and* the king, and that's just a lot for any one person to handle.

The door bursts open, a bitter wind filling the hallway, making me shiver. My mother enters, her face already pinched in a scowl, with Marcus right on her heels. She sheds her winter peacoat and a servant materializes to take it from her. She eyes my civilian clothes and clicks her tongue as Marcus comes forward to hug me. His eyes widen in warning as if I couldn't already tell my mother is in a mood.

"Marcus tells me the two of you called this meeting," she starts as Marcus shakes Archer's hand. "Would you like to tell us why before we go in and see the king?"

Archer swallows hard, finally starting to show some of the nerves I've been feeling all morning.

"I assume it has something to do with the fact that you have been holed up in Katie's room for the past few days." The ice coating her voice is piercing. "Or the obscene public display of affection in the training ring."

She makes it sound like I mounted him in the middle of a class. It was one fucking kiss.

Nothing I say is going to matter. I can tell by her tone that she's already made up her mind that I've gone against orders. It's not like my mother has ever approved of any of my boyfriends, so it shouldn't bother me, but she still gets under my skin.

"What was the one order I gave you, Kathryn?" my mother demands. My hands fist at my side, the air charging as I work to control my magic.

"Misty—" Archer starts, stepping in and wrapping an arm around my waist.

"Your Highness, this is none of your concern," my mother responds, shooting daggers at me.

"Katie was nothing but professional on our mission," Archer asserts. "I pursued her, and I initiated the kiss in the training ring. I understand it wasn't the time or place, and I'm sorry for that, but I'm in love with your daughter."

Three jaws hit the floor. Archer leans over and kisses my temple.

"Don't look so surprised, love," he whispers against my hair. Then, louder, but still to me, "I've been falling in love with you since the moment we met."

I meet his eyes and he gives me a shy smile.

"You--you barely know each other," my mother stammers.

"I understand it seems fast," Archer continues, his focus returning to my mother. "The reason we called this meeting is so that we can tell my father that Katie will be my date to the Solstice ball."

"His Majesty is ready to see you," a guard announces from the huge double doors that lead into the throne room. My mother protests, but Marcus grabs her arm and steers her towards the chamber, giving Archer an approving nod before he leaves. As soon as they're through the door, we both release a sigh of relief.

"Okay, I dealt with your mom...you got this next part, yeah?" Archer says, wrapping me in a hug.

"If you think that's over, you're deluding yourself," I quip before leaning back and meeting his gaze again. "So, you like...really like me."

"Nah, not that much," he teases, and I press up on my toes to kiss him and playfully snap at his lower lip with my teeth. He chuckles against me and then pulls back, grabbing my hand and dragging me through the open doors.

The throne room is unnecessarily gigantic and filled with rows of chairs that typically sit empty since most audiences with the king are private. Gilded beams arch across a high vaulted ceiling, and four black-velvet pendants emblazoned with the Kingdom's crest hang from the rafters. The polished marble is interrupted only by a plush red carpet that runs from the doors to the throne.

The throne is carved from a solitary piece of white opal, which, when hit by the light streaming in from the floor-to-ceiling windows, becomes iridescent and shimmers with a thousand colors. The back gently curves to form three flames that frame the sovereign. The arms are fashioned to look like two magnificent dragons, their mouths agape as though they created the sparkling fire.

The king of the Kingdom of Magic sits atop the throne, a simple gold circlet on his balding head, his blonde hair having receded past its edges. He's wearing a crimson cape above a simple, yet obviously expensive, black tunic and pants trimmed in gold and bear the Kingdom's crest. His stubby fingers, each sporting a flashy gold ring with a different gem, tap against the dragon-head armrest as he watches us enter with carefully masked neutrality.

The king is the polar opposite of his son. Where Archer is tall and lean, the king is a stout man, his stomach protruding even though he's leaning back in his seat. Where Archer is pale with dark features, the King is tanned with light features, giving him the impression of being beige. The only thing they share is their ever-changing hazel eyes.

My mom and Marcus reach the throne and dip into a deep bow, sinking to the floor. They remain kneeling as Archer and I approach and genuflect behind them. I cast my eyes down, studying the black veins that snake through the white marble floor as I wait to be told to rise. A pair of shiny black wingtips stop in front of me, and I tentatively raise my eyes.

"Captain," the king's voice is warm and honied, a deep baritone sound that echoes in the empty chamber. He offers a hand to me, and I allow him to guide me off the floor and to stand before him.

"Or have you been promoted again?" he chuckles, a smile blooming from his thin lips. "It's been a few months, so surely I should be calling you a new title by now." He leans forward to kiss the air by both of my cheeks while grasping both of my arms between his thick fingers. I try to release some of my nerves as I return the gesture.

"No, Your Majesty."

"Leopold is fine, Kathryn. My savior should be nothing but familiar." He flashes me another smile before telling the rest of our party to rise. He approaches my mother and kisses her next. "Misty, have I mentioned how thrilled I am that you've brought your beautiful daughter into the Dragons?"

"Thank you, Your Majesty," my mother says tightly.

"I'm serious!" His eyes rake over me. "Different circumstances and she could be running the other side." My mother's eyes connect to mine, and she gives me a silent warning to keep quiet, but Marcus releases a booming laugh.

"Give it a few years and she'll be in charge of us all." He beams with pride as the king clasps his hand in greeting.

"Let's hope," the king murmurs low enough that I question whether I've heard him correctly. He then turns his attention to Archer, who bows his head again.

"Sir," Archer says coldly. I instinctively reach for him but drop my hand before it moves too far. The king doesn't miss the motion, and his head cocks to the side before he gives Archer his full attention.

"I've been meaning to set up a meeting," he says while he appraises his son, who keeps his head held high and his jaw clenched. "I assumed I had, only to find out that you called this audience."

"Yes, sir," Archer says.

The King turns on his heel and returns to his throne, crossing one leg and resting it on his opposite knee as he settles back into his seat. He laces his fingers together, resting his round chin against them as he waits for us to begin speaking. My mother and Marcus move off to the side so Archer and I stand directly in front of him.

"Why don't I start?" he asks, a cruel undertone in his voice. Archer opens his mouth to protest but then closes it. "I've been brought up to speed on your mission. It looks like you were finally able to tap into your hellfire."

"Hellfire?" I squeak out, and the king nods.

"The Baran line has always possessed that special aspect of our fire magic. Archer only displayed his affinity for it once, but not since. I was beginning to think it was a fluke."

"It appears not," Archer says tightly, the muscle in his jaw working overtime.

You've used it before? I send silently to Archer in our reformed mental channel. He gives me a short nod as his father addresses my mother about the details of our mission.

It's what killed my mother, Archer tells me, and I gasp. No wonder he was afraid of accessing his fire. The king's eyes are now back on us, but he plays off his curiosity behind a mask of boredom.

"Anyway," the king continues, "you've earned your Moment of Valor. I plan to reward you with your medal on the day of the Solstice Ball. We'll have the ceremony in the afternoon since the press will be on-site for the day. Captain Carmichael will present you with the medal, and perhaps make a speech."

I nod in acknowledgment as Archer gives me an apologetic look.

"Another matter. Kathryn," the king continues, his gaze turning to me. "The prisoner from your mission is proving to be a difficult one to crack. Even your mother couldn't get through her mental defenses."

My mother's head dips a fraction of an inch at this statement, her cheeks pinking slightly. Other than myself, my mom is one of the most accomplished users of Mind Magic in the Kingdom. If she can't get through this girl's mental blocks, I can't imagine how strong they must be.

"However," the king continues, "she says she'll speak to you freely."

"Me?"

"She asked for you by name," he says, appraising my reaction. "She said she would tell you whatever you wanted to know, but only you. You'll go down today. This is a matter of utmost importance as I'm sure you can appreciate. I expect an attack on the palace is imminent, and we need all the information you can gather.

"She's being brought to an interrogation room as we speak. You'll be given a list of questions when you arrive down there, and I have a uniform ready for you as well. Though I am curious as to why you and my son are in civilian clothes today. Is perhaps the reason you called this meeting personal?" I look to Archer, who has paled considerably and is lost in his own mind.

"Yes, Your Majesty," I say, taking the reins. Archer gives me a weak smile of thanks.

"I think I'd like to hear this from my son," he cuts me off with a wave of his hand. I take a step towards Archer and nod in encouragement to him.

"Katie and I..." Archer begins and then clears his throat. "I have asked Katie to be my date to the Solstice Ball. And she has accepted." I reach out and grab his hand and squeeze it as the king arches his pale eyebrows. He regards us for a long time and then turns to Marcus and my mom.

"I assume you knew about this?"

"We found out today," Marcus says beaming. "I couldn't be more thrilled for both of them, Your Majesty."

"And you, Misty?" My mother's eyes fall on us.

"I'm processing, Your Majesty," she says, contempt dripping from her words. The king laughs loudly and turns back to us.

"Very well," he says thoughtfully. "I approve of this match." I release a breath of air, tension in my chest uncoiling. "I'll prepare the staff and we'll announce your engagement at the start of the ball."

"Engagement?" I breathe, looking to Archer.

"No, Father," the prince says, stepping forward. "We're not engaged."

"We haven't even been on a date yet." I laugh, but the king scowls.

"Then you don't attend the ball together."

"That's not fair," Archer almost whines, dropping my hand in defeat.

"He's right, Kathryn," my mom pipes in. "When the prince brings an escort to the ball it's saying—"

"I understand what it's saying." I take a step forward and grab Archer's hand again. "Archer and I have no intention of breaking up anytime soon, but it's entirely too early to announce an engagement. The press will get wind of our relationship sooner or later and we would like to control the narrative. We can do so starting at the ball." Archer beams at me.

I didn't think it was possible to love you more, his mind presses into mine. My heart flutters as I meet his gaze. He makes me feel more alive than I ever have before. *Is this love?* There's no way that it could happen this quickly...*can it?*

"A compromise then," the king says, snapping me out of my musings. "You arrive at the party separately. Archer has some duties to perform as the crown prince, he'll attend to those for the first hour, and then you can spend the rest of the evening together. You may announce your relationship to the press, but you will allude to the fact that an engagement is imminent."

Archer eyes me hopefully. I guess it doesn't matter if I enter the ball on his arm as long as I get to be with him for the fun part. Lord knows I do not want to stand on the dais all night and play princess. I nod slowly, and Archer turns and repeats the gesture to his father.

"Wonderful," the king smiles broadly. "On that note, Kathryn you have a prisoner waiting."

And with a wave of a hand, we're dismissed.

Chapter Twenty-Three

I CHANGE INTO MY tunic and leggings and secure my hair in an elastic before rushing down to the bowels of the palace. The clicking of my boots against the stone steps is the only sound as I descend floor after floor to the dungeon. I left Archer with my mother and Marcus, silently wishing him luck for the onslaught of questions he'd no doubt receive about our relationship. He could handle that. I need to handle a Dark Witch.

I step into a corridor, the cold, damp air pressing a sense of dread into my body. The only light comes from a few sconces with low, flickering flames, casting the whole floor in shadows. I move past empty cells, the bars humming with magic suppressants. I instinctively draw my lightning to reside beneath my skin, the current providing me comfort as it buzzes away my nerves.

The dungeon isn't meant for permanent use. It's mostly a holding cell until transportation can be arranged to the prison. A few very unlucky witches have been kept here longer than a day, usually as they undergo questioning and mental interrogation. I can't imagine what it would be like to be stuck down here for longer than that, I feel claustrophobic just walking through the halls.

I make it to the end of the hallway and press my hand against a solid iron door. A soft light emanates from my hand as the lock recognizes my signature and pops open. Fluorescent lighting blinds me, and I blink rapidly as my eyes adjust to the new space. The offices that line the hallway have glass windows and heavy wooden doors. I nod to one of the Dragon officers typing something furiously at his desk as he hastily nods back.

I approach the last door and knock, looking through the window at a burly man with a thick, brown handlebar mustache. He's on the phone, although he must have a spell cast to silence his office because I can't hear a thing he's saying. He holds up one finger through the window as he wraps up his conversation and I tap my foot impatiently. There's no reason for me to have an escort to the interrogation room other than bureaucratic bullshit, which I have zero patience for.

Officer Handlebar ends his conversation and silently walks around me, expecting me to follow. He leads me through another iron door and into a dark observation room with a two-way mirror. I peer through the mirror into the stark white space with a single metal table in the center. The prisoner sits in a folding chair, her long blonde hair knotted and her curls sticking out in multiple directions. Her faded dress is torn, still dirty, and looks looser than when I saw her last. The dark circles under her grey eyes are making her gaunt.

"Have they not fed her? Allowed her to shower?" I scowl at the officer who lingers in the doorway.

"She refuses all food, and when we bring her to the shower, she just stands in the stall staring. The only words she's spoken since she's arrived is your name." I sigh exasperatedly.

"I want total privacy," I tell Handlebar as I roll my shoulders. "No cameras, no agents in here."

"Captain—"

"Someone can view my memories after the interrogation so you can hear everything. But I have a feeling she won't talk with eyes and ears listening in." Handlebar grumbles something, and I fix him with a commanding glare. "Do I need to call His Majesty? Or my mother?"

"No, Captain," he says quickly, and I can't tell which threat scared him into submission. "I'll disable the cameras and lock the door here. Here's the list of questions from His Majesty. When you're done come find me." He backs into the hallway, closing the door behind him, and I glance over the questions briefly before balling up the paper and using my lightning to turn it to ash.

My eyes connect with the prisoner's through the glass, sending a shiver down my spine. I know she can't see me but it sure as hell feels like she can.

I walk into the interrogation room, and the girl emits a strangled sob. She reaches her cuffed hands across the table like she wants to hold mine. I sit across from her in the chair allotted for me but push back out of reach, calling my magic to my fingertips just in case. Even though the handcuffs suppress hers, I don't want to take any chances.

"My Katie," her voice is raspy with disuse and crackles over the words. "You've grown into such a beautiful woman."

"You asked to speak to me." Despite the nagging memory that tries to pull my focus, I keep my voice neutral.

"Yes," she breathes, tears slipping down her cheeks and pooling in her upturned smile. "I couldn't say anything with so many prying ears on our journey here. I know you don't recognize me, but how could you? Father told me—"

"Father?" I cut her off, but she nods excitedly. *It can't be.* I shake my head vehemently. *There's no way...*

"I've missed you so much." She reaches for me again, but I stand, pushing her away and backing up to the mirrored wall.

"What kind of sick joke is this?" I ask no one in particular. "Adriana died the night--"

"The night your lightning emerged?"

How does she know about that? My mother and I haven't told anyone about that night and I just found out that I didn't always have lightning. Unless my father told the Dark Magic Covens...

That has to be it. This is some sort of elaborate ruse to get me to trust her. I gather myself and sit back down across from her, trying to prove she didn't rattle me by fixing my face in a mask of indifference.

"I had to let you believe you killed me," she continues, her voice smaller and oddly sincere.

"If you're really Adriana," I say carefully, "let me see your memories. Something only Adriana and I shared."

"Of course," she closes her eyes, tilting her palms up to the sky like she's an offering. *Fine, whatever works.* Once I prove she's full of shit, I should be able to easily move through her mind and see where my father is hiding.

I extend my mind to hers, finding no resistance, but seeing a memory hovering near the forefront. I decide against bypassing it, allowing my mind to slowly seep into the memory.

I see myself as a child, lying on a stone table, my hands tied down by Dark Magic. The room is the same as I remember, but I'm seeing it through different eyes, eyes that can barely see over the elevated slab. I watch from the sidelines as my father approaches the table and sends magic into my younger self's body.

The memory blacks out for a moment as I close my eyes. Blood-curdling screams assault my ears and physically pain me. The vision comes back into focus when I hear Father curse. He storms from the room, slamming the door behind him.

I approach the table, seeing my younger self writhing in pain, my auburn eyes red and splotchy with tears.

"Adriana," my younger self whimpers, and my hand in this memory reaches out to remove the magical binds.

"My Katie," I murmur, and I pull my younger self into a hug.

"It hurts," she cries, and I make soothing sounds as I stroke her hair.

"I know," I whisper. "But it'll be worth it when you're the queen."

"I don't want to be queen," she cries again.

"What do you want?"

"Ice cream," my younger self says with a sniffle, and I chuckle.

"Then we need to go find some ice cream."

The vision changes to the two of us sneaking out of our house and running down the streets of Salem until we reach an ice cream shop. It switches again to the two of us eating ginormous cones outside the shop on their stone benches. One final switch of the two of us lying to my mother, who asks why we're not hungry for dinner.

I pull my mind out, tears welling in my eyes. I haven't thought about that day in almost fifteen years. Adriana and I swore we would never tell another soul about our ice cream date. She was afraid our parents would be mad that she used her allowance to spoil our appetites.

"Adriana—" I whisper, reaching across the table and grabbing my sister's hands. "You're alive." The words are barely a whisper. "How--?"

"The night you got your Dark Magic, I had a vision that I was going to resurrect the Dark Magic Covens in preparation for you," she explains, gripping my hands tightly, assuring me that she's real.

"You...what?" There's so much in that sentence that I don't understand.

"Oh, I'm a touch clairvoyant," she says, pride filling her eyes. "Unfortunately, I haven't mastered it. My visions are unpredictable at best. I saw myself serving at your right hand, but I also saw that I would have to leave you for that to pass.

"The night your body accepted the Dark Magic, I knew it was time. I found a coven member hiding nearby, and she took me in.

She moved me back here, to England, because she knew Misty would be looking for me. I needed her to think I died that night, so you had to believe it as well."

"You were only eight," I whisper.

"I had a normal childhood," she shrugs. "Then, when I was twenty and fully trained in my magic, I began to gather the covens. I reached out to the leaders who weren't in prison to help me, and we began recruiting new members. We built an entire fortress to house everyone when the time comes. It's truly spectacular; it has meeting rooms, a training ring, and dormitories, completely hidden from magical and non-magical eyes. Some of the most extensive magic I've ever worked is in that building."

"Which is where?" I ask.

"I'll take you," she says with a wave of her hand. "Not everyone is there yet, and they won't be until you call them. That's one of the more ingenious spells I created. Only the leaders of each coven know the location of our fortress, and even if they tell, they can't arrive unless specifically called by you or me...or I guess Father. It's keyed to our blood."

My head spins. The magic she's speaking about is intense Dark Magic. Adriana must be one of the most powerful witches in the world. How is it that she's still locked in this dungeon? How is it that she was captured in the first place?

"The covens are set up around the world, waiting for instruction, getting more powerful each day. Once they were set up, I freed Father and the other leaders from prison." My mouth drops open.

"How—"

"I'll teach you." She grins happily. "As your right hand, it is my job to fill you in on all the gaps in your education. Father predicted this would happen. He knew you'd be an expert at wielding your lightning, but you have so much more within you that I can't wait to unlock. You'll be the most powerful witch in history. I just know it."

"How can you teach me if I don't have Dark Magic?" I ask.

"You do. The lightning is the clash of the Dark and the Light within you," she says like it's the most obvious thing in the world. "But you can call on them separately. I'll show you how as soon as we arrive at the Dark Magic Headquarters."

"Adriana, I'm not going anywhere," I insist, pushing away from her. "And neither are you."

"You're coming back with me. You're our queen. I'll take you to Father, we'll begin the next phase, and with you on the throne—"

"Adriana, I'm not your queen," I say, firmer this time, but she just smiles serenely back at me. "I have no desire to be anyone's queen."

"No? Are you not on your way to being a queen here? Are you not involved with the prince?"

"How do you know that?"

"Clairvoyance. Katie," she tilts her head to the side like she feels sorry for me. Like she's explaining something to a child. "You were made in the image of Finley. You are destined, prophesized to take the crown, and restore honor to our magic. Not through marriage, through conquest."

"Who the hell is Finley?" I demand.

"*Who is Finley?*" Adriana sighs, exasperated. "By the darkness, what did Misty teach you?"

"Not that, clearly," I say with more sass than I intend. "Would you like to enlighten me?" She grows quiet, her eyes flitting closed, and then she inhales sharply.

"No, you'll have to figure that out for yourself. Check the royal library. The information you seek is in there. I'm afraid company is coming."

"Adriana," I implore, "you need to tell me where Father is. What's his next plan of attack?"

"You'll see soon enough. I know you don't trust me yet, but I promise you can. When you need me, I'll be there."

"Adriana—"

"My queen," she stands and walks around the table. Her hands come forward to cup my cheeks as tears spring to her eyes again. "We won't be separated for long this time."

"Separated?" I hear the door to the observatory burst open. Adriana moves to the center of the room and gives me a crooked smile. She raises her bound hands in front of her and then disappears in a cloud of grey smoke just as the interrogation room opens and my mother spills in followed by two other guards.

"Katie," her breathing is shallow like she ran here. "Where did she go? Where's Adriana?"

"She just teleported! How is that possible? She had cuffs on." I ask frantically.

"Search the grounds. She couldn't have gone far," my mother commands, and the guards rush back out of the room.

"How did you know she was Adriana?" I ask my mom.

"She must have planted a vision in my head when I interrogated her." My mother shakes her head wildly. "It just unlocked a minute ago and I ran here as soon as I figured out who she was. My god, I thought she was dead all this time."

"Mom, what was the vision?" Her throat bobs and she pales.

"You were wearing a ruby crown sitting on a throne. You were leading the Dark Magic Covens."

Chapter Twenty-Four

I SINK INTO THE bathtub, letting the warm water and the eucalyptus and lavender bubble bath drain some of the tension in my shoulders. To say the last two weeks were long would be the understatement of the fucking year. Adriana's escape led to extra training, both as a teacher and a student again. My mother decided the best way to combat the Dark Witches would be to learn to separate my magic. It's not going well.

Even today, which was supposed to be a day of pampering before the ball tonight, was taken up by the medal ceremony for Archer's Moment of Valor, which lasted way longer than I anticipated. I *may* have pouted about missing a massage so that Archer would let me use the bathtub in his suite to get ready. I was hoping he'd join me...but apparently, a girl can only ask for so much.

Every stolen second Archer and I have had together these past two weeks has been...honestly, it's been a fucking tease. Every quick kiss, lingering look, even that time he dragged me into a supply closet to reenact the chapter he read to me from *Love Bites* has me going out of my mind.

My hand drifts down my stomach, settling between my legs as I remember the feel of his fingers teasing and stroking and coaxing me higher and higher. A small moan escapes my lips as I circle my clit, imagining Archer in the tub with me, pulling me to straddle him and gripping my hips as he guides me down onto his—

"What are you thinking about?" My eyes pop open to find Archer leaning against the doorway. The sight of him almost finishes me off then and there. He's already dressed in his black tux, the slim cut highlighting his lean muscles.

"You," I answer breathlessly. "And the supply closet." His eyes scan down my body to where my hand has stilled against my sex. "And how you should finish what you started."

"It's not my fault we were interrupted," he purrs, slowly stalking towards me.

I flick a soap bubble at him with my free hand. "You didn't have to answer the door."

"Well..." he slowly removes his jacket and hangs it on a hook. Then he starts on his cufflinks, opening them and setting them on the vanity.

"What are you doing?" I ask weakly, my mouth suddenly dry.

"How did you put it?" he asks with a wry smile, slowly rolling up his sleeves to the elbows. "Finishing what I started."

He crouches down next to the tub, his hazel eyes not leaving mine as he reaches beneath the flimsy layer of bubbles and his fingers follow the same path mine took only moments before.

I groan as he bypasses my hand and slides a finger inside me. "Fuck, Archer."

"I don't have much time," he whispers, his nose brushing against the shell of my ear as he nips at my earlobe. "You think you can come quickly for me, love?"

My brain short circuits and I make a non-sensical sound between a whimper and a word. He chuckles darkly, his breath warm against my skin. "Good, now rub your clit. Let me watch you pleasure yourself."

I'm helpless to do anything but submit. I arch my hips, careful not to slosh water onto his tux until his finger is hitting the perfect spot. I was already so close that in no time I'm seconds away from orgasm.

"Archer?" Jai's voice calls from the suite.

"Ignore him," Archer whispers as my eyes pop open.

"Your dad's throwing a shit fit." Jai's voice is distinctly closer. "You need to get down—Oh fuck." He rounds the corner and I shriek. His eyes widen in horror before he swiftly turns around. "Oh shit, I'm sorry. You uhh... Hi Katie. I didn't see anything I swear."

"I swear to god, Jai..." Archer grumbles, his fingers still inside me. I swat his hand away, my orgasm well and fully out of reach.

"They sent me up here...I didn't know..." Jai sputters.

"Go wait in the sitting room at least," Archer barks, and Jai flees.

"This is twice you've given me blue balls, your highness," I say as he stands, drying off his arm with an apologetic grimace.

"We have the worst fucking luck," he says by way of an apology. I watch, disappointed, frustrated and so unsatisfied as he begins the process of redressing. When he's done, he comes over and kisses me sweetly.

"I'll see you down there, love." He punctuates the statement with another peck before leaving, closing the door behind him.

"Fucking hell," I groan and start actually bathing.

I HURRY DOWN THE hall, my red stilettos clicking on the stones as my gown flutters around my legs. I only slow my pace when I make it to the chamber outside the ballroom, scanning the area for signs of my mother and Marcus who are supposed to escort me inside.

The hall is filled with witches in their finest. I nod politely to a few people I recognize from school and am not ashamed to say I duck behind a pillar when I catch sight of my ex-boyfriend, Rodger. *How the hell did he get invited?* He's the farthest from a courtier that you can possibly get.

"Is there a reason you're hiding behind a pillar?" My mother's voice in my ear has my lightning springing to my hands and I jump as I turn around. Marcus chuckles, all decked out in his white military formals and countless medals.

"I saw a ghost," I murmur to my mom, who is in a simple A-line navy gown. She looks over my shoulder and rolls her eyes.

"I told Archer it was a mistake to invite him," she says with a click of her tongue.

"He what?" I slowly turn, but the offending party has disappeared into the ballroom.

"He's always been a fan," Marcus says with a shrug. I raise my eyebrows at him, silently calling him on his bullshit, and Marcus's lips twitch trying to hold back a smile.

"Kathryn," my mother says, drawing my attention back to her. "You know there are rules of etiquette for how you behave tonight."

"We've been over this," I deadpan.

"No overt displays of public affection," she barrels on, ignoring me. "When you dance, keep to the ballroom styles you've learned, don't dance too close."

"Yes, Mother."

"And for the love of magic, do not talk to any of the reporters." She reaches forward and shifts one of my meticulously placed curls. "I know the king said otherwise, but your mouth has gotten you in trouble before."

"I promise to be on my best behavior," I say with a sickly-sweet smile. She purses her lips in response and stalks off towards the doors, leaving me alone with my stepfather.

"How do you deal with her?" I ask him, letting out an exasperated sigh.

"She means well," he says with a large smile. He holds out his hand for me to take, but rather than begin escorting me in, he twirls me around. "You're going to give poor Archer a coronary."

I laugh as I smooth down the bodice, which is encrusted with ruby-red crystals and hugs tight to my waist. The crystals drip in tendrils down white chiffon that flutters out before pooling at my feet. My hair is down, save for one piece that's clipped back with a silver comb studded with rubies that my mother let me borrow. I fix the curl my mother mussed so it lies off to the side of my shoulder and doesn't obscure the sweetheart neckline...and my cleavage. Which I have to say is fucking on point tonight.

Marcus links my arm in his and we make our way to my mother who is chatting with one of the Dragons officers on duty at the doors.

"Oh, Kathryn," she says as we approach, and she takes Marcus's other arm. "Don't forget to open your Dragons channel."

"I'm not working tonight," I respond coolly.

"It's a no-chatter channel," she shoots back, shifting into her commanding officer voice. "For emergencies only." I roll my eyes but open the channel that links the minds of all the Dragons officers.

"Enjoy your evening," the officer stationed at the doors says before swinging the doors wide.

"Generals Carmichael and Weatherbeak, and Captain Carmichael," someone announces as we step onto a grand staircase that leads to the ballroom.

It's nothing short of a dream. The room is lit with thousands of fairy lights in red, green, and gold, giving the space an unearthly glow. Evergreen wreaths with gilded bows line the stairs. Christmas trees of varying sizes and décor dot the hall, my favorite being the tree made entirely of poinsettias sitting next to the small orchestra. A large banquet table filled with desserts extends the length of one wall, while the other comprises floor-to-ceiling windows that open to a moonlit garden.

The king sits atop a dais adjacent to the stairs and gives me an approving nod as we descend. No sign of Archer, though I've been warned that he would have various 'duties' to attend to before my arrival. I scan the dance floor, filled with couples whirling around to the lively waltz and the clusters of courtiers laughing insipidly at something that I doubt was funny. We descend the last step, and I decide to excuse myself from my mother and Marcus to hit up the dessert table when suddenly, he's there.

"Wow." Archer appears before us, and ignoring both generals beside me, takes my hand in his gloved one. His head dips as he places a kiss against my knuckles that sends a delicious warmth coursing up my arm, into my chest, and pooling in my core. He smiles against my skin as his hazel eyes look up to meet mine, causing my heart to flutter. A strand of hair breaks loose from its gelled hold, and I fight the urge to brush it back into place. There are rules. Rules my mother was very clear on. Rules that—

Archer tugs me forward and his mouth crushes against mine. My body instantly melts into him as his arms wind around my waist and I grab the lapels of his jacket to pull him closer. *Fuck the rules.*

Distantly, I hear my stepfather clear his throat, and feel my mother pinch the underside of my arm. Even with my eyes closed, I see the blinding flashes of cameras going off and am aware of the not-so-subtle whispers wondering how a *soldier* managed to captivate the prince. Still, I don't pull away, savoring the contact I've missed so desperately these past two weeks.

When Archer finally nips my bottom lip, I pull back with a breathless laugh. My gaze is still narrowed to his lips, which are now smeared with my red lipstick. I consider leaving it for a least a dance, but I've pushed my luck enough. I wave my hand in front of his face and the makeup disappears. Archer removes his wand and taps it lightly against my lips, and I feel the tingling caress of his magic, which I assume did the same thing for me.

"Your highness," Marcus finally cuts in, and I don't miss the amusement in his tone.

"Generals," Archer says, with a lazy smile, breaking away from me to shake Marcus's hand and kiss my mother on the cheek...another blatant rule break that makes her squawk. Then he's back at my side, grasping my arm.

"Happy Solstice," Archer directs to my parents as he escorts me towards the dance floor. His arm is rigid beneath mine like he just now remembered he has a protocol to follow, and I can't help but laugh as he holds me away from his body.

Everyone on the dance floor has come to a standstill, no doubt reeling from our earlier performance. Archer ignores it all and leads me to the center of the floor beneath a large chandelier, its light reflecting off the crystals in my dress so that I'm practically glowing. He places a hand on the base of my spine and holds the other out for me to grasp. I barely have a moment to place my other hand on his shoulder before he's whirling me around.

I'm no slouch on the dance floor. Ballroom dancing is something every Dragon officer is required to take as we rise through the ranks to represent ourselves in society. But Archer is stellar.

His body moves assuredly, guiding me through the motions with perfect fluidity. I was trained for this...but Archer was *born* for it.

I allow myself to relax, my eyes taking in the glittering opulence of the ballroom and all the courtiers in their finest as we take another trip around the dance floor. I feel Archer's eyes on me like a laser even as I look around. I'm afraid if I meet that gaze, I'll be completely consumed by the fire that lights his eyes.

The music slows and Archer pulls me in closer, breaking that strict ballroom hold to draw me tight against his lean frame. He leans in so close that when I finally tilted my chin up to catch his eyes, the tip of his nose brushes mine.

"You look so beautiful," he murmurs, his breath tickling my lips.

"You're not half bad yourself, your highness." I bite my lip and he tracks the movement hungrily, emitting a low hum that reverberates in my chest.

I suppose couples eventually join us on the dance floor, but I don't notice. My entire world has narrowed to the man in front of me, to his firm grip on my waist, to his cedar and agave scent that envelops me. I brush my lips gently against his, sighing as he kisses me back briefly.

"Do you have to dance with the other courtiers?" I ask tentatively, really asking if he's planning on following that rule.

"Is that why you didn't set your lipstick?" Archer gives me a knowing smirk with red-tinted lips from our brief brush. "That's quite possessive of you, love."

"Pot. Kettle." I tease and he dramatically inhales in feign shock. "You want to explain how my ex got an invitation?"

"I don't know what you're talking about," he says with a grin before drawing me into another kiss. "Is it bad of me to want everyone to know you're mine?" he murmurs against my lips.

"No," I reply, sliding my arm down and around to his back so I can lean my head against his shoulder as we sway.

"Good," Archer places a kiss in my hair. "Because I don't plan on letting you go."

The music stops, the conductor turning to the crowd as we all politely applaud him. If I hadn't been focused solely on my prince, I don't think I would have seen the slight nod of his head or the light that passes over his eyes. When Archer notices me staring, he smiles widely.

"I have a surprise for you," he whispers, and the orchestra starts up again. I recognize the melody instantly.

My lullaby.

No. Our song.

I don't know when it switched, maybe when we were in the cave, but somehow Archer turned a song meant to drive away nightmares and pain and turned it into something so much more.

Tears prick my eyes and emotion chokes my throat as his eyes search mine expectantly. I have no words for the surge of emotions I feel towards this man, my prince. That's a lie. There are words. But *those* words get lodged in my throat.

"I didn't mean to make you cry," Archer whispers, his face concerned as a tear falls from my lashes.

"It's not..." I swallow hard. "It's perfect."

"You're perfect," he says earnestly, and I fight the urge to laugh in his face at the cheesiness of that statement. Instead, I kiss him again.

I mean for the kiss to be light, a small way to express my feelings for him even when I can't voice them. But Archer seizes control, his hand dropping mine and cupping my cheek before threading into my hair and tugging me closer. I gasp as he uses his grip on my waist to tug me flush against him.

"I need you," he growls against me, as his hand skims down the exposed skin on my back, leaving a trail of goosebumps in its wake. "*Now.*"

"If we leave together..." My head reels at the thought of the headlines. Archer grunts in agreement, and swallows thickly.

"The garden," he murmurs. "Take the path on the far right to the wall. There's a walkway hidden by ivy. I'll meet you there in ten minutes."

I slowly run my thumb along the curve of Archer's mouth, the lipstick marring his soft lips magically vanishing as I pass. When I pull away, he swallows *hard* and adjusts his pants before leading me off the dance floor. He holds my hand as we head in separate directions, grasping my fingers and keeping his eyes on me until we can no longer reach. I wait for the paparazzi to turn their attention to the prince before discreetly slipping through the large doors and into the winter air of the garden.

The garden is an elaborate maze of hedges that stand eight feet tall, the center of which is a fountain laden with sparkling jewels. I skirt past the couples milling about searching for a secluded corner and walk along the right edge of the maze towards the castle wall. Night-blooming roses hang from a trellis on the outer edge of the garden, their petals open in the bright moonlight.

It takes me a minute to find the ivy along the castle wall at the opposite end of the garden. I cast a glance around, making sure no stray paparazzi followed me from the ballroom before I slip into the dark, narrow passageway between the hedges and the outer wall. The moonlight barely filters in here through the thick ivy growing overhead, and I doubt anyone would know about this passage unless specifically told.

I'm only a few paces in when strong hands grip my hips and spin me roughly, pushing my back against the wall. My breath catches as lips find my own in the darkness, and I arch into the kiss, flicking my tongue against something hard and metal. *The fuck—*

I push the man away and cast a ball of light to illuminate the hallway. *Rodger.* His blue suit is open at the collar, revealing a peek of the tattoo that snakes up his neck. He pushes a hand through his mud-brown hair, which is longer since I last saw him.

"Hey babe," he purrs and takes a step towards me again. His eyes scan me, lingering on my breasts. "Miss me?"

"Fuck off," I hiss. "What do you want?"

"I think that's fairly obvious," he cages me in and leans down again like I'll somehow fall under his spell again. I let him invade my space and then I slap his face, adding lightning to my palm so it leaves a good sting. He reels back, his hand coming up to cradle the spot which is rapidly turning red.

"Do it again," he groans, his eyes lighting. I surround myself with an invisible shield, so when he advances the next time, he collides with the air around me.

"You're no fun," he tsks. "You could have at least tied me up."

"You'd like that." His responding smirk is enough to let me know I'm right. "You gonna tell me why you followed me back here? Or do I have to search through your nasty-ass thoughts?"

"That's the hard limit, babe," he teases, but I detect an iota of fear in his voice. "Are you going to act like you weren't trying to make me jealous out there?" He gestures wildly to the ballroom.

I laugh like it's the funniest joke I've ever heard. "I didn't even know you were here."

"Bullshit," he charges my shield again and bounces off it. "You—"

A rustle of ivy cuts him off, and my eyes pop open. *If Archer finds me back here with Rodger*...I shudder.

"You have to go," I say. Rodger opens his mouth to protest, but I throw lightning at him, binding him to the hedges. Then I cast a shield around him, weaving in an invisibility and muting spell so his protests are effectively cut off. I extinguish the light just as Archer steps into the corridor.

"Love?" Archer whispers. I take a few steps further down the passage, so he hears my heels. The wall behind me gives way into a small alcove, and I press into it and wait.

"Are you hiding from me?" Archer asks, his voice husky, almost predatory. "I'd think after your bath you'd be eager—"

I reach out just as he passes the alcove and grab his arm, pulling him against me and kissing him savagely. He pushes me further back, and my back bumps against something smooth and cold.

"What the hell—" I call light again and find myself against a glass case that holds a silver sword with a ruby in the hilt. "That's a random place for a sword—"

Archer cuts me off by claiming my mouth again, and all thoughts in my mind are silenced by the heat that scores through my body. His hands skim my waist while mine immediately fist into his raven hair. Our tongues dance and I groan, wordlessly begging him for *more*. In one smooth motion, he grips my ass and hoists me up as I wrap my legs around his waist. He pushes the fabric of my dress up, so my legs are bare around him, and I roll my hips against his rapidly hardening erection.

"Archer," I gasp as he gently nibbles and kisses my neck.

"Fuck," he groans in my ear before nipping down on my earlobe and thrusting his hips against me. I let out a breathy moan which drives him into a frenzy. He grinds into me relentlessly, making the crystals of my dress bite into my skin in the most delicious way. Suddenly he's on the move, my legs still wrapped around him. I trail my lips across his jaw as he carries me to the end of the corridor and starts ascending a spiral-iron staircase. At the last minute, I remember I've restrained Rodger, and wave my hand quickly, dropping the various spells as Archer kicks open the door at the top of the stairs.

I squint against the bright light as Archer lowers me to my feet. He shuts the door behind us and covers it with a tapestry pushed to the side.

"You have a secret entrance to your room?" I ask, taking in my surroundings. He nods, giving me that sexy as hell smirk as he shrugs off his jacket. "What was the point in me watching you if you could escape out the back?" He wraps his arms around me, and I playfully swat at his chest.

"I'm sorry," he murmurs, his eyes hooding as he places a kiss in the crook of my shoulder. His jaw skims along my collar bone, and I throw my head back to give him better access. His fingers draw lines of fire up my skin as they wrap around my back.

I move out of his grasp, turning my back to him. "Unzip me?" I brush my hair to the side as his hands quickly grasp my zipper. He resumes kissing my neck and my shoulders as it slides down my back. Once it's down, I turn back to him holding my dress up with my hands as my eyes flit pointedly to his chest. He loosens his tie, tugging it over his head and his hands move down the buttons of his shirt as I let my dress drop, revealing my white corset and matching lace panties. His jaw slackens and I bite my lower lip as he shrugs his shirt off.

"You're perfect." His voice is thick with desire. I step out of my dress and sit down on the edge of his bed, crossing one leg over the other as he quickly removes his belt and slides his pants down until he's only in his black boxer briefs. I swallow as I take in the length of him, rock hard and practically uncontained by the thin fabric. I scoot back on the bed, my thighs falling open as he approaches slowly, stepping between them. His throat bobs as his knuckles brush against my jaw.

He guides me to lie on my back and hovers over me, tenderly tucking a lock of hair behind my ear. When he kisses me again, it's like he can't get enough, like he's savoring every second. His hands fall to my breasts and my nipple hardens as he gently pinches. I gasp at the hurt, but he drops down and sucks, turning the short-lived pain into pure ecstasy.

I writhe under him as he continues lower, hooking his fingers around the edge of my panties. I lift my hips and he slides them down my legs, dropping to his knees between my thighs. His eyes are molten as they connect with mine and we don't break the intense gaze as he draws a finger down my center.

"Fuck," he breathes as he finds it slick for him. His fingers continue long, luxurious strokes, skirting around the one area I want him to touch as he nibbles my inner thighs. I squirm, trying desperately to push him to where I need contact. He pauses his exertions to give me a smirk that has me whimpering in anticipation, before plunging a finger inside me as his mouth captures my clitoris. My body bows off the bed as his finger mercilessly pumps me, and his tongue rolls over the bundle of nerves. I feel my body tightening I climb higher and higher.

"Archer, please," I moan, and he slides another finger inside me. I explode around him, crying out in ecstasy. He continues to wring out every last moment of pleasure that my body can give him. I throw my hands over my face as I shudder, coming down. He stands, looming over me, and with his free hand pins my hands above my head.

"Let me see you," he whispers, as an aftershock rips through my body. His mouth captures mine and his tongue pushes inside just as his throbbing cock nudges my entrance. I gasp as he stretches me, slowly adding more length with each gentle thrust that he gives me until he's completely seated inside. I adjust to the size of him before I drive my hips to meet his, begging him to move.

He rewards me by slamming into me, swallowing my scream with a kiss. I wrap my legs around him, my stilettos digging into his hips as I pull him deeper. I'm building again as he slams into me with relentless pace, my body crying out for release. He reaches between us and his thumb rolls over my clit as he slams into me one final time as his own orgasm finds him. The sound of him crying my name sends me over the edge again.

He collapses on top of me, burying his head in my neck as we both try and catch our breath. We're still connected when he pushes himself up and kisses me sweetly, the look on his face pure satiated wonder. An easy smile blooms across my face as I run my fingers through his hair.

"Wow," I whisper finally, and his laugh rumbles through me in every part of our bodies that are still connected. Archer slowly retracts from me and rolls onto his back, pulling me with him so I'm cradled against his chest. I sink into his hold, nuzzling against him.

ALL UNITS ATTENTION! ALL UNITS. I wince and grab my head as the shrill sound of my mother shouts down the open

Dragons channel. *Does anyone have eyes on the prince? He's been missing for ten minutes.*

"It was longer than ten minutes..." Archer grumbles next to me and a laugh escapes my lips. I guess my mother included him on that channel.

I have eyes on the prince, I respond down the channel.

"A lot more than just eyes," he teases.

All units stand down, my mother's voice sounds judgmental even when she's not actually talking. *Archer is needed by his father's side for photographs. Please return to the ballroom A-S-A-P.*

I sigh, readying myself to get up, but Archer tightens his hold on me. *I'm feeling...under the weather.*

"Liar," I flick his nose and he captures my finger, placing a kiss on the pad.

I'll be retiring for the evening. There's a lengthy pause before my mother confirms the message and wishes Archer a speedy recovery.

"So, we're retiring for the evening?" I ask as my hand makes long strokes down Archer's abdomen. "Because I had some other ideas." I flash him a devilish smile which he meets with one of his own.

"I can be persuaded," he says stealing a swift kiss.

"Good," I push away from him and bounce to my feet, moving to where my dress remains in a heap of fabric. I step back into my dress and rush back to him, giving him my back. "Zip me up."

"Why?" Archer asks while indulging me.

"I'm going downstairs to get us some of those pastries." Once my dress is zipped, I make my way to the hidden stairwell and push aside the tapestry. "Seriously, how did you not tell me about this?" I don't pause for an answer, but Archer's laughter follows me all the way down the hallway.

Chapter Twenty-Five

ARCHER'S HAIR TICKLES MY nose as his lips move along my jawline, alternating between soft kisses and little nibbles that have me waking in more ways than one. I let out a soft moan of appreciation before my eyes flutter open to find his.

"Morning, love," he murmurs. I grip his bare shoulders, pulling his naked body against mine and delivering a kiss that has him humming in anticipation. We barely slept last night, and I still can't get enough. Seemingly of their own accord, my legs open wider, and I thrust my hips to meet his in an invitation. I whimper as he pulls back, teasing me as his hand palms my breast.

"Someone's impatient," he purrs, and I nip his shoulder in response. As he chuckles, I wrap my legs around him and flip us over so I'm straddling him.

I slowly slide myself down his body, trailing kisses down his stomach and coming to a pause between his thighs. He props himself up on his elbow to watch, his eyes latching to mine as I hover over his quivering member.

A click of a door from the sitting room has me bolt upright.

"Did you hear that?" I ask and Archer curses as I hop off the bed and grab his shirt, throwing it on and hastily buttoning it up.

"I will murder the asshole who comes in here," Archer growls, sitting up. I hold up a hand as the footsteps approach his bedroom door, and I place myself between him and the impending threat, lightning blooming from my palms. He has the sense to wrap the sheet around his waist and with a nod from me, calls a ball of fire to his hands, waiting for my signal. The handle turns slowly, and then the door is flung wide open.

There's a high-pitched squeal before a blur of blonde hair tackles me, pushing me back to the bed and flopping on top of me. Archer jumps up, the sheet forgotten, and aims as my attacker begins to cackle in glee. I'm overwhelmed by the familiar scent of rosewater, and the sight of sapphire eyes.

"Edina?" I gasp.

Chaos erupts as Archer launches his fireball at my best friend. I panic and send my lightning to intercept it, and the resulting blast knocks us all sideways. Edina shrieks as she douses the blaze with her water magic before it can cause too much damage. Archer, eyes wild in confusion, ping-pongs between the two of us.

"Holy shit," Edina breathes, throwing her face into my shoulder at the sight of the prince in all his naked glory. "You must be Archer," she wheezes as her whole body shakes with laughter.

Archer looks completely and utterly confused.

"This is my friend," I hastily explain.

"Her best friend," Edina amends, sitting up but keeping her eyes snapped shut. Archer clasps a hand in front of his junk, which is still hard as a rock for the record.

"How did you know I was here?" I ask.

"Your mom," she responds simply.

"My mom?"

"Umm...I'm just gonna..." Archer points awkwardly to the bathroom and slips inside, his exposed skin now a bright shade of crimson.

My best friend runs a hand through her long blonde hair, pushing it away from her face and folding her legs, causing her super skimpy dress to ride way up. "How badly did I interrupt?" she asks, pointedly regarding my attire.

"It's fine," I shrug. "His best friend interrupted us yesterday, so...payback."

She laughs heartily and cups my face in her hands, kissing me wetly on both cheeks. "I've missed you, babes." She pulls me back into a hug, and this time I return it.

"Why are you here early? Not that I'm complaining." I settle back to the bed, curling my legs beneath me, and propping my arm against the headboard.

"Long story," she says, waving me off.

"You should have at least come to the ball."

Edina looks around at the discarded dessert plates, our formal wear piled on the floor, and the picture frame lying shattered on the floor beside the wall Archer fucked me against when I returned to the room. "Looks like you didn't stay very long, anyway" she chides.

"Accurate," I admit.

"Just saying, I called it. I said you'd be in bed with him within the month." Edina reminds me and I stick my tongue out at her. "Mazel tov, by the way," she says fanning herself.

"You gonna tell me what's going on?" I ask, and she bites her lip. I know her tells too well, and there's no way Edina shows up a day early wearing last night's clothes without something being up.

"Fine," she sighs and leans in closer to me. "I met a guy at a bar a couple of nights ago, and he invited me back to his place. No big deal."

"Were you kidnapped or something?" I ask, alarmed. She shakes her head.

"His place was in Faerie." She winces at the admission and my mouth drops open.

"You met a Fae? In Salem?" I whisper-shout at her, and she nods.

"But he wasn't like the Fae they teach us about in school," she says defensively. "He was...gorgeous."

"Did he have wings?" I ask with a grimace. "Or horns."

"Wings, yeah. He glamoured them away when he was here, though."

"When he was *here?*" I ask pointedly, and Edina blushes. "*You realm jumped?*"

Realm jumping was outlawed years ago because time operates differently in different places. Witches would take a portal to Faerie for a week's vacation, and they'd come back having missed the whole season. And that was if they made it back at all. The Fae are notoriously tricky and often trap or enslave the humans that make it to their realm. All but three of the portals were closed a while back, and those are only approved for royal use.

"It was so amazing, Katie," Edina gushes. "It was the most beautiful place I've ever seen. Better than my parent's island in the Maldives. And Puck—"

"I'm sorry, Puck?" I scoff. "Like from Shakespeare."

"Who was apparently a total diva if Puck's to be believed," she says with a hair toss. "Anyway, it doesn't matter. It's not like I'll see him again."

"Why?" I ask. I expect her to tell me that he wasn't up to her usual caliber, or that she isn't one to be tied down. Instead, she looks...*disappointed*.

"I left," she says simply. "He asked me to stay, and I jumped in the portal and came right here since I wasn't sure how much time passed."

"Oh shit." My eyes widen, and she rubs the back of her neck.

"Yeah, the Dragons guarding the portal put me in a holding cell," she tells me. "I told them you'd vouch for me, but they called your mom."

"Fuck, fuck, *fuck*," I swear. "You didn't tell her—"

"Do I look like an idiot?" she asks, shaking her head. "I told her I took the portal from Salem and then listened to her thousand-word lecture on dropping in unannounced. She let me go when I promised not to take the portal again."

The water clicks off and I hold up a hand for Edina to pause.

Don't say anything else right now, I send through our mental channel.

Why? she asks, her nose crinkling.

Why. Edina and I have always had issues with following rules. And with that comes an understanding that we'd inevitably bail each other out of tight situations. But Archer's not like that. I think the most rebellious thing he's ever done was kiss me last night at the ball.

Let's just keep this between us, I respond. She gives me a wary look but then nods.

Archer emerges with a towel around his waist in a cloud of cedar and agave scented steam. He runs his hand through his wet hair and smiles brightly at Edina.

"We haven't officially met," he laughs and Edina scoffs.

"Archer, this is my *best* friend, Edina," I dramatize with an eye-roll. She extends her hand to Archer, and he flips it over, planting a kiss on the back of it. *Kiss ass.*

"It's nice to finally meet you," Archer says smoothly.

"Sorry about the blue balls," Edina says, a smirk playing across her lips.

"My friend did the same to Katie yesterday, so I guess it makes us even," Archer winks, and Edina looks at me wide-eyed.

"Is this real life?" she whispers, and Archer looks at me questioningly.

"I said the exact same thing," I chuckle and crawl over the bed towards the prince.

"One night and our minds are melding," Archer says in a creepy voice, and I laugh as I wrap my arms around his neck and kiss him deeply.

"Oh god," Edina groans. "I'm too hungover for this. I'm claiming the room across the hall. Call me when you're done."

She hops off the bed and strides across the room, slamming the door behind her.

"Thank fuck," Archer says, dropping the towel and scooping me in his arms. I squeal as he drops me back on the bed and lowers himself over me. "Now... where were we?"

Chapter Twenty-Six

"I DON'T WANNA," EDINA whines, her voice echoing in the otherwise silent library. The librarian, an older witch with a rat's nest of grey hair and an honest to God humped back shoots her a glare through the stacks. Edina ignores her and slumps down in one of the chairs at a research table, throwing the large tome in front of her with a clanging thud.

The library is lined with shelves that stretch four stories high to a glass ceiling, which bathes the entire room in the pale winter sunlight. White ladders are positioned around the stacks, and subsequent signs are posted that caution against sliding down the aisles. The center of the space is left open save for the large oak research tables and the plush midnight-blue rug beneath it.

"That's what you get for showing up early," I whisper-shout, smiling sweetly at the librarian. "This is the first day I've had off since I spoke with you-know-who, and I need to research."

It turns out we needed permission to enter the Royal Library because not just anyone is fit to read the books stashed in this *hallowed* space. Archer was able to get us a pass while his father was commandeering his afternoon for some royal appearance. After he left, I caught Edina up on everything happening with

Adriana. I held nothing back, so when I told her I needed to research this Finley person, she jumped at the chance to help. That was before her post-Faerie jetlag hit and she started behaving like a toddler.

"I can't believe she's alive," Edina says, absently opening the large volume in front of her and beginning to scan the pages for the name.

"Just one of the many mind-fucks I've been dealt recently." I open my book, a genealogy of the royal families, and begin scanning the list of names until my eyes are crossing. I'm about to give up and move to a different book when I come across the name Finley directly under King Darius's name in a list of Light Witches.

"Fuck. Katie, look at this," Edina knocks her chair back and it topples behind her, earning a *shush* from the librarian. "Seriously? There's no one else here!" Edina calls out, giving the librarian a gesture better suited to her hometown of Manhattan.

I stifle a laugh as Edina places the book before me, hovering over my shoulder and pointing out a passage. "It says Finley was the lead commander of Carman's army in the Four Kings War. King Darius murdered her at the final battle."

"That doesn't make any sense." I push her book aside and show her the name in my book. "This says she was King Darius's daughter."

"Maybe it was two different people."

"That seems like too much of a coincidence," I say, putting my head in my hands. *But why would Darius's daughter be the commander of his opponent's army?*

"Maybe she jumped ship," Edina suggests. "That would make sense why Adriana wants you to emulate her." She pushes her book aside and heads into the stacks. When she emerges, she has a stack of textbooks about The Four Kings War. "At least we have a direction now."

After another hour of fruitless searching, I'm about to give in to Edina's incessant whining for coffee and go grab us lattes when I come across something. I almost miss the reference in my skimming, but my eyes snag on the word *lightning.*

"Holy shit," I breathe. "E, listen to this." She looks up from her reading, shaking away the glazed look in her eyes.

"Darius's daughter, Finley, was a celebrated warrior and was often tasked with keeping the peace in her father's name. One day, she faced off against a werewolf in a gruesome battle and was almost killed by a vicious bite to her neck. The healers managed to stave off death, but the bite left Finley unable to use magic. Darius declared war on the weres and Queen Aldonza, who defended them.

"At a war meeting, Finley met Queen Carman, who promised a broken, depressed Finley she could restore her magic in exchange for commanding Carman's armies. Finley signed away her life to service of the Queen without a second thought.

"The Queen worked for days, infusing Finley's body and mind with the Dark power that lay at her fingertips. It took ten

ten-minute sessions, but Finley's magic was restored. However, her magic was not the Light Magic she was accustomed to. Because Carman's magic was Dark, the two forces combined, making Finley the first-ever recorded lightning wielder.

"Oh shit," Edina murmurs, giving my hand a gentle squeeze as I continue.

"Carman worked with her to control the magic, learning to separate both Light and Dark forces within her as well as use them in a combined effort until she became the most powerful witch in existence. It was then that Carman offered her aid to Aldonza in the war against Darius. Together they had a mighty army of Magical Creatures and Dark Witches, led by Finley and her electricity.

"Five years into the war, Darius learned who the Dark Magic commander was, and struck out to kill Carman for the injustice she had brought upon his daughter. Carman battled him for days, their powers evenly matched, neither one yielding. It wasn't until Finley stepped on the battlefield that it was over. She threw her body in front of Carman, protecting her savior from a killing blow from Darius. When the blow struck and Finley fell, the King of Light Magic broke. He sobbed over her body, begging Carman to end his life so that he might join his daughter. For all her faults, Carman loved Finley in her own way, and she too was broken by her absence.

"It goes on to talk about how King Baran took over and killed Carman and Darius," I say, scanning the rest of the page, trying desperately to figure out what this all means. "It reads like a fairytale, not like a history lesson."

"Finley had both Light and Dark Magic," Edina confirms. "And her death is what tipped the scales so that King Baran could take over."

"But it doesn't say anything about the prophecy." I flip through more pages, hunting for any mention of the words my father so painfully reminded me of.

"We'll figure this out," Edina reassures, wrapping her arm around my shoulders and tipping her head to rest against mine.

"Come on," I sigh heavily. "I owe you coffee." Edina's face lights up and she practically dances out of the library as we leave in search of caffeine.

AFTER OUR COFFEE, EDINA decides she needs a nap, so I leave her in Archer's spare room while I head down to headquarters to check on Deavers. The healers still haven't figured out what's keeping him in his coma-like state, so I try to visit him every day.

I absently tap the wooden armrests on the chair in the corner of the sterile white room, watching the rhythmic rise and fall of Deavers' chest. I'm so close to a solution, I can feel it. I squeeze my eyes shut, trying to grasp the idea that keeps eluding me when I sense something with my Mind Magic. Dark smoke dances like a wraith above Deavers', but it retracts into his mind when I reach for it.

"The fuck?" I swear under my breath, and send my mind out again, this time reaching directly into Deavers' mind.

His mind is completely shrouded in that black smoke that hangs like thick curtains around a cracked mental shield. I try to enter through the crack, but the smoke senses me, and coils around Deavers' mind. I pull my mind out, opening my eyes and checking that his vitals have remained the same. When I'm convinced my intrusion didn't hurt him, I enter again, this time surging forward so forcefully that I spear straight through the smoke and into Deavers' shield. The smoke tries to follow me, but I throw up my shield, protecting his mind and my back.

Deavers, I call as a myriad of memories and visions try to bombard me. *Deavers, can you hear me?*

Captain? The voice is weak, but I surge towards it. I explore every inch, sending the golden light of my Mind Magic through him, seeking out any irregularities.

It's me. I'm going to try and wake you up.

I've been trying, Captain. Even though it's just a thought, he sounds defeated. *I can't breach the spell surrounding my mind. I was close...but the healers' Light Magic made the spell tougher somehow.*

I'll figure this out. I have to go, but I won't leave you in here for long. I feel him shudder as I pull my mind out.

What kind of spell can't be healed by Light Magic? Or worse, is made stronger when attacked with Light Magic. I think back over the few healing courses I took, but they were all quick solutions to patch wounds on a battlefield. And I highly doubt my lightning will be helpful in this situation.

The solution hits me with the force of a moving train. *I have to use my Dark Magic.*

I try to swallow the lump forming in my throat. This is just the kind of sadistic thing my father would plan to force me into using my Dark Magic. It feels so much like a trap that my gut reaction is to leave the room.

"Fucking hell," I silently curse my father and Adriana for good measure. I focus on the pit in my stomach where my magic resides and push away the lightning which rises to meet me.

I let myself embrace the chaos that surfaces when I have the least amount of control over myself. The part of me that takes risks and makes bold choices. I delve into my magic again...and there it is. Directly next to my kernel of sunshine is a black shadow.

I retract despite myself, visions of my father coursing through my mind and making me tentative. *I need to do this.* I need to grab my Dark Magic so I can help Deavers. I steel myself and reach for my shadow. As if it senses my apprehension, my Light Magic wraps around the darkness, creating lightning before my eyes. *It's trying to protect me,* I realize. Just like it did that first day my magic combined, my sunshine is protecting me from the unknown.

I shake away the nerves and really look at my magic as they separate again. My Dark Magic is...beautiful. The black is iridescent, shimmering with starlight that projects a prism of colors when it brushes against my Light Magic. It's as pure as the sunshine that resides beside it.

I know at that moment that my Dark Magic isn't malicious. It won't hurt me because it isn't bad, and it's as much a part of me as my Light Magic. When I reach for it again, I welcome its presence, encouraging it to help me. I feel it surge to the forefront, leaving my pulsing Light Magic behind, and when I open my eyes, that black shadow is wrapped around my hand.

I innately know what to do and I lay the hand that's enveloped in Dark Magic on Deavers' shoulder. He inhales sharply, his back arching up off the bed and I use the space he's created to shift my hand down his back, sliding down until I feel the scar that signals where he was hit with this spell. I pull back and a trail of smoky grey magic seeps from his body, following me, latching to my shadow.

I extend my mind into Deavers', watching as the smoke surrounding his mind starts to recede, like water flowing down an open drain. I watch until I can clearly see his mental barriers before retreating into my body. With one final, hard yank, the last of the smoke recedes and his body slumps back onto the bed. The magic disappears into the air, and I hold my breath as I wait.

After the longest minute of my life, Deavers' eyes drift open and find mine.

"That was badass, Captain," he murmurs, a smirk playing across his lips. My breath leaves my body, and I throw my arms around him.

"I'm so sorry—" I start, but he pushes me away with a scowl.

"Seriously, Captain?" he asks, his voice still thick with disuse. "You just saved my life."

"It's my fault you were hit."

"I owe you everything," he says, gripping my hand tightly. I purse my lips, uncomfortable by the gratitude, but I squeeze his hand back.

The sound of footsteps in the hallway has my eyes widening in panic. I used Dark Magic on a Dragons officer. It doesn't matter my motives. "You can't tell anyone about this." I plead, my voice dropping to a whisper.

"Never," Deavers swears, and I throw myself back into the chair just as the healers burst through the doors.

Chapter Twenty-Seven

THE EARLY MORNING LIGHT trickles in through Archer's heavy drapes and I reach across the bed, seeking out my prince and sighing when I find him stretched out next to me. I fell asleep before he made it back to his room last night, barely managing to change into one of his t-shirts before I passed out. I'm not sure if it was the lack of sleep the night before or using a new facet of my magic, but I was wiped out.

I crack my eyes open, watching Archer's serene expression before rolling into him and cuddling into the spot right above his heart. His arm reflexively closes around me, pulling me in closer as he places a sleepy kiss on the top of my head before drifting off again. I smile against him, completely content.

I don't know why this relationship feels so different, why I feel so at ease with Archer even though we've known each other for such a short time. I can't shake the feeling that this relationship is so much more significant than anything I've felt before. It's...terrifying and wonderful, and I'm conflicted between guarding my heart and jumping in headfirst and enjoying the free fall.

The door pops open and Edina appears backlit by the light in the adjoining room looking entirely too perky for this early in the morning. The pink silk camisole she stole from me is too short on her, exposing her pierced navel. She throws her arms in the air, waving around a bottle of champagne.

"IT'S MY BIRTHDAY BITCHES!" I sit up just in time to see the cork fly into the picture that Archer just rehung, shattering the glass, and waking him. She tips the bottle into her mouth and then climbs on the foot of the bed, holding the foaming alcohol over my mouth until it tips in.

"I didn't know it was your birthday," Archer says before Edina turns the bottle to him, and he's drowned in champagne.

"Well, *technically*," she stretches out the word for about ten seconds, "It's tomorrow. But when we were kids, I hated that my birthday was on Christmas Eve."

"She didn't like other people getting presents on her birthday," I explain.

"So," Edina continues, flipping me off, "Katie decided we'd celebrate the day before." She salutes me with the champagne bottle and takes a long swig.

"Happy birthday, E." I wave my hand for a refilling spell before she can polish off the remainder.

"Thanks, babes," she says, settling back on her heels while I slide back against the headboard next to Archer. "So, what's the plan for tonight?"

I give her an over-the-top wince. "About that—"

"What?" she asks, her eyes going wide.

"This year is a little different," I say slowly. Because Archer and I are both targeted so heavily by the Dark Witch Covens, I decided to throw her a party at the Dragons' headquarters rather than going out. "But there's booze, soldiers, and a six-tiered cake." Edina squeals in delight.

"Your dress is hanging in my wardrobe," I continue, "It's the blue one. And Archer and his friend Jai will bring you to the pit tonight since I'm staying over there to set up. Actually," I grab my phone off the nightstand checking the time, "Jai is on his way here now to keep you company while we're training. So go change out of my lingerie...which you can keep by the way."

"Thanks," she says, tossing her hair over her shoulder as she hops off the bed and heads to the door, swaying her hips as she goes. "I can't wait! See you tonight."

Once she's gone, Archer leans over and kisses my shoulder. "That was your lingerie?" he murmurs against me, pulling the neckline of his t-shirt down so he could have more access to my skin.

"E always steals my clothes while she's here." I laugh. "She has an entire wardrobe up at Marcus's cabin, but obviously nothing here so..."

"She can have it," Archer interrupts, his gaze so heated it has my breath quickening. "I like seeing you in my clothes." He kisses me greedily, and despite the sentiment, he tears the shirt from my body with record-breaking speed.

I DODGE A BOOMERANG of fire as it circles my head, waiting for it to re-enter my eye-line before lassoing it with lightning and hurling it back at Archer. He dives out of the way of the fire, but I snag his ankle with my lightning, and he hits the mat with a *thud*. Before he can scramble back to his feet, my lightning coils around his body like a snake, immobilizing him where he lies.

"Fuck me," he swears.

"Again?" I chide winking at him. "Do you yield?" He growls but nods his head and I release him from my coils.

Archer's control of his fire has gotten so much better in the few weeks we've been training. He hasn't beaten me yet, but he's become a worthy opponent. The one thing that's been bothering me is that he hasn't used his hellfire since Sicily, which is worrisome, especially if he can't control it.

I motion for a break and hop out of the training ring, grabbing the flame-retardant suit I bought and slipping it on as Archer grabs a drink. I'm not sure how much help the suit will be; everything I've read on hellfire says that one touch of the element is deadly. It's rumored to devour your soul the second it touches your skin, which I'm sure is just superstitious bullshit. That being said no one who has been attacked with hellfire has survived, including Archer's mother whose element *was* fire.

I hop back in the ring, and Archer drags his eyes down my body in the skin-tight suit.

"We're going to summon your hellfire today," I announce, hoping the bravado in my voice is enough to inspire confidence.

"No," Archer says, turning away. I grab his arm before he can hop out of the training ring.

"Listen," I say softly. "You saw what we're up against, the power the Dark Witches have." His face pales considerably, and I know he's replaying our battle in the sky.

"Your hellfire is a last resort," I reassure him. "But it's a weapon that can literally incinerate the opposition. We might need it, and I want to make sure you can control it if we do."

Archer looks at his hands with disgust, and I recognize the fear of being ruled by an element. I know that fear all too intimately, and the only way to combat it is to learn control. I never want him to feel powerless again, not while he can wield a weapon that is power incarnate.

"I just want to start with you calling a flame to your hand," I plead with him. He holds my gaze for a long time before solemnly nodding.

"Back up," Archer insists, and I cross to the other side of the training ring, prepared to dive under the platform if need be. A flick of my hand has the doors to the pit slamming shut and locking so that no one innocently pokes their head inside.

Archer takes a steadying breath and closes his eyes. He turns his palms up towards the ceiling and splays his hand out flat. It shakes with concentrated effort, and a muscle in his neck begins to tic.

"Breathe," I instruct.

"What if I hurt you?" he asks, his voice is strangled and his eyes wild with worry.

My eyes widen as the realization washes over me. He's not unleashing the flame...he's *trying* to keep it inside. I've known that Archer was holding back for some time, but I had no idea that he was actively trying to repress his magic. Everything I've seen has only been a fraction of what he can do. The thought is...thrilling.

And terrifying.

But there is not one inch of my body that believes that Archer would hurt me. Even when he was lost to his power, he kept me safe.

"You control your power, not the other way around," I tell him finally, giving him a confident smile. "Own it, your highness."

Archer scoffs, but that act gives him a breath he so desperately needed, and his shoulders relax. Instantly there's a ball of white-hot flame in his hand. It's the perfect teardrop shape, hovering directly over his palm and glowing like a comet. Archer breathes again and the flame stays the same size.

"It's beautiful," I murmur, taking a half-step closer. "Make it bigger. Double it in size." He nods and it jumps in size quickly, but Archer reins it in. "Now shrink it back."

"It's pulsing," he whispers, his eyes transfixed on the flame as it shrinks back down. "It looks like a heartbeat." He smiles as the flame morphs into an anatomical heart, complete with valves and everything.

"I think it's cued to your heartbeat," I say, taking another step closer to him and watching as the pulse of the flame picks up again. "I want you to create a ring of fire around us."

"I'll destroy everything," he whispers, the flame pulsing faster still.

"The room is made to withstand the heat. It'll be fine. And I trust you." I take hold of his elbow as Archer's eyes link with mine and the hellfire spreads around us.

As the ring closes, sweat beads along my forehead, the sheer heat of the fire overwhelming. And it's bright, like trying to stare directly into the sun. So instead, I look at Archer, my heart rate increasing at the sight of him glowing with the release of his power.

"Banish it completely," I whisper as a drop of sweat slides down my temple. Archer closes his eyes, and the fire disappears. It's not until a cool breeze caresses us that he opens his eyes, whooping in excitement. He picks me up, spinning me around and I laugh, sharing in his triumph.

"Amazing," I praise, right before stealing a kiss. Archer deepens it, pulling me closer to him, his tongue sweeping across mine.

"Thank you," he murmurs as I pull back slightly.

"Now," I say, running to the edge where I've stashed some supplies. "Let's spar."

I levitate two bricks into the ring and murmur a duplicating spell. The bricks multiply until I have enough to magically stack into the shape of a man. Okay, man is a bit of a stretch, they're two giant blobs stacked on top of each other, but it'll do the trick.

"How?" Archer asks skeptically.

"Easy," I step behind my stone man and transfer my lightning, so it dances around the rocks. "I want precise blasts, don't just unleash waves. Aim for the chest."

"I'm not shooting with you back there," he says crossing his arms.

"If you focus it shouldn't hit anywhere near me."

Archer releases a breath, relaxing his shoulders and calling a baseball size flame to his hand. He lobs the hellfire at the stone man and my eyes widen as it collides with the "chest," leaving a scorch mark in the dead center.

"Again. Aim a little to the left this time, at the heart," I command. Another direct hit.

I cast another duplicating spell, this time erecting two more men.

"Three on one." He strikes in quick succession, hitting all three targets just as my lightning reaches him. Hellfire explodes from his arms, wrapping around his body, protecting him from my bolts.

He turns to me, flames dancing across his hazel eyes.

"Good. Extinguish it," I call, but Archer doesn't respond. "Archer." He launches a ball of hellfire at the stone man closest to me. I scream and scuttle backward as it connects, and the bricks explode in a cloud of dust.

Archer's eyes widen in panic, and he shakes himself as the flames disappear. Panting, I stand and slowly cross to him, tentatively wrapping my arms around his neck.

"Did you not hear me again?" I ask softly, but he just blinks rapidly. I gently take hold of his jaw, tilting his head down so he's forced to meet my eyes. "It's okay. I didn't have to use Mind Magic this time, that's progress." He nods once, the only sign he can hear me.

"The more we practice—"

"Right," Archer says, disoriented. "Can we be done? I...I think I'm just tired."

"Of course." I pull him in closer to me and he stiffens before sinking into my hold and burying his face in my neck. "Go nap," I murmur. "I have to start setting up for the party."

He releases a long sigh and then straightens, pecking me on the lips before climbing out of the ring without another word.

Chapter Twenty-Eight

HOURS AND HOURS AND *hours* of preparation later, I've completely transformed the pit into a winter wonderland. The floors are covered in a fine layer of powdery snow that the Water Elementals spelled to be slip-resistant and icicles that can't melt hang from the ceilings. Some Earth Elementals helped me grow white-barked trees along the black walls and draped them in fairy lights, turning the room into an enchanted forest. I even enchanted the ceiling so that when you gaze upwards you see snow falling.

The training ring has been raised ten feet off the ground and is turned into an ice-skating rink complete with a sweeping ice sculpture staircase on either side. Underneath the ring is the dancefloor, the DJ playing some mortal favorites and some from the Kingdom. A six-tier red-velvet cake is in the corner of the room, frosted and dusted with white sugar so it sparkles.

I make my way over to the bar, which is naturally made of ice, and swipe a martini glass, waiting for the dry ice inside to stop smoking before I down the contents. The bar is completely stocked, but I take extra pride with the signature cocktail...a blue martini in the exact shade of Edina's eyes.

I tasked the O'Malley twins and Jai with inviting any witches who might want to attend, so even though the party has barely started, the place is filling up fast. Edina was told to arrive about twenty minutes ago, which means she'll be here soon, ready to make her fashionably late entrance.

I smooth down the material of my dress, pulling down my neckline a smidge in anticipation of Archer's arrival. I opted for a velvet, forest green mini-dress with long sleeves. The short hem of the dress and the four-inch peep-toe platforms I'm wearing show off my toned legs, making them look way longer than they are. I left my hair down in simple curls and chose a delicate silver necklace that Edina bought for my birthday to complete the look.

"Hell of a party," an accented voice grumbles in my ear.

I turn to thank the person and tell them to back the fuck up, but the words die in my mouth as I come face to face with the werewolf from the woods in Italy. The one who saved my life and also caused one of the biggest fights Archer and I have been in.

"What are you doing here?" I hiss as he runs his hands through his shoulder-length hair and flashes me a smile that has my body reacting in ways I can't explain. My eyes dip to his broad chest; I can just glimpse a hint of his tanned skin from the few buttons undone in his navy shirt.

"Is that the kind of welcome you give someone who saved your life?" he asks, shoving one hand in the pocket of his fitted jeans. His golden eyes crinkle in amusement.

"It's not safe for you in London," I whisper. He chuckles, placing a hand on the small of my back and steering me towards the dancefloor. I dig my heels in and grab his forearm, his corded muscles straining under my hand. *Seriously, who has muscles like that on their fucking forearm?*

"Relax, little witch. I won't be here long." I have half a mind to slap the smirk off his face, but then he leans into my space and the fight drains out of me. "I have a message for you," he whispers.

"A message," I repeat, distracted by the scent of rain and earth and the unnatural heat I feel radiating from his body.

"And it'll look a lot less conspicuous if we're dancing while I relay it. Wouldn't want that *prince* of yours to get the wrong idea." He spits the word prince like it's a curse and I balk at his tone.

This time, when he guides me forward, I follow.

A slow song starts playing and the werewolf wraps an arm around my waist. He's so much taller than me that even in heels he needs to bend significantly to be able to whisper in my ear. The stubble on his jaw brushes against my sensitive skin as he turns to me, sending shivers down my spine.

"You look beautiful tonight," he murmurs, and I pull back watching as his eyes drop to my mouth, which has popped open. An all-male smile slowly crawls across his face. "Course I prefer what you were wearing the last time I saw you," he says with a wink.

"That's your message?" I recover quickly, laying on a heavy layer of sarcasm. I swear the werewolf's eyes flash in amusement for a quick second, but the emotion is gone quickly.

"Your sister says she's proud you used your Dark Magic," he says softly, and the breath leaves my body. I push away abruptly, but he keeps hold of my hand, spinning me into him so that my back is pressed to his front.

"You're working with her," I confirm, cursing myself for ever doubting Archer when he questioned the nature of this man's intentions.

"Not even a little bit," the wolf states, his breath hot in my ear. I glare unbelieving at him over my shoulder. "I met her an hour ago when she showed up in my woods and kidnapped me."

"She what?"

"She grabbed my hand, told me she needed me to deliver a message, and then teleported us to London." He shrugs like being kidnapped by a wanted Dark Witch is a regular occurrence for him.

"Why would she send you?" I ask.

"She said something about being a touch clairvoyant, and this was the only way she could see that you would listen."

I roll my eyes, but for some reason, I believe him. Based on what I know of Adriana as an adult, it sounds like the kind of impulsive crap she would pull.

"Was that all she said? I feel like that's a lot of trouble to go to—" He flips me around again, so we're face to face.

"She also said, 'The time is close for you to join us. When the one you love the most has nowhere else to turn, call and I'll bring you home.'"

What the hell does that mean? "Anything else?" I ask, hoping for at least one more clue, but he shakes his head.

The one I love the most. The one I love the...*holy shit.* Tomorrow, Edina, my parents, and I are leaving for Marcus's country home. It would be the perfect time to plan an attack on the palace, on Archer. Adriana would know we're official; it's been in the papers all week. *Fuck me*, I need to report this to my mother.

"Thanks," I murmur, distractedly pushing away. The werewolf's arms tighten around me, his eyes flickering with concern. "I should—"

I don't finish my train of thought as his eyes glow and some of the tightness in my chest eases. I should go tell my mom, but I find myself entranced as the werewolf's face softens and his fingers toy with the end of my hair. It should be uncomfortable, but it's oddly...not. I can't help but feel at ease around this man, which makes no sense at all.

"Can I ask you a question?" I say softly, my arm shifting around his shoulder as we continue to dance. "Is this...I mean—" His eyes meet mine expectantly and I swallow hard.

"How does the bonding spell work?" I manage. "The one you performed in the woods."

"It's a bond between two souls," he says simply. *Souls, not minds.* "I can't explain how it's done exactly. It's an instinct all weres have. But every bond is set up differently depending on what's needed."

"And you set ours up to take some of my pain?" I ask, and he nods. "Did you just do it again?"

"Yes."

"But I wasn't in pain," I prod, and he considers that.

"Our bond is...different than any other I've experienced." As he speaks, I feel it, like an invisible tether between the two of us, urging me closer.

"Whoa," I breathe as I feel his confusion through the tether. He must feel my emotions as well because his pupils dilate.

"I shouldn't be able to feel emotions other than pain," he says thoughtfully. "I also used the bond to locate you tonight. Adriana told me your approximate location, so I knew to come to the Dragons headquarters and to the bottom level. But I followed the bond to find you."

"And that's not normal?"

"It shouldn't be," he sighs. "Some wolves bond this way, typically with their children, but I didn't set up our bond for tracking."

"Maybe you did it wrong," I snark, and he barks a laugh that sounds like an actual bark.

"Maybe it's because you're a witch," he quips, and I purse my lips choosing to ignore that.

"Does it have any range to it?" I ask, and he shrugs. "So, if I'm in danger..."

"Hypothetically, I'll be able to feel it and find you."

"And what if you're in pain?" I ask.

"I don't know if it works both ways," he admits, and then smiles, tugging me even closer. "Would you come to save me, little witch?"

An evil idea sparks in my head. I slide my hand down the muscular planes of his chest, and he inhales sharply, his eyes sparking with desire. I pause when I reach his peck, and then pinch his nipple, hard.

"Ow, fuck," he swears as a siren starts blaring in my head. The bond between us pulses painfully and I feel the most intense pull to soothe the werewolf. It shouldn't make me laugh, but needless to say, I'm cackling as he tries to hide his own laughter.

"You're a fucking animal," he laughs, and the vibration runs through me.

"You're one to talk," I tease, and I'm granted with that laugh again.

"Now can I ask you a question?" he asks, leaning in closer, and my mind runs wild with possibilities as I nod. "What kind of cake is that?" he asks, his eyes lighting up and making me laugh again.

"Red-velvet," I answer. He growls and bares his teeth in a gesture that's so purely wolf it's comical.

"Red-velvet is bullshit," he grumbles. Then he leans in and kisses my cheek, and my laughter dies as I feel a blush bloom beneath his lips. "I have to go, little witch," he breathes against my skin before backing away.

"I still don't know your name," I call after him, but he's already disappeared in the throng of bodies. I shake the encounter from my mind, choosing to firmly ignore the feeling of disappointment that's settling in my stomach.

A chorus of "HAPPY BIRTHDAY" echoes through the hall as Edina enters the party, looking stunning in the powder-blue shift dress I bought for her, her blonde hair in loose spirals. She squeals in delight at the winter-scape I created for her and breaks free of Jai and Archer's arms when she finds me in the crowd.

"Katie, this is spectacular," she breathes, pulling me into a hug which I return a little too tightly. When she pulls back, she notices that the smile I'm giving her doesn't reach my eyes, and her face falls.

What happened? she sends to me mentally as Archer comes up behind me and wraps his arms around me. I shake my head, not even needing to use our connection to voice that I'll explain later. I fix the smile back on my face as I kiss him. She lingers for a moment, but then nods and grabs Jai to escort her to the bar.

"You wanna dance?" Archer whispers in my ear. I nod and let him lead me towards the floor, but not before I catch a glimpse of golden eyes before they disappear in the crowd.

Chapter Twenty-Nine

WE STAYED AT THE party past dawn and managed to crawl back to the palace for a minute of sleep before we needed to be up and ready to go again. Today, Edina and I are meeting with my mom and Marcus to make the trek to Marcus's country house. It's our Christmas Eve tradition to spend the holiday out there, just the four of us. I had hoped I could convince Archer to join us this year, but apparently, the dinner his father has planned for him is mandatory.

I stand under the scalding shower relishing the heat, letting the pounding of the hard water run over my hair and skin. I'm using Archer's shower, which is so luxurious that it makes me forget the fact that I prefer baths. The tiles and the floor are a dark grey giving the impression I'm in a high-end spa. The showerhead has these different settings, so the water comes out in different ways; right now, I'm taking advantage of the rainfall feature, but I make a mental note to find time to take a steam. Along the wall behind the showerhead is an array of dispensers containing shampoos, soaps, and a selection of tonics to cure anything from a hangover to the flu.

I prod the shampoo dispenser, inhaling deeply as cedar and agave permeate the steam, and scrub my scalp, infusing Archer's scent into every inch of my chestnut hair. My eyes drift closed as I dip my head under the showerhead and a delighted gasp escapes my lips when a set of large hands rake through my hair. I whirl around and Archer pushes me back against the cold tiles, his mouth finding mine while his fingers are still tangled in my locks.

"What are you doing in here?" I ask, throwing my arms around his neck as his one hand slips down to my waist.

"While I adore Edina," he murmurs, his fingers idly twisting the wet strands of my hair. "Since she's arrived, we've barely had a minute alone."

"She gets dibs," I flick his nose and he in turn places a kiss on the tip of mine.

"As she should," Archer says with a devilish smile. "But I'm guessing she won't be joining you while you're in here."

"I wouldn't count on it," I scoff. "The girl has no boundaries."

"Good thing I locked the door," Archer growls, as he tightens his grip on the hair on the back of my neck, making me gasp.

"I have an hour," I breathe, letting my hands slide down to his chest. I groan as my fingers trail down the subtle cut of his muscles. He presses in closer to me, his arousal pressing against my thigh. My breathing quickens as I reach to the shelf beside me.

"What are you doing back there?" His eyes are hungry, but he's completely still as he watches me pump conditioner into my hand.

I chuckle darkly, rubbing the thick mixture in my hands. But rather than running my hands through my hair, I wrap my hand along his hard length. The conditioner makes my hand slide over him easily and he hisses, throwing his head back into the hot water. I pump my hand up and down, faster and faster, my leg hooking around his to keep him close to me. He swears and calls my name like it's a prayer.

In one fluid motion, he grabs my wrist and gracefully spins me around, so my back is pressed against his chest. The water spills between us, heating my blood as he grinds against my ass and uses his knee to gently nudge my thighs apart. His teeth graze the column of my neck while one hand cups my breast and the other slips between my legs. His fingers simultaneously roll over my nipple and clitoris, making me cry out as a wave of pleasure crashes over me. He continues working his hands in a magical combination until I'm panting with need, my body sagging against his as I get closer and closer to the edge of ecstasy.

"Archer," I gasp, and he slides two fingers down my center and inside me, fracturing me into a thousand pieces. I'm still in the careening depths of my orgasm when he removes his hands and bends me at the waist, not wasting a second before slamming his hard cock inside me.

"Fuck," I swear, reaching out to brace myself against the wall. The bitter cold of the tiles mixing with the scalding hot water sends my senses into overdrive. Archer reaches around and begins stroking my clit as he slams into me at a relentless pace. His other hand fists into my hair, pulling me up so my back arches as he uses my hair to guide our pace. The pain mixes with the pleasure in the most delicious way and soon I'm building towards another orgasm. I match his thrusts, grinding back into him as I feel him tense as his release builds in time with mine.

"Come with me," he pleads, and the suggestion is enough to have me shattering again, screaming his name as I topple over into oblivion. Archer slams into me twice more before shuddering in his release and then sagging against me. We hover there catching our breath, bent over as the water cascades off Archer's body onto mine where we're still connected.

"I love you," Archer murmurs into my hair before kissing the sensitive spot behind my ear. I shiver happily and turn to him, drawing him forward into a long, slow kiss.

"So, was this my Christmas present?" I chide, grabbing the conditioner to put in my hair this time.

"No, that's on the bed."

"I don't have time for another round." Archer swats at my ass and I squeal. He reaches behind me, grabbing a luffa and his body wash, lathering it up. "You didn't have to get me anything," I add.

"I wanted to," he says thoughtfully. He nudges me out of the direct stream of the water and runs the sponge over my body in small circles. I stand there watching his eyes light with desire as he moves down my body, lingering for far longer than necessary over my breasts. I moan as he skims his hand alongside the brush.

"Don't start something you can't finish," I warn, and he lowers the luffa reluctantly to my stomach.

"You're the one with the tight schedule. How bad would it be if you were...twenty minutes late?" The glint in his eye is pure lust, and it instantly has my insides tightening again. But then my mother's face set in disapproval flashes through my mind and it's like being doused with ice-cold water.

"Come on," I sigh, and he groans as I pluck the luffa from his hands and start washing for real. "I want to give you your present before I go."

Archer leans in and places a kiss at the corner of my mouth. "You're—"

"Don't finish that sentence," I say, placing a finger on his lips.

"Why?"

"Because you were going to say something super cringe-worthy like 'You're my present,' or 'You're all I wanted for Christmas'. And then I'd have to break up with you out of sheer embarrassment."

Archer's laugh bounces off the tiles, echoing around us, wrapping me in the melody and bringing a stupid love-sick smile to my face.

"Fair enough," he chuckles, his laughter only ending when his lips meet mine.

AFTER WE'RE BOTH, RELUCTANTLY, dried off and dressed, I sit on the edge of Archer's bed with a small box in my hands. My eyes bounce between Archer, who is only wearing a pair of grey sweatpants because *he's evil* and apparently has been reading some of the romance novels on my shelf, and the corner of the gold wrapping paper that I've torn loose. The box is small enough that I'm pretty sure it's jewelry and my heart is thudding in my throat. There's been so much talk about the two of us getting engaged between his father and the papers, but it's way too fast. It hasn't even been a month.

The gift I bought him, with its colorful snowman wrapping paper is balanced on his leg. I nod to him to open my gift first, and I set my present beside me and fiddle with my Christmas-red sweater instead of the paper. He hesitates but then rips into it with such vigor that I can't help but smile. A laugh escapes from him as he uncovers the first present.

"My own copy?" he exclaims, pulling out the book I bought him. I specifically made a trip to a mortal bookstore to buy him a copy of *Love Bites*, the book he read to me when I was sick.

"I figured you can use it to occupy your time while I'm away." He nods excitedly, putting the book on the desk and pulling out the other item in the box. His face morphs into a wistful expression as he pulls out the gold picture frame and studies the image of the two of us dancing at the Solstice Ball, staring into each other's eyes like the world would end if we broke apart.

"I know it's not much," I murmur as he continues to stare at the photo. He leaps up, rushing towards me and cupping my face in his hands.

"I love it." He bends over me, pushing me back slightly on the bed as his mouth meets mine. "Thank you." He whispers in between a succession of light kisses that make my heart flutter. He pulls back and sits next to me, wrapping an arm around my waist as he silently nods towards my present.

I pull back the gold foil, gingerly removing a grey velvet box. I bite my lip as my finger strokes the soft material, finding the lip and pushing it open. Sitting on the white satin lining is a necklace and my breath releases in a *whoosh*. It's stunning. The pendant is a silver heart surrounded by a layer of alternating rubies and diamonds. I reach out to touch the delicate piece and I can feel the hum of magic, unlike any magic I've ever encountered.

"This necklace," Archer begins, "Is part of the crown jewels. It originally belonged to Queen Aldonza, but most recently, it belonged to my mother." He removes the necklace from the box, gently handling the silver chain and finding the clasp.

"You're giving me your mother's necklace?" I ask in awe as I give him my back and lift my hair from my neck so he can put the necklace on me.

"Before she died, my mother told me I would know who to give the necklace to when the time was right. When I was trying to decide what to give you, it was the only thing that seemed right.

"Legend says," he finishes with the clasp then places a kiss to the back of my neck, "that once you find your true love, the magic in the necklace mimics their heartbeat."

The necklace settles in the hollow of my neck. Time slows, one second stretching on for eternity as we wait for the verdict from this magical jewelry. Just when Archer's eyes drop in disappointment, the necklace thumps. My breath rushes in as my hand flutters to the pendent, which is now beating in a rhythm that's different than my heartbeat.

"Holy shit," Archer and I say in unison before he pulls me in for a slow, passionate kiss.

"I love you so much," Archer murmurs, pulling me onto his lap.

My breath is coming in too quickly like it can't decide which heartbeat to follow. I open my mouth to say something, anything, but most specifically the words Archer is so clearly hoping for. Only a squeak comes out.

"Do you like it?" he asks, his eyes landing on the thudding necklace. I swallow hard and let a forced smile creep across my face.

"I do." I lean in and give him a quick peck, throwing my arms around his neck as he rubs soothing lines up my back. "Merry Christmas, your highness."

"Happy Christmas, my love."

Chapter Thirty

"So, you had a panic attack?" Edina asks, pushing the door of the mortal coffee shop open as we exit back into the winter air.

As soon as we got to Marcus's cottage, I convinced Edina to take a walk with me to the village main street. I had to promise her coffee to get her to come, but I needed to talk away from the prying ears of my mother. I spent the entire walk to the coffee shop updating her on everything that happened at the party before she arrived, and on Archer's present.

"No...not a panic attack. I just..." Edina regards me over her ridiculous frozen coffee drink...which I'm not convinced has actual coffee in it. It's red and has whipped cream and crystalized sugar on top.

"Couldn't breathe," she finishes for me. "When you found out Archer is your true love. I mean that would be my reaction to any kind of love, so I totally get it."

Edina chuckles as I sip my black coffee, letting it warm my soul.

"But why?" I lament. "I don't get it. Archer makes me so happy."

We walk in silence through the town which looks like something out of a cheesy holiday movie. There's snow on every rooftop, and the white Christmas lights twinkle even though the sun hasn't yet set. Each streetlamp has an evergreen bow tied to it and there is a large twenty-foot tree in the center of town. All we need are carolers...and there they go, in period clothing and everything.

"Do you really want me to answer that question?" Edina asks tentatively, once the refrain of *Good King Wenceslas* fades into the background.

"Just say it."

"Fine." She pauses, pulling me off to the side of the street. "I like Archer. He seems nice. And I love that he *adores* you. Seriously, he looks at you like the sun shines out of your ass."

"But?" I ask.

"But...he's really intense. You've been together for all of two minutes and he's already giving you his mother's necklace and telling you he loves you. It's a lot of pressure."

"I mean yeah, it's intense, but it's...it's good," I say defensively, trying to hide the fact that her words sting.

"Then why haven't you told him you love him? The necklace proves you do, right?" Her sapphire eyes pierce through me.

"I—" I falter because I don't know why I haven't said it. Any time Archer said it to me, it just hadn't felt right to say it back. "I just need more time." She sighs and pats my arm before tugging me along to keep walking.

"With reason. You've dated some douchebags in your time, that's for sure."

"Like you're one to talk," I snap back. The two of us both burst into laughter.

"Maybe the universe is putting us through our paces. And one day we'll wind up with two awesome guys who are sexy as hell and worship the ground we walk on." She gets a dreamy look in her eye and for a second, I have a feeling she's already met someone who may fit the bill.

"Is that smile about Jai, by any chance?" I prod, acting like I didn't see him sneaking out of her room this morning.

"No," she scoffs. "I mean he was a good time, but he's too far up Archer's ass."

"So? Isn't that the dream? Us winding up with best friends?" She rolls her eyes and then winces when she realizes I saw. "What was that?" I demand.

"Nothing," she breathes. "I'm hungover. And for some reason, my back is killing me." She rolls her shoulders, her face scrunching up in pain.

"Don't bullshit me, E. You don't want Jai because you don't think I'm going to wind up with Archer."

"I just..." Edina continues with an exhale. "I feel like Archer is just looking for a queen. And--" she breaks off, looking at me with pity in her eyes that sparks my rage.

"And?"

"You're too special for that life," she exclaims, and I tug on her arm getting her to stop on a side street with very few people. "If that's what you wanted, to be a princess and sit by his side while he rules the Kingdom, I'd be fine with it. But last year you told me you wanted to make general by the time you're thirty."

"I still do."

"Do you think you can do that while being with him?" she asks, her eyes not leaving mine, not giving me a second to look away and ignore this warning. "You're too fucking talented to spend your life planning parties and organizing charities. You should be the one running the Kingdom—"

"I don't want to run the fucking Kingdom." I get in her face, feeling my lightning crackle around me.

"Well, you should." She jabs her finger into my chest, not even wincing as the electricity licks at her skin. "I met some of the sergeants from your mission last night and they would follow you into the depths of hell. You're a born leader, Katie...not some prince's trophy wife."

"So, you think Archer is just using me?" I grit out through clenched teeth.

"No, I think he genuinely cares about you. But I also think he realizes you're a catch and wants to quickly lock it down. Didn't he even say that his dad wanted the two of you together from the very beginning?" She grabs my hand, pulling me closer to her. "I want you to be happy. I just don't want you to lose yourself in the process. And I'm worried that's what's going to happen."

Edina knows she's preying on my biggest fear right now, and it's not okay. I'm not okay with her throwing all my insecurities in my face, even if I know she means it with the best intentions. I direct my fury, my confusion, and every other emotion she's dragged up and I throw them back at her.

"It won't," I spit. "And maybe you shouldn't offer relationship advice until you've had one that lasts longer than a night." Edina's jaw goes slack, and I instantly want to take back every word.

"Just answer me one more question," she says, her eyes hardening. "Did you tell Archer about using Dark Magic?" I let the silence speak for me. I didn't tell him, I didn't tell anyone but her, but she knows this.

We make it back to the cottage and Edina groans in pain, dropping her drink so it splatters on the cobblestones.

"I'm gonna be sick." She takes off, running up the uneven walkway and throwing open the large wooden door. I hesitate outside the cottage, taking in the frosted trellis covering the stone walls. I'm not sure if she'd even want my help at this point.

I push into the drafty hallway, not bothering with the light as I trudge up the stairs. My room connects with Edina's through the bathroom, so I ignore my door and head to hers. The doorknob is unnaturally cold, so much so that it hurts to the touch.

"E?" I call as my hand turns the frozen knob. A strangled sob is all it takes for me to fling the door open to help my best friend. But when I see her room, I'm frozen in place, my eyes bugging out of my head.

"Oh fuck."

Chapter Thirty-One

THE BEDROOM IS ENCASED in ice. It spreads over the floral wallpaper, sparkling in the sunlight that peeks through the encrusted windowpane. I watch as the ice on the ceiling melts and quickly solidifies into a terrifying spike. I take a step forward, but the thick sheet covering the beige carpet has me tripping over my feet and steadying myself on the wardrobe.

"Katie," Edina gasps from where she sits on the bed, hugging her knees to her chest. Tears spill down her cheeks and turn to ice before plunking down on the comforter. Her grey sweater is completely shredded around her, and she keeps tugging at the remaining material in a failed attempt to keep her skin covered. Her blond waves are pushed back behind her pointed ears.

Pointed ears.

My breath wheezes out in a visible cloud as she leans forward revealing a pair of delicate, iridescent wings. They have gently rounded edges, and glitter with a swirling snowflake pattern that stretches across the entire wingspan. They flutter briefly as more ice blasts from her delicate frame, coating the mirror opposite her.

"Holy fuck." I swear, my eyes transfixed on her wings. "How—"

"He said I was, but I didn't believe him," she wails into her knees, and I skate across the ice to wrap her in my arms. She stiffens as my hands approach her wings, but then melts into me. Her breathing is too shallow, and the ice around us thickens as she panics. I gently rub circles over the non-winged portion of her back until the air warms ever so slightly.

"Who said what, E?" I whisper.

"The Fae I met, Puck. He told me I was Fae, but I didn't believe him." She hiccups and I stroke her hair, my hands grazing over the points in her ears as I pass. "He told me my powers would manifest on my twenty-first birthday."

"But you were fine this morning," I state, shifting as the ice beneath me begins to melt, soaking my leggings.

"I officially turned twenty-one at four o'clock," she chokes out. I glance at the clock in the room; it's five after. "He said he could sense it."

"He came for you," I murmur, realization dawning on me. Somehow, they realized Edina was a changeling and they came to collect her.

"He was mad I was leaving, but I told him I couldn't miss Christmas with you. Not if..." She trails off and my chest seizes in panic.

"Not if what?"

"Katie, they want me to go to Faerie," she says softly.

"No," I insist. "Absolutely not. You're not leaving. We'll figure out a way for you to stay."

"How?" She pulls away, her eyes emblazoned. "We can't go back to the palace. I'll be killed. I can't even leave this room. And this power..." On cue, icicles explode from her body, and I duck to avoid being impaled as they soar across the room and imbed themselves in the wall. "Katie, I'm scared."

I pull her back to me again. "I'll help you figure out the magic, how to hold it back. But I'm not letting you banish yourself to another realm where you don't know anyone. You've heard the stories, E. The Fae are—"

"Don't you dare finish that sentence," she grits through her teeth, pulling away. Her wings beat furiously, despite the quiet tone of her voice. "Look at me, Katie. *I* am Fae."

My lips chatter in the cold, but I don't move as I try to figure out how this could be happening, and how I can help now that it has. I'm at a loss for words.

"Are you going to turn me in?" Edina asks in a scary calm voice, her entire body going completely still.

"What?" I snap, shocked. It comes out harsher than I intend. "Edina, you're—"

I reach for her, and she *flinches.* I pull my hand back but meet her sapphire eyes with mine.

"You're my sister," I remind her, pouring all the love I feel for her in those words. "I'm on your side, *always.*"

She visibly relaxes and flops down on the frozen mattress, staring up at the ceiling. "What do we do," she asks, and I sigh, flopping back next to her, keeping distance from her wings.

"Maybe we could try the werewolf?" she asks tentatively. "He's a Magical Creature. Maybe he knows somewhere safe I can go?"

I tentatively reach down the bond I felt yesterday and give it a mental tug, but nothing happens.

"I don't know how to contact him...unless you feel like hurting me." Edina chuckles, but I'm about thirty seconds from grabbing one of those icicles and jabbing my hand if this is our option.

"If I can get to the portal..."

"How are we going to get you to the portal?" I ask. "Going to the palace would be suicide. And then what? You're just going to walk into Faerie and say, 'Hey, who wants to adopt a changeling?'"

"No. I'd fly obviously," she says dryly, but a smile ticks the corner of her mouth, and then we both laugh. We laugh like she hasn't sprouted wings and isn't doomed to be hunted in this realm unless she can learn to glamour her wings away. It's only thirty percent hysterical panic fueling this moment.

"We will figure this out," I vow.

"We have no one else we can go to."

"E, I will figure something out, I swear. I love you more than anyone in the world—"

The realization knocks the wind out of me. This is what Adriana was talking about. *When the one you love most has nowhere else to turn.* It wasn't about Archer; it was about Edina.

"Fuck me," I swear.

"If you think it would help..." Edina says with a laugh that I don't return now that my mind is racing.

We can go to the Dark Witch Covens. And they'll help us if I agree to be their queen. It means turning my back on everything I've built...my family, my career, my relationship, but it's the only way I can keep Edina safe. And I would do anything for this girl...*this Fae* in front of me.

"I know what we have to do," I say, squaring my shoulders.

"Girls! Time to cut down the Christmas Tree!" Marcus calls from downstairs. Edina's eyes widen in panic.

"Here's the plan," I switch to my captain's voice, a voice my best friend has never heard, and I would never have ever imagined using towards her. "I'll go cut a tree with my mom and Marcus. You stay here. See if you can thaw the room and pack your stuff. We'll leave tonight. I'll make an excuse why we can't stay." She nods and stands reluctantly.

"Where are we going?" Edina asks, already moving to the wardrobe.

"We're going to call my sister."

Chapter Thirty-Two

CONVINCING MY MOTHER WE needed to return to the palace was easier than I anticipated. I told her I had a bad feeling and needed to protect Archer and the king, and she agreed immediately, praising my work ethic, and giving Edina and me two brooms to get back faster. Which is how we're currently standing on a hilltop a few miles from the cottage, looking out over the sleepy countryside dotted with Christmas lights. A light snow falls around us, though I'm not sure whether it's Edina's magic or if it's natural.

Edina's ice, much like my lightning, is cued to her emotions, so as long as she remains calm, she can keep it under control. We practiced a bit of Battle Magic before we left, and found her water is working the same way, except it's now frozen and about ten times more powerful.

"What do we do now?" Edina asks, adjusting the knit beanie so it covers her ears. Her wings are folded beneath a puffy coat, but her eyes still glow with power.

"Hang on a second," I tell her, whipping out my phone. The werewolf said all we needed to do was call Adriana...and I doubt he meant just by shouting her name at the sky. I scroll through my contacts, and of course, Adriana's name is in there. "When did she get my phone?"

"Babes, she can teleport," Edina points out and I roll my eyes.

I'm about to dial her number when my gaze snags on Archer's contact, who I haven't told I'm leaving. I left a note for Mom and Marcus in their presents, so they'll know everything once Edina is safe, but Archer... He deserves more than me disappearing without a goodbye.

"One second," I tell my best friend. "I just have to..." I trail off, pointing to the open message to Archer.

"I'm here if you need me," she says, stepping away to give me privacy.

I take comfort in the faint pulsing of my necklace, internally cursing myself for finding it so stifling just hours before. It seems so stupid that the biggest problem in my life was that I couldn't admit my feelings. Because of course I have feelings for Archer, of course I--

My phone pings, drawing my attention. A new message from Archer is open in my palm as if he felt me thinking about him. Not that I can tell him any of my newfound revelations, not when I'm about to disappear and may never see him again.

Archer

Marcus told me you were coming back...did you leave yet?

Well...I didn't see that lie backfiring. I take a deep breath and force my fingers to move.

Katie

No.

Archer

Good. Father and I are at the safehouse...the generals were insistent. Some kind of threat to the palace. But come to Edinburgh instead *wink emoji*

Katie

I can't...

Listen, Archer. Something's happened.

Archer

What's wrong?

Katie

I can't go into detail...but I'm going away.

Archer

When are you coming back?

I feel myself losing my nerve and my lip is quivering, but I press on.

Katie

I'm not.

The read receipt feels like a punch in the gut, and tears fall freely down my cheeks as the three bubbles appear and disappear as Archer types. Edina appears beside me, resting her hand on my shoulder.

"We don't have to do this," she whispers. But I shake my head. This is the only option.

Archer

Where are you?

Katie

I have to go. I'm sorry

I close the message and call Adriana's number. It only rings once, and then the air in front of us swirls with dark smoke.

"You got my message," Adriana pops out of the smoke and practically leaps into my arms. I tentatively return the hug, awkwardly patting her on the back. When she pulls away, I can't help noticing how much better she looks from the last time I saw her. She's wearing a simple, grey sweater underneath a black blazer and fitted black pants. Her blonde curls are clipped so they're off her face, and the pumps she's wearing make her look like a kick-ass executive, opposed to the deranged-mental patient look she had going on in prison.

She surveys my puffy eyes with curiosity, her head cocked to the side like she's not sure what to make of it. "Did you tie up that loose end?" Adriana asks. Even though there's no hint of malice or taunting in her voice, I feel a surge of anger towards my sister. *Does she not realize I'm giving up my entire life for a cause I don't believe in?* I feel the lightning crackle around me, and Adriana must notice because she takes a half step back. At least she has the sense to be afraid of me.

Without waiting for an answer, she turns from me and surveys Edina. Adriana strides over to her, lifting her face and peering into her eyes. They stand like that for a long minute, and I take the time to silence my phone, which is vibrating like crazy with unread messages.

"You'll be safe in our home," Adriana says, more to me than to Edina, finally breaking the weird eye contact. "Are you ready to go?" She extends two hands, one to each of us, and my heart pounds wildly. Edina takes her hand and they both look expectantly at me.

"I won't take her without you," Adriana says, regarding my hesitation.

"What are the terms of this agreement?" I ask. I know this is the only option, but everything in my body is fighting being taken to my father, to the Dark Magic Covens.

"We'll negotiate once we arrive," she responds simply, stretching her fingers wider willing me to take her hand. I hesitate for one more second before taking it, her hand warm against mine.

We're overtaken by grey smoke that swirls and squeezes until it feels like my lungs will pop from the pressure. I let out a small whimper as it envelops my body, but as quickly as it came on, it's gone, and we're somewhere completely new.

"So fucking cool," Edina mutters.

"I can teach you both," Adriana replies. "Teleportation was originally a Fae skill taught to Dark Witches. You both should be able to master it easily enough."

I take a minute to look around our new location, blanketed by fog that reeks of Dark Magic. As my eyes adjust to the thickness of the air, I realize we're in a valley. Mossy rocks rise above us before descending into deep ravines. Adriana approaches the formation closest to us and lays her hand on the greenery that surrounds its base. The moss clears at her touch and the rock rearranges itself, revealing a dark doorway.

"Welcome to the Highland Coven." Adriana smiles widely and plunges into the darkness. Edina grabs my hand, and we follow her under the mountain.

We trudge after her, down a dark corridor that's carved from the walls of the mountain and magically lit with an eerie green light. The whole place is humming with Dark Magic, and I can't even imagine the scope of power it took to build it. We come to a fork in the road and Adriana quickly moves to the left, not even bothering to look over her shoulder to check on us.

"Where are we going?" I finally break the silence, quickening my pace so that Edina and I fall directly at her heels. I have a feeling if we get lost in this labyrinth, we may never see the light of day again.

"To the throne room." We hit another fork and this time she takes a right, but I get a glimpse down the left corridor, which opens into a large training facility. I hear grunting and the clash of metal.

"What was that?" Edina whispers.

"The leaders of the covens and some of their seconds have assembled," Adriana answers, steering us up a small set of stairs set into the wall. "They're training with swords, seeing if they can get the metal to wield spells in place of a wand."

Holy shit, that's brilliant. I make a mental note to bring that to Marcus before remembering I won't be returning to the Dragons. I huff out a frustrated breath.

The hall opens into a giant cavern, the ceiling extending up to the very tip of the mountain and the whole space illuminated with that same green light. Fifty witches in matching black robes stand in perfect lines, and they all shift to face us, even the children in the back row who stand on their tiptoes. One child breaks rank and approaches, deftly whipping off our coats before running to the far end of the cavern and disappearing down yet another corridor.

Adriana moves us to the front of the room to a small stage set with a glass throne that glows electric under the green lights. The throne crackles with hidden power, but I can't discern if it's coming from the chair itself or the silver and ruby diadem that is on the seat. I look to Edina to see if she's as drawn to the throne as I am, but her eyes are on the crowd, who watch the two of us with wide eyes.

Adriana pauses before the dais and drops to her knee, orienting her body so that she faces me. As one, the entire congregation kneels. Adriana's eyes flit up to Edina momentarily, before a cloud of smoke flutters around her, forcing her to kneel as well. She lands with a thud and a cry in front of me, her eyes flashing.

"She doesn't kneel," I command. Adriana sighs but releases the power surrounding Edina, who quickly gets to her feet and stands at my side. "Get everyone else up too."

"They'll obey their queen. You just need to command them," she says.

"Who am I negotiating with? I'd like to see them so we can get this over with." I feel a prickle of awareness at my back before hearing the footsteps. The hairs on my neck stand at attention and I whirl around to come face to face with my father.

His black cloak is open around his shoulders, revealing the button-down shirt and tie combo he wears. He's put on more bulk since I last saw him, but he still appears malnourished and frail. His silver hair is pulled back in a low ponytail, and he flashes a sinister smile in my direction that has my magic ready to pounce.

"Negotiations are simple, Kathryn," my father coos. "We need you to put on the crown and sit on the throne." I wait for more, but that's all he says. His auburn eyes drill holes into mine as he waits for my answer.

"You want me to...sit? Seriously?" I deadpan and Edina scoffs beside me.

"Once you sit on the throne, the prophecy will be enacted," Adriana explains from her kneeling position. "You will be visited by Queen Carman, the last Dark Magic Queen, and she will show you the way to lead the Dark Magic Covens to victory over the Elemental Witches. Then you will be our queen."

"Not just sitting then, is it?" I counter, and my father shoots a glare at me. "Sitting on the throne is agreeing to be your queen."

"And in return, we will protect your *Fae* friend." My father's voice drips with disdain. "She will have a place here until we can find a way for her to return to Faerie safely, or until we win the war and then you can decide what to do with her."

"Because I'll be the Queen of the Kingdom of Magic, in this hypothetical world where we beat the Elemental Witches." I scoff, but I can tell my father is serious. Part of me wants to tell him to fuck all the way off, but I need to play along. I need to ensure Edina's safety.

"No one harms her," I reiterate.

"You have my word on behalf of all the covens." My father extends his withered hand towards me, his face illuminated in the creepy green light making him look nightmarish. I gulp hard, my eyes connecting with Edina.

Katie, don't, she murmurs through our mental connection. *We'll find another way.*

I reach out and shake my father's hand. No turning back now.

Adriana stands and snatches the diadem off the throne, the large ruby at its point glistening. As she approaches me, my father grabs Edina's hand and escorts her to the front of the line of kneeling witches. He sinks to one knee, and this time, Edina kneels of her own accord.

"Please kneel and receive your birthright," Adriana says in a clear voice, and I fight the urge to roll my eyes. I slowly drop to my knee before her and bow my head.

"Long live the Heir of Carman, Queen of the Dark Magic Covens. Queen Kathryn!"

"Long live Queen Kathryn," the cavern echoes as Adriana lowers the diadem to my head. She steps back and the slight weight settles onto my head. I'm struck with the feeling that it was always supposed to be there, supposed to be mine.

"Take your rightful place on the throne and receive its blessing."

The word *blessing* doesn't sit well, and I have a feeling Adriana may have been simplifying her prior explanation.

I slowly walk to the throne pausing when I reach it to look at the coven, who are all staring at me expectantly. My fingers fidget with the hem of my sweater, and I keep thinking I'm incredibly underdressed to meet a queen, even if she is just a memory. I release a shaky breath and lower myself to the edge of the seat.

Then everything goes black.

Chapter Thirty-Three

MAGIC CRACKLES IN MY veins from an ancient source. It's infusing into me from the throne, rushing to meet and meld with my magic, embracing the Darkness and the Light and intensifying the lightning. It's so painful my back spasms, and I shudder as the current surges through me. The power moving through me is more than I've ever felt; it feels like I could crack the world in two with a flick of my finger. I inhale sharply and more enters my lungs.

I vaguely hear something happening in the world around me, but my eyes must have closed because I can't see. I hear a scream somewhere beyond, but I can't tell if it's male or female, pain or pleasure. I'm lost to the power flooding into me from the throne. My father's experiments were a freaking lullaby compared to this hell. As suddenly as it began, it recedes from sharp pinpricks to the sweet kiss of an ocean spray. And then, there's a solitary voice. A sweet voice, that sings to the magic within me.

"Open your eyes," the voice commands. The room around is pitch black, the only light comes from the throne which is now glowing as lightning crackles inside the glass. It's empty, save for one person. Although I'm not sure person is the right word. She lingers in a wisp, her form seeming to solidify and fade at random intervals.

What strikes me first is how much she looks like me. She's wearing black armor, with giant shoulder spikes and she holds a helmet under her arm. She has long chestnut brown hair that hangs in loose waves past her waist. When she smiles softly at me, it's like looking in a mirror; the way her eyes slightly crease in the corners, the slight imprint of a dimple on her cheek.

"It's about time." Her tone is melodic, jovial. A smile spreads across her lovely face, completely lighting up her eyes, which are the same green as my mother's.

"You're not Carman," I whisper. It's not so much a question, but I still look to her for the answer.

"That's correct. Who am I, Kathryn?" She cocks her head to the side, a gesture I've used so many times in my life. She waits for me to answer, and the name forms on my tongue.

"Finley," I croak.

"Thank goodness you're smart." I hear a distant scream again and look wildly around, but Finley ignores it. "I've waited for so long for you, Kathryn."

"I...I'm so confused." I sink back on the throne, unsure if I should be going towards this person...ghost...*vision thing.* "I thought I was supposed to find out how to—"

"Bring victory for the Dark Magic Covens? Yeah, I'm not sure why the prophecy was interpreted like that." She runs a hand through her hair in the most pedestrian way. I swear my head is about to explode. Another scream sounds, and this time Finley takes notice.

"I only have a few minutes," she says quickly. "But there's much I need to tell you, so listen carefully." I nod, sitting forward to the edge of my throne as she begins.

"You know that I'm the daughter of King Darius and was born with Light Magic. During a battle, I was gravely injured, and it threw off the balance of the Kingdom of Magic."

"A werewolf attacked you, right?"

"No," she growls through gritted teeth. "My fiancé was the Pack Master, the head of the werewolf packs, and I was well respected amongst their kind. An Elemental Witch struck us both and somehow made my injuries look like a werewolf bite. My father wouldn't hear it when I told him who really hurt me, and he declared war on the Magical Creatures. Because of me. I was destroyed when he started attacking the people who had shown me nothing but kindness.

"Carman came to me with a plan to stop my father. She heard a prophecy that said a woman who contained both Dark and Light Magic would be the only one who could restore balance to the Kingdom. She infused me with her magic, and I became the commander of her armies. Together we fought for our cause alongside Queen Aldonza's army of Magical Creatures.

"When my father realized I was the one leading the forces against him, he turned on the Dark Magic Covens, yet another faction of magic, widening the divide even more. And then..." Finley sighs, the weight of the world on her shoulders.

"And then he killed you," I finish for her. A tear escapes Finley's disappearing eyes.

"It was a mistake. He was aiming for Carman, and I intercepted him. He felt such guilt after that he wanted to die. He asked Carman to kill him, but she refused. She said we needed to restore the balance that existed for many years. But then King Baran came and killed him anyway. When she watched Darius die, Carman knew there was no hope for her either. My death was the final straw, the last thing that tipped the scales to a world unbalanced. Thus, the prophecy you know was born.

"*Made in her Image.* A girl of Darius's bloodline, someone born with Light Magic.

"*Made from Magic.* Carman has immense power even beyond the grave. For generations, she would appear to Dark Witches in proximity to Darius's line and grant them visions on how to infuse someone with her magic. It took centuries, but finally, your father understood what was needed to create her heir."

Finley's eyes meet mine, the glowing green connecting to my auburn. While she's completely stoic, I can see the plea in her gaze.

"Kathryn, the Kingdom of Magic is on the brink of a catastrophic war that threatens to destroy magic entirely. Baran's ancestors, while well-meaning, have shunned Dark Magic and the Magical Creatures, making them desperate. You are the only one who can restore balance to the Kingdom. *Made to Conquer, Made to Rule.*"

"How—"

"You'll need allies from all factions of magic even to stand a chance of restoring the balance of power. Begin with the Dark Witches and the Magical Creatures. Then, you'll need to find the pieces of the blood oath; only then will you be recognized as the true monarch."

"Blood oath?"

"When the four kings and queens swore to rule together, they each imbued a drop of blood within a silver piece to solidify a blood oath. They kept their piece on them at all times, so that no one could ever become the sole ruler of the Kingdom of Magic. But if you have all four—"

"Then they'll just let me rule?" I ask, and she chuckles darkly.

"The pieces are enchanted to belong to the rightful ruler. You'll still need to fight for your throne, but it will help convince those who don't trust a Dark Witch."

"Where do I find them?

"Unfortunately, I don't know what or where two of them are." Finley smiles at me. "But I do know that you're currently wearing the other two." I balk and my hand immediately goes to the locket at my throat.

"Aldonza's locket," I whisper. Finley nods up to the tiara currently on top of my head.

"And Carman's Diadem." Another scream sounds from off in the distance and my entire body tenses.

"I don't want to go to war against my people. The Elemental Witches are my family, my friends," I tell her frankly. Because I can see nothing worse than having to fight against my mom, Marcus, and Archer. Not to mention all the soldiers I've trained. Another shriek, this one I recognize. *Edina.*

"You already have," Finley says as she looks at me sadly. "Use the power that was given to you, embrace it all, don't be afraid of it. Restore the balance." She fades away completely, leaving me in the darkness for one second before I'm thrust into the middle of chaos.

Chapter Thirty-Four

EDINA IS STANDING OVER me, shaking my shoulder with trembling hands.

"Katie! Katie, please," she wails right before slapping me hard across the face. I jump up, throwing her away from me as my hand flies up to my stinging cheek.

"What the hell—" My jaw hits the ground as I take in the scene in front of me.

It looks like someone took off the top of the mountain. Chunks of rock fall from the edges of a gigantic hole, crashing inside the throne room and sending out violent tremors. The green glow mixes with moonlight, which now floods the underground space. Screams echo off the walls from every direction.

Gone are the perfect lines of subservient witches; some are flat out running for hallways that head out of the chamber, others are clumped together in a rough battle formation. Dark Magic is flying towards the space underneath the hole, but I can't see what they're squaring off against. I make my way off the dais when it hits me in a wave, making my stomach turn. The smell of charred flesh...a scent that haunts my nightmares. I scan the crowd and find Adriana at the front, throwing Dark Magic at a single figure covered in white flames.

"Archer?" I gasp, and Edina nods. *Holy shit.*

"He saw you on the throne and went fucking ballistic. He killed the entire back row before we could react." Edina shouts, hot on my heels as I push around the Dark Witches that are scattering.

"How did he get past the wards?" I ask as I reach the group that is making a stand. They part for me but don't stop sending off spells in Archer's direction. Edina jabs a finger towards the hole.

"He obliterated the mountain with that crazy-ass fire! How did he even know we were here?"

"I swear I didn't tell him," I yell over the sounds of the battle. A blast of hellfire shoots in the air like a geyser and we both duck instinctively. I throw up a shield around the group immediately surrounding us.

"You need to stay back here," I tell Edina. "Don't let him see you."

"Like fuck I will." The look in her eyes is rage and vengeance and suddenly I understand why witches are so afraid of the Fae. "My magic is ice. I'm going with you."

"E—"

"Katie, there were kids in the back row."

"How many--?" I ask as a lump forms in my throat.

"Enough," she says, shaking her head solemnly.

She's right. Any casualties in war are terrible, but children—A wave of guilt crashes over me. If I hadn't listened to Adriana, if I had waited five seconds to sit on that damn throne, I could have stopped this. I've been a queen for mere minutes and already *children have died* on my watch.

Archer's words echo in my ears... *I will burn the world down for you.*

I cast one more pleading look at Edina, who I know is resolved to help, before snaking back into the crowd. They part for us until we make it next to my father and Adriana, pushing our way between them. I survey their shield briefly, noting the gap off to our right where a witch is crumpled to the floor, her body a burned husk.

Archer is completely encased in the hellfire. It swarms over every inch of his body, the flames coating his arms, licking up his chest, and reflected in his eyes making him look like a demon. He roars and the fire spills from his mouth, making a line at the shield, right towards Adriana. Edina reacts quickly, sending ice to encase the hellfire and it goes out with a satisfying hiss. Her eyes widen when she realizes the scope of her new magic, and I give her a thankful nod.

"ARCHER, STOP!" I scream. He falters, then lets out a blast so strong that the entire mountain quakes. The fire collides with the shield and explodes, throwing everyone to the floor.

"Archer," I whimper as I stand, my ears ringing. He's still aflame, and his sights are set on me. I don't even think he realizes who's in front of him.

"Please, stop," I beg, hoping I can reach my prince. His head cocks to the side and the flames dim momentarily.

I watch as Archer's eyes drag up and down my body. I follow his gaze and I realize my magic surrounds me in every form. Light Magic, my sunshine, coats my skin. The iridescent black of my Dark Magic swirls around it, and where they intersect, lightning crackles. The whole display surrounds my body like armor. Archer growls, his hellfire flaring again.

"It's me, your highness, Katie. I know you won't hurt me." And to prove it, I force my magic to seep back inside me, absorbing the power that surged unbidden to protect me. Archer falters and I think for a minute he's coming back to me.

And then everything goes to shit. My father stands, springing up from the floor with entirely too much grace for a man of his age, and sends a blast of Dark Magic barreling straight for Archer's chest. Archer roars in anger as he blocks the curse with a swipe of his hand and sends a wall of hellfire great enough to envelop everyone in the cavern.

I don't think before jumping in front of the coven, throwing my magic wide so it protects the witches laying sprawled throughout the throne room. The hellfire and my magic clash in a sonic boom that rattles the remaining ceiling. I put up a shield around the entire cavern to keep anyone from being hit by falling debris, but the shield takes my concentration from Archer.

I don't see the lone, targeted flame streaking towards me, on a collision course with my heart, until it's almost on me. Edina screams from where she lies on the floor, alerting me just in time. I jerk my body to the side, but I'm not fast enough to dodge the flame and it slams into my shoulder.

I've experienced a lot of pain in my life, but I have never experienced agony like the strike of pure hellfire. My world erupts in stars as the flame burrows into my shoulder, searing every inch of the flesh it connects with. Between the pain and the smell of my flesh dissolving, I'm heaving. And then, when I think it can't get any worse, it starts to travel up my neck, the tendrils of flame reaching for my ears, my hair, my face. I scream, trying every spell I can think of to put it out, but nothing stops the creeping hellfire. It reaches my locket and the chain breaks under the pressure of the heat, the charm falling at my feet.

"Katie," Archer gasps, and the fire disappears, but the burning is still spreading.

"What have you done?" my father cries, his hands pulling at his hair in a moment of desperation. He throws a spell in Archer's direction, but I don't see if it hits as my vision temporarily darkens.

Adriana is at my side in a flash, bracing me from an inevitable fall and my eyes drift open again. She places a hand on my cheek, muttering a spell under her breath. The burning halts at her touch but begins receding down my arm and across my chest instead.

"I'm holding it off from reaching her brain," she says, turning to Edina and beckoning her over with one long finger. "We can't let it get to her heart. You need to use your magic."

"I—" my best friend approaches me, tears blooming in her eyes as I can feel the fire-less burning snaking down towards my chest, making it hard to breathe. "I don't know what to do. My powers are new. I don't know how to control them."

"You can do it," Adriana assures. "I've seen it."

She grabs Edina's hands, guiding them to my chest. "Katie, you need to access your Light Magic. Send all your Light to your heart to protect it." I do as she says, diving deep into my belly and wrapping a hand around my kernel of sunshine, which is much bigger than a kernel now. I direct it to my heart, wrapping it in the bright light not a second too soon. I feel the singeing pain reach the muscles around my heart before my Light Magic stops it. I inhale sharply as it moves again like it's seeking a way in.

Adriana guides Edina's hands and begins whispering something to her. Bright blue light coats Edina's hands, followed by the most delicious cooling sensation across my skin. I fight to keep conscious, swaying backward only to be held upright.

"Stay with us, Katie," Adriana whispers.

There's a pulse of blue light, followed by a gasp, and then I fall into oblivion.

FOR THE LOVE OF *magic, my head is pounding.* I roll over to check my phone, opening my eyes as little as possible, but my nightstand isn't where it should be. *Where am I?* I flip over and my hand lands on unnaturally freezing skin next to mine. My eyes fly open and connect with Edina's sapphire blues, which are puffy and rimmed in red. She's curled next to me, her delicate wings tucked behind her. She releases a sob when she meets my open eyes and flings her arms around me, causing me to hiss in pain.

"Shit, babes," Edina exclaims. "I'm so sorry."

The room spins as I push myself to a seated position. Edina's icicle fingers prop me up, steadying me as I sway under my blankets. When it passes, I realize the room is designed to look exactly like the bedroom I had as a child in Salem, with pale blue walls and gentle white curtains, but there are no windows. One wall is completely lined with bookshelves, and another has a white vanity with a large oval mirror.

"Adriana?" I call, suddenly remembering where I am. *We're with the Dark Magic Covens.* Because Edina is Fae. I was crowned queen....and then my memory is fuzzy.

"My Katie," she coos, plying her body from a grey armchair across the room. "You're awake."

"Something's wrong," I murmur. Even without the dizziness, something is off. The two women exchange a glance. "How long was I out?"

"A few hours. How much do you remember?" Edina asks gently. I reach through the corners of my mind, pulling apart memories. I see Finley, and her message about the prophecy...and the battle. *The battle.* The vision of Archer shooting hellfire at me surges to the forefront.

"Shit," I swear. *He attacked me with hellfire.* I don't think he knew it was me at the moment, but he could have killed me. He *meant* to kill me. "Where is he?" Another exchanged glance.

"He escaped on a broom," Adriana says finally, her shoulders sinking with the revelation of this failure. "While we were tending to you, he flew out of the hole in the ceiling."

"Fucker didn't even stay to see if you survived," Edina growls. "I swear to whatever Fae gods-I'm-supposed-to-believe-in-now when I find him, I'll cut his balls off." I manage a chuckle, but it feels hollow.

"How am I alive? Hellfire..."

"Is a death sentence," Adriana finishes. "We're not sure exactly. We think it was the combination of your Light Magic, Edina's Faerie Magic, and my Dark Magic."

"You saw how to save me," I remember, and Adriana nods.

"But not how it worked. I just saw everyone combining power."

"How did he find us?" I ask no one in particular. Adriana reaches into her smart black pants pocket and removes a blackened phone that looks like it was electrocuted. It takes a minute for me to realize that the phone is mine.

"We think he tracked your phone," she murmurs. So, this *was* my fault. I was going to blame myself anyway, but there's something about knowing the truth that makes it so much worse. "It got damaged when you sat on the throne, which is why we think he blasted through the mountain. It lost signal and he thought—"

"It doesn't matter what he thought," I spit, and thankfully Adriana backs off. I instinctively reach for my necklace but find thick white bandages wrapped down my neck, across my chest and shoulder, and down to my elbow. "How bad is it?"

"We don't have a healer yet," Adriana says softly.

"But we used whatever healing spells we knew and put salve on it," Edina supplies. "It will probably scar, but it'll look so badass." I nod absently.

"Something is...wrong," I mutter. "I feel...empty. Like something's missing"

"Missing?" Edina echoes. "Your necklace? Adriana grabbed it after it was burned off you. Is that what you mean?"

"No, it's not that. Although it's good you grabbed it. We'll need it," I comment. Adriana gasps, her eyes glazing over.

"Oh no." She shakes loose the vision and grabs my head in her hands. "Katie, shock me."

"What?" I push her off me. "I'm not using my magic against you." *Is she serious right now?*

"Do it," Adriana commands sternly, and I sigh. *Fine. She wants lightning... I'll give her lightning.*

I reach into myself, pulling my magic forward. Except nothing comes. My face falls and my entire body starts shaking. I try again, reaching down into my depths. I search for my sunlight, for the darkness, for anything, but come up empty. My eyes connect with Edina's just as Adriana lets loose a keening wail loud enough to be heard in London.

"My magic is gone."

End of Book One

Want More?

Made to Conquer (Book 2: Made from Magic Series)
Coming September 2022 and available for eBook preorder now!

Need to talk about that cliffhanger? Join our readers' group or
follow me on TikTok!
ALSO!
Bonus chapters from the werewolf's POV are available for free
when you sign up for my mailing list.
All links can be found at https://www.marianneascott.com/

Acknowledgements

First of all, if you've made it this far, THANK YOU! Thank you for taking a chance on a new author and for helping me realize this dream.

To the best writing partner/sounding board/plot-hole cannon a girl could ever ask for...the elegantly fuckable R.E. Sommons (I take no credit for that last description, that's her brilliant writing). Thank you for every note, every hour spent listening to me dissect the magic system only to scream "there's a spell for that" when I couldn't answer the question you asked, and every counseling session when the imposter syndrome was rough. Thank you to my first beta reader Jillian Melko, for being the only other person I felt comfortable enough to send this book to. I am so unbelievably lucky to call you my friends and to have you in my life.

To all those who have helped me along the way, including my amazing editor Paige Lawson who made me sound way smarter than I am, and Cassidy Townsend for listening to my ramblings about the cover and turning it into something truly stunning.

Thank you to my husband for creatively checking in with me during my five-year hiatus from writing, constantly reminding me of what I wanted even when I thought I didn't want it anymore. Thank you for knowing me better than I know myself, and for jumping on board and helping with all the behind-the-scenes things that go into self-publishing that I wasn't prepared for.

And last but not least, thank you to my family who are literally the most supportive people in the entire universe. I'm seriously so lucky to have not only my parents and brother, but my entire extended family and the wonderful family I married into rooting for me. I hope you know how invaluable your support has been.

ABOUT THE AUTHOR

Marianne A. Scott is a Sagittarius and a Ravenclaw...which should tell you all you need to know.

She enjoys writing fantastical stories adjacent to our world because she's secretly hoping that one day a rift will open between realms and magic will be real.

When not writing, you can find her with her Kindle and a latte, sitting opposite her husband in their New Jersey home. In her other life, she teaches tiny humans how to sing, passing along her love of musical theater to the next generation.

Printed in Great Britain
by Amazon

11112658R00181